IF ONLY

Lottie moved a step nearer, powerless to resist the magnetic pull of their attaction. His arms closed about her, urging her still closer until her arms went around his neck. She arched her back, pressing her body tightly against him. She was not surprised by the hardness of his muscled body. What caught her unawares was the softness of her own. She had done a man's work for so long, she had thought her femininity a thing of the past, yet of its own volition her body yielded to his, bending and accepting comfort.

"Ah, darlin' girl," Sean whispered, his lips descending on hers, robbing her of her last rational thought.

There was such sweet tenderness in his kiss she felt tears gathering in her eyes. Yet there was an edge of mastery as well, a combination of power and hunger that left her breathless.

<u>BOOK YOUR PLACE ON OUR WEBSITE</u>
<u>AND MAKE THE</u>
<u>READING CONNECTION!</u>

We've created a customized website just for our very special readers, where you can get the inside scoop on everything that's going on with Zebra, Pinnacle and Kensington books.

When you come online, you'll have the exciting opportunity to:

- View covers of upcoming books
- Read sample chapters
- Learn about our future publishing schedule (listed by publication month *and author*)
- Find out when your favorite authors will be visiting a city near you
- Search for and order backlist books from our online catalog
- Check out author bios and background information
- Send e-mail to your favorite authors
- Meet the Kensington staff online
- Join us in weekly chats with authors, readers and other guests
- Get writing guidelines
- AND MUCH MORE!

Visit our website at
http://www.kensingtonbooks.com

The Man For Her

Alice Valdal

ZEBRA BOOKS
KENSINGTON PUBLISHING CORP.
www.kensingtonbooks.com

Chapter 1

1886

A glaring sun bore down on the small mining town of Prospect, bleaching the color from the landscape and sapping the strength of its citizens. The streets were nearly deserted as people huddled indoors or in patches of shade, seeking respite from the unrelenting heat.

Only Lottie Graham was out and about, hurrying across the unnaturally quiet main street, her worn boots kicking up small eddies of fine white dust. The heat and the dust filled her nostrils and choked her throat. It was late August and Prospect was desperate for rain. *But not just yet,* Lottie prayed, even as she wished for a breath of wind.

She gained the boardwalk and continued on her way to the Mercantile, her footsteps echoing sharply in the still air. A group of men sat in the shade of the Gold Nugget Saloon, their chairs tipped back and their hats pulled low over their eyes. Their sprawled legs barred her progress, forcing her to step off the walkway or pick her way carefully over their outstretched feet. She could feel their eyes upon her as she stepped down into the dusty road. A rude guffaw hit her like a fist to the solar plexus, making her stomach clench, and humbling her pride.

She gritted her teeth and hurried on, casting an anxious eye to the sky. Leaden gray clouds boiling over the mountain peaks held a storm that could break at any minute, and the bulk of her grain harvest still stood in stooks in the open fields of Pine Creek Farm. *Blast Jack Williams and his broken-down threshing machine. The crop should have been safely in the granary by now.*

She approached the entrance to Barclay's Mercantile, and two women gossiping in its shadow flattened themselves against the weathered board and batten, whisking their skirts tightly against their legs as though fearful of contamination from the slightest contact with Crazy Lottie.

Turning a hard stare upon them, she charged, unseeing, through the open door of the Mercantile, and jostled hard against someone entering from the other side.

"I beg your . . ." She looked up, the apology dying on her lips, as she gazed into eyes as blue as the Irish Sea. Eyes that could fill with passion and darken to the deepest hue of midnight. Eyes she had dreamed of for ten long years. The room began to whirl about her, the floor tilting up at a bizarre angle, the shelves seeming to buckle and heave before her eyes.

"Ma'am?" The Irish lilt was right but the voice was too deep.

She stared at the stranger. He was the same height, about six feet, but he had broader shoulders than the man she remembered. The blue eyes looked out from a more rugged face and there was no smile to curve the wide mouth. She had been mistaken. The room took on its proper form and her heart died within her . . . again.

"I beg your pardon," she whispered, becoming aware of his hands on her arms, steadying her. She tried to step away, but her legs would not obey her wishes. Memory held her fast. Grief rushed to her throat, and filled her heart with tears. She stood frozen within the stranger's grasp.

A shrill titter behind her alerted her to the women who had followed her into the store. She could practically feel their eyes boring into her back, seeking new fodder for the gossip mill. Mary Jane Lewis and Thelma Black had been insolent troublemakers in her schoolmarm days. They hadn't improved with the intervening years.

She straightened her shoulders and freed herself from the comforting grip of the stranger's hands. "My apologies, sir." She spoke firmly, then turned and walked away to the end of the store, composing herself.

She stared hard at the shelf of dry goods along the rear wall, willing away the mist from her eyes and from her mind. A bolt of heavy yellow silk shone like a gold nugget among the homelier cottons and worsteds that surrounded it. A lifetime ago, she'd had a yellow silk dress, soft and feminine, hugging her breasts and swirling in sensuous folds about her ankles. She'd gone to dances in that dress, had laughed and dreamed and loved.

She looked down at the men's black trousers and plaid flannel shirt she wore and wished, just for an instant, for the fine clothes of her youth. It was a foolish thought and instantly repressed. She was a farmer now, with cattle to sell and supplies to haul.

Her days as a fine lady in tight-waisted dresses and high buttoned boots had long since ended.

"Ladies?" She heard Jed talking to Mary Jane and Thelma, doling out the sugar they'd come to buy.

"There's a dance at the hotel on Saturday night," Thelma said. Was her voice deliberately loud? "Everyone will be there."

"Not everyone," Mary Jane snickered, her irritating giggle clawing down Lottie's back. "Only ladies in dresses are welcome."

"Oh, Mary Jane, you're awful." She heard the spiteful glee in Thelma's words. "Only a crazy woman would dress like a man."

"Was there anything else, ladies?"

"No, Mr. Barclay, I guess not, unless you have some new ribbons."

"Sorry. Maybe you should try that new millinery shop."

Lottie didn't know if Jed had deliberately sent the women on their way, but she was grateful to him when she heard the door close behind them.

"Want something else, Lottie?" the proprietor called. She shook off her brooding and turned to the business at hand. Heading to the front of the store she kept her eyes lowered as she passed the stranger studying a row of new boots. Unaccountably, she wished he hadn't been witness to Thelma and Mary Jane's rudeness, though why she should care was a mystery.

She reached the front of the store. "No thanks, Jed." She kept her focus on the storekeeper. "Just the supplies I ordered before."

Jed Barclay stood behind a long wooden counter lined with jars of candy and spices and pickles. Behind him a wall of shelves held tinned goods, sacks of flour and sugar, tea and coffee, and other staples of a mining camp.

"How are you doing with that list?" She forced a wooden smile to her lips, keeping her back to the man who had surprised her.

Her scalp prickled with perspiration, and not just from the oppressive heat. She strained her ears, listening for his movements, wondering how close he was. She turned sideways to the counter, letting her gaze drift casually around the store before she found him lounging negligently against the doorjamb, his thumbs hooked over his belt, totally at ease in his big, rangy body. His collar was open at the neck, giving her a glimpse of fine black hair that curled at his throat and no doubt spread across his chest and perhaps down onto his belly. She drew a sharp breath and jerked her eyes upward.

She'd already noted the breadth of his shoulders but now she studied him more carefully. She hadn't been mistaken in her first impression. He was raw and rugged and strong enough to sweep a woman off her feet and carry her away on his whim— and the woman would be grateful. She caught her thoughts up short as a flush spread down her throat and over her bosom, tightening her nipples until they pressed hard against the fine cotton of her undershirt. She slouched, making sure her man's shirt hung limp and loose about her body. Could he tell she wore no corset?

She twitched her shoulders, impatient with her own foolishness. She wanted to be on her way, back to the security of Pine Creek Farm, away from the man who disturbed her hard-won peace. She turned her back on him, concentrating on her business with Jed. "My supplies?"

"All loaded and ready for you, Lottie." Jed passed a handwritten account slip to her. "Thought you might be in a hurry. There's a storm brewing."

"Thanks, Jed." His unexpected thoughtfulness touched her, threatening to break through her tough facade. She glanced quickly over the list she held gripped tight between her fingers, checking the figures and totting them up in her head, keeping her focus on the details of survival. "Still no nails?"

"Nope." Jed shook his head. "My stock's running low on other things too." He waved to a half-empty table. "Not many shirts left or boots. The supply wagon from Vancouver should've been here a week ago but . . ." He raised his hands, palms upward, and shrugged expressively.

"Then we'll just have to endure without, won't we." She straightened her shoulders, as though accepting a heavy burden, and dug into the pocket of her woolen trousers for a wad of money. Peeling off a handful of bills, she pushed them across the counter. "That should settle my account, Jed. Thanks for loading up for me. You're right about the storm."

In all the time she'd talked to Jed, she'd been uncomfortably aware of the stranger behind her. He was beyond her vision but she could sense his eyes upon her. He had a right to be curious, she supposed, in light of her ridiculous swoon when they had collided in the doorway.

She risked a second glance behind her and saw him leaning against the doorjamb, surveying the half-empty shelves of Barclay's Mercantile. His hat was pulled low, but not enough to hide the brilliant blue of his eyes. She caught her breath and abruptly dropped her glance. A stubble of beard didn't hide the too-thin cheeks, hollow under high cheekbones. His clothes hung loosely on his tall frame. His boots were worn down at the heels and curled up at the toes. He looked hungry.

Pity prompted her to offer him a meal, but she quickly subdued the impulse. Prospect had seen thousands of strangers from every land and clime, all with their heads stuffed full of dreams, and their pockets lined with nothing but hope. One more blue-eyed Irishman heading for the gold fields was no concern of hers.

Raising her eyes to study his face once more, she caught his eye. Heat flared in her cheeks as he boldly returned her stare. With a defiant lift to her chin she challenged him with her eyes for a full minute but he didn't flinch. Flustered, she turned on her heel, all thoughts of pity vanquished by the proud light in the Irishman's eye.

"I'll be on my way then, Jed." She strode out the side door of the Mercantile, stepped easily up into the wagon, and took the reins. She clicked her tongue and the horses moved forward. From the corner of her eye she saw the stranger come to the doorway and watch her off. Stealthily, she reached under the seat for her rifle and placed it across her lap. If he thought she was a helpless female alone in the wilderness, he was in for a surprise.

Sean watched the odd woman until she disappeared from view. She was not a sight to delight the eye, yet he had felt a spark of connection when he had touched her arm. She had felt it too, he knew. Her barley-brown eyes had flamed with light as brilliant as the sun. For a brief instant, she had gazed at him as though she glimpsed paradise. Just as quickly her eyes had darkened, the flicker of joy extinguished. The change had hurt him, made him feel guilty, even though he couldn't name his crime.

He shook his head to clear his fanciful musings. "Strange woman," he remarked to the shopkeeper.

"Crazy Lottie?" Jed bit off a plug of tobacco, rolled it around in his mouth, then squirted a stream of tobacco juice into the spittoon behind the counter. "She's a bit odd, but harmless enough."

Sean pursed his lips, recalling the haunted look in her eyes. No doubt she had known sorrow and trouble, but he had caught no glimmer of madness in her face. "Crazy?" he asked.

"That's what folks around here call her." Jed leaned a beefy forearm on the counter and continued. "Happened before my time, but the story is, Crazy Lottie was once the schoolmarm here. A fine young lady from Toronto she was then. Met a fellow, got in the family way. The chap went off prospecting and was never seen again. Story is, she got a little tetched in the head then. O' course, she had to give up schoolteaching. Couldn't have her corrupting the young 'uns. Kept pretty much to herself then, but always insisted her lover was coming home." He opened a cash drawer and counted Lottie's bills into it. "She runs Pine Creek Farm now. Her and Michael."

"Who's Michael?" The question shot out, more sharply than he'd intended.

"Her son. Must be nine, ten years old, I guess. The father never did return."

"You mean she runs a farm all alone, with only a ten-year-old boy to help?" Admiration mixed with incredulity in the question.

"Yep." Jed nodded. "Sometimes she gets help for haying and harvesting. You looking for work? She might give you a few days."

"No!" Sean rejected the suggestion almost violently. He hadn't traveled across an ocean and a continent to grub dirt on someone else's farm. He'd had enough of that in Ireland. He was here to make his fortune. There was gold in the Kootenays. Gold nuggets glistening in the streams, gold dust swirled into piles at the edges of the rivers, grains of gold buried in the sand of the creek beds. Anyone with grit and determination could become a millionaire, and Sean O'Connor had plenty of both.

"No," he repeated with more deliberation. "I'm not looking for work. I'm looking for a cousin of mine, passed through here some years ago. Name's Patrick Malone. Ever hear of him?"

"Nope"—Jed shook his head—"but I'm a bit of a newcomer. Might try the assay office."

"Been there." Sean shook his head. "No luck."

He was disappointed but he wasn't surprised. It had been ten years since Patrick had written, and the registration on his gold claim had long since lapsed. Looking for him in Prospect was like looking for a particular tree in British Columbia's vast forests. Best to get on with his own plans.

He shrugged. "Well, I guess that's that then." He picked up a set of gold scales, testing the weights in his hand. "Know how I could go about staking a claim on the Wild Horse Creek?"

"Another one, eh?" Jed chuckled to himself and chewed some more. "Afraid you're a bit late, son. Every inch of that creek has been staked long since and most of the claims is pretty well played out."

The lightly spoken words slammed into Sean's soul, freezing the breath in his throat. His mouth filled with the cold, metallic taste of dread. His stomach churned. He fought to draw breath into lungs that seemed to have closed up. Rage, raw and savage, burned in his chest. He wanted to lash out, to catch an indifferent world by the throat and shake it. His hands balled into fists, ready to fight, but there was no enemy to strike. Only smiling Jed Barclay who shrugged him off and said "too late."

Just once, he wished that famous luck of the Irish would smile on him. He might as well joust with the wind.

"There must be some place," he said, following Jed's example and leaning against the counter, trying to appear casual, trying to still the trembling in his limbs. After all his striving and sacrifice, he couldn't abandon his dream without a fight.

"Most fellows are heading out to the Big Bend now," Jed said helpfully, "up along the Columbia. They used to say it was all played out, but there's been some good pay up there lately. Better'n here anyways."

It was a chance and he clutched at it. "How far?" he asked, trying to sound nonchalant.

"A month or more if you go by horseback. But if you take a paddlewheeler up the river, you could get there in a little more'n a week. Course, it'd cost you some."

"How much?"

The answer made his heart sink. The cost of transportation and the extra supplies he'd need would stretch his hoard of cash to the utmost.

"How much for this lot?" he asked, shoving a carefully written list across the counter, and finding himself holding his breath as Jed totaled the numbers. To relieve his tension, he walked to the end of the counter and examined a small stack of buffalo robes. "Much call for these?"

"You're new to Canada, I'd say." Jed glanced up from his list.

"I was passed at Montreal," Sean growled, his hands balling into fists again as he remembered the indignity of the medical exam, remembered the poor souls who were ill and quarantined at Gros Isle. The poor beggars probably died there.

"Oh, I don't doubt that," Jed said, chewing on the end of a pencil, then using it to jot down a number on the list. "It's just you've never lived through a winter in the Rockies. It gets colder'n a witch's heart. Down to forty below some days. Cold enough to freeze your lungs. Ice in the creeks, snowdrifts as tall as a house. Whiteouts, snow blindness. A man could walk off the edge of the mountain and nobody'd ever find him."

"You figure that's what happened to Lottie's lover?" For a moment he forgot his own problems as the odd woman's haunted eyes flashed into his mind.

"Could be." Jed chewed some more on his pencil and shook his head. "Gold fever takes some men that way. They lose all sense, blundering up and down every godforsaken creek in the country, not eating, not sleeping. Ain't nobody crazier'n a man with gold fever, if you ask me."

"Surely a man would know enough to take shelter," Sean protested.

"Not them." Jed shook his head and spat again. "Ever hear of Fisherville?" He stopped adding and bit off another plug of tobacco, leaning his girth more firmly onto the counter.

"No."

"Town of about five thousand souls, just a little ways from here." He jerked his thumb vaguely toward the north. "Well, that bunch of loonies found they was sittin' on a gold vein and they burnt the whole place down. Houses, stores, church, school.

Whole town went crazy. Dug up the streets, destroyed everything. Happened about twenty years ago, and there's nothing left there now but the stove from the general store." He shook his head again and went back to his sums. "You want to be careful, young feller. Gold fever can kill you."

He pushed Sean's list back across the counter. "There you go. I got nearly everythin' you need."

Sean looked at the total and felt a sick knot in his stomach. He had been so careful. Done without, traveled steerage, even gone hungry, but it wasn't enough. His savings would buy him supplies, but not transport and not food for a four-week trek through the mountains.

He studied Jed's face, looking for guile or deceit. He was a good judge of character, separating almost intuitively the rogues and scoundrels from true men. In Jed Barclay he saw only an honest, good-hearted man who had told him God's truth and destroyed his last hope.

"What can I do without?" he asked, his pride hurting. He hated to beg. Once he'd left Ireland he'd sworn never to dip his head to any man again, and yet here he was, haggling with a stranger over a few pounds of flour.

"Nothing," Jed replied unhesitatingly. "That list of yours is already a few rations short."

"What?" He forced the word out through tightly clenched teeth.

"Forty mesh screen for one thing."

"I've got screen," he growled, his frustration growing with every minute.

"You got ten mesh," Jed agreed, "but there's been prospectors roaming over this territory for nigh on twenty years. Chances are you'll be working old diggings, taking the dust and flour instead of coarse.

Now don't get riled up," Jed interrupted himself when Sean made an impatient gesture. "There's plenty of wealth there. You just got to be patient. But make sure you stay away from China diggings. Once those fellers been over a creek, there's nothing left."

"China diggings?"

"Creeks the Chinese have worked. Those fellers is so quiet and secretive you hardly know they're here, but once they've been through a creek bed, there's not a fleck of gold left. Still, there's places they haven't been."

A tiny flame of hope flickered in Sean's black world. Patrick's claim had been in the Big Bend, and if he knew his cousin, there would still be plenty of wealth in the tailings. Patrick was a reckless, dash-away sort who hadn't the patience for fine sifting. He might even find his cousin there. He fanned the spark, feeding the flame with even the smallest slivers of faith.

"Add the fine mesh," he said, gesturing to the list still on the counter, "and take off the coffee. That get me there?"

"You go off to Big Bend with nothing more'n that and you're just begging for trouble." Jed was adamant. "Like I said, if you need money, Lottie might give you some work. There's a hailstorm brewing up or my name's not Jed Barclay. Lottie's oats is still in the field. She's been waitin' on Jack Williams and his crew to do her threshing. You take my advice, you'll go out there now, make a deal with her. She needs help, you need a grubstake."

Sean had only half listened to Jed's long speech. He'd been too busy brooding over the impossibility of getting to the gold fields. He'd been so sure

Prospect was the end of his quest. But when he heard "grubstake" he snapped into focus. "What did you say?"

"Lottie. The woman who bowled you over in the doorway. She's got a big house and a good farm, and she needs help. She's a mite particular about hired hands but if I was you, I'd get out there and ask her to take you on. Build up a decent grubstake before heading north. If you're still bent on prospectin', that is."

A weight of despair settled on Sean's shoulders, diminishing him, bending him down. Once again he was a supplicant, dependent upon the goodwill and largesse of a rich man—or, in this case, a woman, and a crazy one at that. Yet he had no choice. He slapped his hand against the counter in frustration.

"It's only for six months, lad," Jed chided him, straightening the tins of tea rattled loose by his temper.

"Sorry," Sean muttered, unclenching his fists while his belly tied itself into an even tighter knot. "How do I find her farm?"

While Jed sketched him a rough map of the way to Pine Creek Farm, Sean schooled himself to accept the unavoidable, subduing his rebellious pride. He took small comfort from Jed's repeated assurance that a delay of a few months didn't mean the end of everything.

"You'd better get a move on, if you want to beat that storm." Jed pushed the map across the counter.

"Thanks," Sean grunted. He picked up the scrap of paper, studied it for a moment and then stuffed it into his pocket. "I'll see you in the spring." He went off to retrieve his horse from the livery stable and try his chances with Lottie.

*   *   *

An hour later Sean shivered in the saddle and wished he'd expended some of his carefully hoarded dollars for a hot meal in Prospect. In the time it had taken to reach here, the temperature had dropped at least ten degrees. He crested the top of a rise and reined in his horse to take his bearings.

He gazed down at the homestead spread out below him, Pine Creek Farm, if he'd read Jed's map correctly. Beneath the roiling clouds the valley looked unnaturally peaceful. A big, rambling house with garden and orchard, barns and outbuildings, cattle dotting the pastures. Fertile soil and a creek to guarantee water. Just the sort of place many a man dreamed of. But not him.

He fingered the empty poke in his pocket. Gold. That's where his hope lay. Enough gold to buy luxury and ease and security. If hard work and perseverance meant anything, he'd fill that pouch and more besides. He'd be as rich as any of the strutting English lords who turned up their noses at their poor Irish tenants.

A rumble of thunder brought his attention sharply back to the scene before him. He looked again at the pastoral landscape and saw a team of horses with a wagon, plodding around a field of grain. A black and white dog loped along beside. Lottie and a boy were forking stooks onto the wagon but it was slow work. If they were going to beat the storm, they needed help. Digging in his heels, he urged his horse forward at a canter.

He was within shouting distance of the wagon when Lottie dropped her pitchfork, dragged a rifle from the grain rack, and leveled it at his heart.

"Stop right there!" she hollered, sighting down the barrel.

Surprise made him pull so sharply on the reins,
his horse reared and nearly threw him. "Whoa,
easy girl," he muttered to the mare, squeezing his
knees tight and slacking off on the bit. He held his
mount in check with one hand while he raised the
other in a gesture of surrender. He didn't much
like having a gun pointed at him, but he had to admire the grit of the woman holding it. Her fiercely
protective attitude toward what was hers found an
echo in his own soul. If ever he came across the good-
for-nothing snake who had deserted her, he'd enjoy
handing him a beating he wouldn't soon forget.

"Could you point that thing somewhere else?"
he said, sliding out of the saddle and raising his
other hand.

The rifle didn't waver. "What do you want?" she
demanded, holding her ground, her finger curled
around the trigger.

"A job." He nodded toward the dark clouds and
the field still only half emptied of its crop. "Looks
to me like you could use a hand."

The gun wavered and he knew he'd struck the
right note. If there had been no clouds overhead,
he had no doubt she'd have sent him packing, but
her need to save her crop gave him an advantage.
She glanced toward the boy, then sighted the rifle
again.

"Who are you?"

"Name's Sean O'Connor, ma'am." He touched
a finger to his hat brim. "Newly arrived from
Ireland. Jed Barclay told me you might be looking
for help."

Lightning crackled along the ridge of the mountains, casting an eerie light over the valley. Lottie
jumped slightly, her face paling.

She's afraid of the storm, he thought, and unaccountably wanted to take her into his arms, stroke the tangled hair out of her eyes and quiet her fears. Instead, before she could regain her poise, he reached out and took the gun from her hands, tossing it onto the wagon seat.

"You drive the team," he said to the boy standing nervously beside his mother. "I'll load."

"Ma?"

Another crack of thunder split the air. The nervous horses stamped their feet and tossed their heads, rattling their bits and harnesses. "That team's set to bolt any minute," he challenged her, "best not be wasting time."

"All right," she capitulated, "for today only. I'm not making any promises."

"Fair enough." He tied his mount to the back of the wagon and bent his back to fork the first stook onto the half-full load. Inexplicably, he felt a smile pulling at his mouth. Lottie Graham was a woman to be reckoned with, but he'd won the first battle. He found himself looking forward to the war.

The sky grew blacker and a few fat drops of rain fell as they made their way around the field. From shivering with cold, Sean now felt the sweat pouring off his face and down his back as he forked sheaves onto the wagon at a killing pace. Each minute counted. Each sheaf meant food for the winter. He'd known enough of famine to treasure every kernel of grain, even if it wasn't his own. He stopped to mop the sweat out of his eyes.

Whump, whump. Two stooks landed on the wagon. He looked up to see her glaring at him, her eyes wide, hair slipping in disheveled tresses from under her hat. Dust mixed with sweat on her face gave her the look of a wild woman, but the straight line of her nose and the fine curve of her jaw signified a lady. She was a strange one, all right—part ruffian and part aristocrat. He hid a grin and bent to his task with renewed vigor, tossing stooks onto the load at a frantic rate. No woman, crazy or not, would outwork Sean O'Connor.

The sky was nearly as black as night when she yelled "That's it!" and leaped onto the wagon, snatching the reins from the boy's hands and turning her horses toward the barn. "Hyah, hyah!" she yelled, slapping the lines and urging the team into a gallop as the first hailstones struck.

Sean jumped for the back of the load and hung on as they raced hell for leather toward shelter, the dog streaking along beside them. Water and hail pelted from the sky, soaking him through to the skin in minutes, taking his breath away with its fierceness.

Rain in Ireland had been a gentle blessing from the heavens. Here the deluge streamed from the skies over Pine Creek Farm as though driven by the devil himself. Whipped by wind, studded with ice, the storm lashed between the mountain peaks, filling him with reckless exhilaration.

For the first time in his life he felt completely free. He turned his face to the sky, letting the rain strike him with all its power, taking that power for himself. He threw back his head and let out a wild whoop into the teeth of the storm, issuing his own challenge to the land as the horses pounded through the open door of the barn.

Lottie hauled on the reins and the team pulled to a halt, their heaving flanks running with sweat and water. The deafening roar of hail and rain pounded on the roof; thunder rolled down the mountains and through the valley. The horses fretted, stamping their feet. The din was magnificent.

"Yippee! We did it, Ma." The boy cheered before jumping down from the wagon and running to swing shut the barn door.

"Whoa, laddies," Lottie crooned to her horses, leaping lightly from her seat and securing the reins with a quick twist about the brake handle. "Easy now." She patted their great, broad backs, murmuring her soothing words, rubbing her hands down their foam-flecked necks.

Her soft words and gentle hands as she soothed her team held Sean in thrall. Standing perfectly still, he listened. Her voice, a pool of quiet and calm in the midst of the storm, filled him with a deep yearning. No woman had ever spoken so tenderly to him, never offered comfort or praise or love as generously as Lottie did to her horses. He had known women to tease and cajole, cry and demand, offer themselves for pleasure and scream in rebuke, but the deep tenderness he beheld in Lottie Graham was something he'd never known.

"You going to stay with us?" Michael asked.

Reluctantly, Sean turned his eyes from the mother to the son. Where Lottie was all shades of brown—golden-brown hair, barley-brown eyes, sun-browned skin—Michael was a study in contrasts: black hair, blue eyes, fair skin, cheeks flushed red from exertion and excitement—rather like Sean himself.

"Could be," he replied, sneaking a look toward the enigmatic woman who held his fate in her hands. Jed had said she was mighty choosy about her boarders. "I'm looking for a place to stay over the winter."

"There's more work in the summer," Michael pointed out, his air of maturity and ownership bringing a smile to Sean's face. Clearly the lad had inherited his mother's spirit.

"Come spring, I'm heading for the gold fields," he replied, giving the boy the courtesy of an explanation. "I'd go now, but I need to build up my grubstake."

"Gold!" Michael yelped, forgetting all about being a grown-up. "Are you a prospector? Do you have a claim? My pa's a prospector . . . at least, Ma says he is." His face fell. "He ain't been home since I was born."

"Michael, don't say ain't and come help me unhitch the team." Lottie's sharp command sliced through the dust-laden gloom of the barn.

"Let me," Sean offered, reaching to unhook the traces while Michael cast a perplexed glance toward his mother.

"No!" she blazed, interposing herself between him and Michael, as though shielding the boy from a threat. Her eyes burned with defiance. He could sense her body trembling. "Tend to your own," she all but hissed at him. "I'll look after mine."

She stood a whole head shorter than he. She was slight—no match for his larger build—and her rifle was out of reach, yet she faced him with all the fury and determination of a grizzly defending her cub. He shook his head in amazement. She was the oddest creature he'd ever met, yet he couldn't help but admire her. Whatever her peculiarities, Lottie Graham was no coward.

For a moment they faced each other, challenge and defiance in their stance. Then Sean turned away, pulling off his dripping hat and hanging it on the wagon rack. If she was too pig-headed to accept his help, she could struggle alone. In fact, he was glad she'd rebuffed him.

With quick, sure movements he stripped off the mare's saddle and blanket, dropping both over a convenient sawhorse, then stooped and picked up a handful of hay to rub down the sturdy little mount he'd bought in Gold City. She wasn't the thorough-bred he had dreamed of in Ireland, but she was tough and strong, a bit like the strange woman un-harnessing the team of Clydesdales. The type who could survive in this unforgiving land.

"There's a currycomb and brush in the tack room."

He looked up to meet Lottie's unyielding gaze. Her eyes, as they rested on his unshaven face and worn clothing, held distrust and hostility, yet warmed with gentleness and approval as she assessed his horse.

"You'd better give her a feed of hay and oats as well." She jerked her head toward the horse stalls at the stable end of the barn.

Small wonder Pine Creek Farm prospered, Sean thought, leading his horse into an empty stall, if its owner cared so diligently and passionately for all her stock.

The horse stalls were sturdy and clean, two empty ones for the team, and two others holding riding horses.

"The gray's mine." Michael had followed him. "His name's Cloud. I wanted to call him Silver, but Ma said no." He glanced over his shoulder as though making sure his mother was out of earshot. "Ma has some funny ideas sometimes."

"That a fact?" Sean slipped a rope halter over the mare's head and tied her loosely into the extra stall.

"Yeah, but she don't mean anything by it. Just, sometimes I think she misses my pa."

"What's his name?" Sean jerked his chin toward the glossy chestnut beside Cloud.

"That's Titian." Michael grimaced, drawing a smile to Sean's lips.

"You don't like it?"

"It's a dumb name for a horse," Michael declared with the same stubborn scowl Sean had seen on Lottie. "Ma used to be a schoolteacher," he added, as though that would explain her failings in horse naming.

By the time the horses were brushed down, fed and freshly bedded, the hailstones were no longer thudding against the barn roof, but the deluge of rain continued unabated.

"You told my son you were looking for a job." Lottie faced Sean across the hay manger, her features indiscernible in the shadows, but the strength of her hostility plainer than daylight.

"Yes, ma'am. I'm looking for work to keep me over the winter." He stood straight and tall, looking her in the eye. Asking for a job was not the same as begging for a hand-out.

"Then you're bound to go prospecting," she stated, her voice laced with scorn and pain. "Just like thousands of fools before you."

"There's nothing foolish about ambition," he retorted, stung by her contempt.

"You call it ambition. I call it foolishness. Chasing after gold, hoping for a miracle, expecting a fortune to just appear at your feet." She slapped her hand hard against the rough board of the manger. "You prospectors don't know anything about ambition or the hard work it takes."

"I'm a good worker," he protested hotly. "I saved your harvest. I'm stronger than you or the boy. I'm honest and decent. You've no call to insult me."

"By telling the truth?" Her lip curled in scorn. "Better men than you have disappeared into these mountains and never been seen again. I'll not have a *prospector*"—he heard the sneer in her voice—"on my farm."

"Maybe he could find my pa." Michael's voice from the shadows startled him. For a moment he had forgotten that he and Lottie were not alone in the dusty, dim interior of the stable. "Maybe if he told him he'd seen us, been here, Pa would remember and come home. Maybe he got hurt or something out there and forgot where we live. If Sean found him—"

"That's enough." Lottie rounded on her son, her voice so cold it made Sean shiver.

But the boy persisted, his voice rising in agitation. "If you asked in the gold fields, maybe someone would remember. His name's Patrick Malone."

Chapter 2

Sean stood in the open doorway watching Lottie and Michael battle their way through the rain to the house. The boy's innocent words had robbed him of his power to move. The sneaking worm who had left Lottie Graham to raise his son alone was his very own cousin, Patrick Malone.

The boy, Michael, had the look of Patrick about him, no doubt about that. The blue eyes and ink-black hair were family traits repeated over and over through the generations. He carried them himself. No wonder Lottie had looked at him as though he were a ghost. He and Patrick had often been mistaken for twins when they were boys together.

The poor woman, still believing her lover would return, had thought for one brief instant that he had. His heart clenched in pity as he recalled the joy in Lottie's face and how quickly despair had followed.

For the first time in his life he cursed Patrick. His cousin's heedless ways had brought pain and

hardship to an innocent woman and his own son.
He would have cursed the evil chance that had
brought him to Pine Creek Farm too, but he knew
from long experience that such an exercise was a
waste of energy. He gritted his teeth and accepted
the inevitable. He and Patrick might pass for twins
on the surface, but in their hearts they differed.
Light-hearted Patrick would go adventuring, but
steadfast Sean would do his duty by Lottie and
Michael.

When his flamboyant cousin had shaken the
dust of famine-stricken Ireland from his boots and
set out for adventure and prosperity, it was Sean
who'd been left with the burden of a sickly family,
weighed down with too many children and a feckless father. He'd protested but Patrick had a tongue
that could charm the angels out of heaven. "It's only
for a year," he'd said. "By then I'll be rich. We'll all
be rich. You can join me. Travel first class." He'd
allowed himself to be persuaded. Patrick had set sail,
and Sean had returned to the mean little cottage
with its leaky roof and dank walls.

A year passed and then another and another,
but no packets of gold flowed home to Ireland.
Instead, he'd watched while Patrick's mother birthed
and buried four more children before succumbing
to weariness and poverty herself. After the funeral
he'd eyed the ships, full of emigrants leaving Dublin
for the colonies. With all his heart, he'd longed to
be among them, but his cousins—Mary at sixteen
and Ryan at twelve—still needed him. When Mary
finally married and gave Ryan a home, Sean was
free at last.

He'd sold everything he owned and booked
steerage on a steamer bound for Canada and the
gold fields. In all the time he'd been waiting for

Patrick to make good on his promise, there had been but one letter. The letter that had brought him to Prospect and, in a cruel twist of fate, had blighted his hopes once more.

He looked toward the house that sheltered Lottie and Michael, and shook his head in bitter disbelief. Once again Patrick had foisted his responsibilities onto his cousin's shoulders.

His glance traveled across the rain-swept yard to the big, rambling house. A long verandah graced the front of the two-story structure. Beneath a gabled roof, gingerbread details adorned the eaves. In the fading light of evening, a lamp burned in the front window. *A fine house,* he thought, *and a good farm.* Patrick had struck it rich in British Columbia after all.

He looked behind him. The barn was sound and filled with sweet-smelling hay rising to the rafters in two mows. He pushed away from the open door and walked the length of the barn floor between the mows. At the end of the barn he found an empty granary, awaiting the threshing crew and the harvest from the sheaves now stacked between the mows. Pine Creek Farm was well prepared for winter. His anger cooled a little. Whatever else he'd done, at least Patrick had left Lottie well fixed.

He strolled back to the horse stalls, admiring the team of chestnuts, with their deep chests and powerful haunches. No doubt Patrick had chosen them, he thought with a wry smile. Beautiful horses and pretty women had been a trademark of the man who was more brother than cousin. For a brief moment he feared for his boyhood friend, then cast the thought aside. Patrick survived. He always did. No doubt he would turn up one day, full of sheepish apologies and a handful of new promises.

* * *

Inside, with one ear cocked to the storm, her nerves wound as tightly as the sheaves of grain in the barn, Lottie fed Michael his supper and left him at the kitchen table to do his lessons. She pumped water into a basin, added hot water from the kettle on the stove and set about washing up the day's dishes.

Trying to calm her overwrought emotions, she hummed softly to herself, old hymns from her days in the parsonage. "Unto the hills around do I lift up my longing eyes." She recited the words, looking through the window toward the mountains, knowing their outlines so well she could see them even in the gathering darkness. But tonight not even the mountains and the psalms could bring peace to her soul.

The trip to town had been hard enough. She hated walking down the main street of Prospect. Hers was an old scandal, but women like Mary Jane and Thelma still took delight in turning up their noses at her. And then there were the loungers outside the Gold Nugget making her feel dirty with their lewd stares and laughter.

She clenched her hands so hard a cup slipped out of her grasp and splashed soapy water as it dropped into the sink. She took a deep breath, willing herself to be calm, and fished it out of the pan again. There wasn't a merchant in town who wasn't glad to have her custom, she reminded herself, her mouth tightening in grim satisfaction. Whatever else had happened to her in these mountains, she'd survived and turned Pine Creek Farm into the most successful homestead in the territory.

She placed the last cup carefully on the drainboard, then picked up the dishpan and carried it out the kitchen door, emptying the water quickly and hurrying back inside to escape the wind and rain. But she couldn't escape the storm in her heart. Meeting with Sean O'Connor today had brought back all her memories of Patrick. Reminded her of all she had lost as though it were yesterday instead of ten years since.

She'd fled the town, hurrying back to her beloved Pine Creek Farm, seeking its safety and security. The farm was her refuge, a legacy from Patrick. Now it too had been invaded. A prospector sheltered in her barn.

"I'm done," Michael announced, pushing his books aside.

"So soon?" She sat down at the table beside him, forcing her thoughts away from Sean O'Connor. She glanced through the exercise book containing his arithmetic. "Even the long division?"

"Want to test me?" He grinned at her.

"Divide four hundred and forty-eight by thirty-two." She passed the notebook back to him and watched while he grasped his pencil and wrote down the numbers, his tongue coming out between his teeth as he wrestled with the figures.

"Fourteen," he crowed after a moment and showed her the page.

"Very good." She ruffled his hair and closed the notebook. "You pass. Here." She handed him a tea towel. "You can finish drying the dishes and put them in the cupboard."

"Aw, Ma, that's girls' work."

"And tending cattle is men's work, but I do that, so you can dry dishes."

He took the towel from her hand and slouched across the kitchen to where their few dishes waited on the drainboard. She could see the first faint glimmerings of the man he would become in the set of his shoulders. She studied her "little boy" and marveled at how fast he was growing up. His pants legs were too short. By the time he was sixteen he'd be tall and broad and handsome, drawing the girls to him as easily as flies to honey, the spitting image of his father.

She left the kitchen and walked purposefully into the parlor, moving without hesitation to the window that overlooked the orchard, drawn irresistibly to the Sweetheart Tree. Even through the curtain of rain she could see it at the end of a row of apple trees, a small, weathered bench nestled against its trunk. When Patrick had gone, she'd found her comfort there, touching her fingers to the bark where he'd carved their initials, remembering his tender words and the gentle touch of his hands.

While Michael had grown in her womb, she'd rested on the little bench, watching for Patrick and reliving the joy of their brief love affair. She'd pressed her hands to her swelling belly and waited. Patrick had promised to return after one last trip to the gold fields. He'd vowed never to leave her again. She blinked against the unexpected tears and turned her gaze to the meadows, drawing her strength from the land.

Unwillingly she returned to the kitchen, looking out the window that faced the barn. She'd told Sean O'Connor he might stay there until the rain stopped, but she wished she hadn't. Even out there, out of her sight, he was too disturbing. She turned from the window, disgusted with herself. He was nothing but a gold panner, a drifter. And yet, she'd caught a glimpse of pain in his eyes and felt pity.

"All done." Michael tossed the tea towel carelessly onto the table.

"Bedtime, then." She picked up the towel and hung it to dry over the handle of the oven. "I'll be up in a minute to hear your prayers."

"You don't need to. I'm big enough to do it myself."

"Don't you want me to tuck you in?"

"Aw, Ma. That's for babies."

"All right, then." She sighed and held out her arms. "Just give me a hug before you go up." Her son gave her an awkward pat on the shoulder, then raced up the back stairs. She heard his feet clattering down the hall to his bedroom and the slam of his door.

It was only a natural progression in his growing up, she tried to assure herself; he hadn't really turned his back on her. But she couldn't help feeling hurt. They'd been so close. A flash of lightning lit the room, and the sharp crack of thunder made her jump. She hurried to the window and looked toward the barn, peering into the darkness to discover its shape. She hated thunderstorms. The noise set her nerves on edge, but worse was the dread of a lightning strike on the buildings or stock.

The rain continued to pelt down in torrents, forming puddles on the path that led from the house to the barn. Thank God her grain was safely inside. God and Sean O'Connor, honesty forced her to admit. Without him, they'd never have made it. Was he sleeping peacefully in the soft, sweet-smelling hay, she wondered, or was he like her, awake and prowling the night, watching the storm?

She tried to shake off her heavy mood. He was warm and dry. She owed him nothing more. In fact, he should be grateful she hadn't turned him

off the place immediately when he began talking
of gold. She stalked away from the window and into
the pantry, carrying a kerosene lamp with her. She
measured out flour and yeast and water. Work, she
reminded herself, kneading vigorously at the dough,
work was her salvation. If she toiled hard enough,
pushed her muscles to the screaming point, kept her
mind numb with fatigue, then she wouldn't think,
wouldn't remember, and the stranger in her barn
would not destroy her peace.

She set the bread into pans and placed them in
the warming oven to rise. But tonight her labor
had not brought relief from her care. She could not
shut her mind to the knowledge that a prospector
lay only a few steps from her door. He'd looked so
big and sure of himself in Jed's store. He would set
off in the spring, his heart high, but like most of
the others he would return broken, weary, and more
wretchedly poor than when he began. She would not
have Michael corrupted by such as Sean O'Connor.

Lightning flashed. Thunder cracked directly overhead, rattling the windows and sending a shiver down
her already taut nerves. Were the horses frightened?
Would Sean O'Connor soothe them as Patrick had
with a word, or the touch of his hand?

Patrick. Always her thoughts returned to Patrick
Malone. She went out onto the verandah, trying to
clear her mind of such useless muddle. Even under
its covering roof she felt the lash of wind and rain.
Not the tiniest glimmer of starlight pierced the darkness. She should at least have left a lamp for the
man in her barn.

She returned to the kitchen and looked at the
pot of beef stew on the stove, filled with vegetables
from her own garden. A loaf of fresh bread rested
in the breadbox, and the pantry shelves groaned

under jars of preserves. It wouldn't hurt to at least feed him. She could take his supper to the barn.

Quickly, before she could change her mind, she filled a bowl with stew and placed it in a shallow basket. She sliced off a thick piece of bread, slathered it with butter, and added it to the basket along with a jar of raspberry jam, covering the whole with a cloth.

"I'm taking supper to Mr. O'Connor," she called up the stairs to Michael as she pulled on a coat and scarf.

"Want me to do it?" Michael, fully dressed, bounded to the top of the stairs, his eyes gleaming with excitement.

"No." Already she regretted her generous impulse. "You're supposed to be in bed," she said, and sighed when she saw the rebellious set to his mouth. "I'll only be a few minutes," she added, picking up a lighted lantern and stepping out into the storm.

The journey to the barn was a scant thirty yards, yet it seemed to take hours, turning the short distance into an ordeal as the wind whipped at her head and rain stung her eyes. The lantern swung wildly in her hand as she struggled against the elements. When at last she reached the barn, the wind blew so strongly she had to put down the basket and lamp and use both hands to wrestle the door open a crack. But once opened, the wind whipped the handle from her grasp, slamming the door wide against the wall, allowing the storm to gust inside.

Scrambling to hold the door and the dinner and the lantern, she was knocked off balance when a stronger gust of wind snatched the door from her grasp and slammed it against her. She was sent sprawling to the ground. The lantern, torn from her hand, crashed to the floor. The wooden bung she'd used to replace a lost screw cap bounced loose, spilling oil and flame onto the dry wooden boards.

In seconds she was living the farmer's worst nightmare: fire in the barn. With a choking sob she threw herself onto the flames, beating at them with her hands, trying to smother them with her body. She felt the heat stinging her flesh, smelled the charred wool of her garments, heard the ominous snap and crackle as wisps of dry straw caught fire. In a frenzy she whipped off her coat and used it to beat back the flames. She must keep them out of the hayloft, must keep her horses safe, must save her harvest from the consequences of her own carelessness.

She heard the horses whicker and stamp their feet, already sensing danger. Rain poured down outside, soaking everything in sight, but inside the barn all was snug and dry a tinderbox and she had struck the match. Sobbing and panting, she battled the fire, throwing every ounce of her strength into the task, but the kerosene flowed easily along the uneven floorboards, running down into every crevice, setting a new flame for every one she smothered.

Her hands were so raw she could barely hold the heavy coat, and still new flames flickered around her. The fire was gaining ground. She would lose everything. Everything she had worked for. Everything she had so carefully built in memory of Patrick and as an inheritance for her son. All of it, her life's work, would disappear in one catastrophic inferno.

She couldn't bear it. She could not withstand another tragedy. She sank to her knees as the fire burned toward her.

"Patrick!" His name rose on her lips in a desperate cry. How could he have left her alone so long?

Left her to face hardship and sorrow and now death, alone.

"Lottie!" Strong hands grasped her shoulders, pulling her back from the fire, forcing her away from the heat. "Run, girl; get away from here." Sean O'Connor was there, beating the flames with wet sacks. He had taken off his shirt and she saw his naked torso running with water and sweat. The flickering light sent macabre shadows dancing along his arms and shoulders, picking out the play of his muscles as he pounded at the fire like a demon. Helping her, supporting her, an ally. She was not alone.

Her panic subsided, and she was able to think and move once more. Seizing more sacking, she ran to the other end of the stable and out into the rain, soaking the burlap in muddy puddles, then ran back again, handing fresh supplies to Sean. Together they battled the fire, pitting all their strength against it.

"Latch the door!" Sean shouted, as the wind rattled it on its hinges. "Don't let the wind blow into the loft!"

Heedless of the flames that licked about her feet, she dashed to the hayloft door, using all her strength to drag the sliding bolt into its locked position; then, carrying the used sacking, she sprinted once more for the horse stalls. She dashed out into the rain, welcoming its cooling deluge, soaked the sacking again, and raced back to Sean in time to see him smother the last of the flames.

The fire had flared and died in only minutes, yet for Lottie it had seemed a lifetime. Faint with relief, her knees buckled and she sank into a trembling heap on the floor. Tears started from her eyes and poured down her face unchecked. Gently, Sean took the wet sacks from her hands and laid them over the still smoldering embers.

Then he knelt beside her, whispering, "Sh, sh, it's all over now."

She felt a fool, ashamed of her weakness, despising herself for breaking down before this outsider. And yet, was he truly a stranger? From the beginning she had felt a kinship with him, a soul-deep connection, as though they had shared a lifetime of pain and sorrow. Did that explain her almost uncontrollable desire to throw herself against the bulwark of his chest and sob out her grief and terror? Appalled at herself, she raised her hands to cover her face, to hide herself from his probing yet tender gaze.

"Ah!" she gasped, snatching her hands away from contact with her face, holding them out before her, agonized by the pain.

"Let me see," Sean commanded, taking her by the wrists, turning her hands palm up. "It's too dark," he muttered. "We'll have to get you to the house. Can you stand?"

She nodded, so shocked by pain and the touch of his hands she couldn't speak. But her tears stopped and she struggled to her feet, aided by his arm about her waist.

She should protest, she thought, explain to this interloper that she could manage alone, remind him that he was to be off the place by morning. But she was powerless in the face of his kindness. His strength, so much greater than hers, overwhelmed her defenses, sapped her determination and bade her surrender her will to his. Meekly, she obeyed.

Once inside the house, Sean's quick glance took in Lottie's home. The kitchen held a fine black cookstove complete with warming oven and reservoir. A scrubbed wooden table sat in the middle of a plank floor, surrounded by chairs on three sides and a long bench on the fourth. A hand pump by the sink struck him as a rare convenience, and a jar full of autumn flowers on the windowsill opened his eyes wide. For all the difficulty of her life, it seemed Lottie still treasured beauty.

Through the doorway on the far side of the room, he caught a glimpse of the parlor. From where he stood he could see rows and rows of books, extending beyond his vision. A whole wall of shelves was weighted down with handsome, leather-bound volumes, their spines gleaming with gilt letters.

He felt Lottie shiver and quickly drew her to the table, pressed her into a chair, and brought a lighted lamp closer. "Dear God," he muttered, examining her burns, taking exquisite care not to cause her more pain. "Is there a doctor in Prospect?"

"No," she whispered, glad to discover she could speak, though she still seemed trapped in a gauzy, fog-shrouded world where the only reality was Sean's touch and his voice and the solid strength of his presence.

"These burns must be tended," he insisted.

"Ma?" Michael called from the top of the stairs. "Ma, are you all right?"

The spell was broken. She felt the searing pain of her hands but she would not let Michael know of it. "Of course," she called back, rising to her feet, putting the kitchen table between herself and the seductive presence of Sean O'Connor. "Go to sleep, Michael. You've school in the morning."

"Aren't you coming up?"

"Later. Say your prayers and turn out your lamp."

The effort to speak normally cost her dearly. When the door to Michael's room clicked shut, she sank back into her chair, fighting the faintness that brought a sheen of sweat to her lip.

"Daft woman," Sean muttered, bringing her a glass of water.

"Haven't you heard?" she whispered. "I'm crazy."

"Love turns us all to fools," he replied, holding the water to her lips. "I don't pay much heed to gossip." When she had finished drinking, he put the empty glass on the table. "Your hands must be cleaned and dressed," he said. "If there's no doctor, I'll have to do it. Where do you keep your medicine chest?"

Too exhausted to argue, she nodded toward the pantry. "In there," she said. "There are bandages and an ointment Sadie Gardener gave me."

It took only minutes for Sean to find the necessary items and return to the table with them. "I'm afraid this will hurt," he said, his mouth compressed in a tight line.

His hands were calloused and rough, yet his touch was as gentle as a mother's. Even so, she winced as he began cleaning the deep burns on her palms. "Who's Sadie Gardener?" he asked, not raising his eyes from his task, but she could see the line about his mouth grow white.

"My only friend in Prospect," she replied, allowing his question to distract her from the pain. "She midwifed me when Michael was born. She's been here for over thirty years and knows all about home remedies."

She flinched as he applied ointment and then wrapped her right hand in cotton bandages. "That ointment," she gasped, fighting against the agony, "is made from a native Indian recipe. Sadie claims it will cure anything."

Sean grunted an inaudible reply, placed her right hand in her lap, and repeated the process with her left. By the time he had finished, she was shivering with pain and shock. She noted his hands also trembled as he replaced the salve and bandaging in the medicine chest.

Without asking, he bent, swung her up in his arms, and carried her into the sitting room, where he laid her down on a sofa. He took a knitted blanket from the back of a rocking chair and spread it over her, tucking it in well. He left her briefly, only to return with a hot water bottle that he placed against her back. "I saw it in the pantry," he explained when she raised her brows in surprise.

The whole situation was absurd, she thought, the taut muscles in her neck relaxing as warmth eased her shivering. She should be ordering him off the place, not lying like a helpless invalid, accepting his care. And yet . . . just for tonight, it felt so good to be cosseted. Just for tonight, she would allow herself to be treated like a lady.

She looked up to find him towering over her, studying her face, watching her with thoughtful eyes. She looked away from that penetrating gaze.

"Why were you in the barn tonight?" he asked at last.

It seemed a lifetime since she'd lifted a bowl of stew for the stranger in her barn. She shook her head slightly. "I was taking you some supper," she said, a bubble of hysterical laughter forming in her throat. "You didn't get it."

"No." His smile matched hers, shaky and wan and brave.

He took a step backward and collapsed into an armchair, feeling as though he'd just gone eight rounds with the Dublin Bruiser. The fire had tested his physical strength, but it was nothing compared to the emotional storm this woman raised in him with her simple kindness.

When his Aunt Bridget had taken him in—a five-year-old orphan added to a home already filled with too many children and not enough to eat—he had known hard charity, but he had never met compassion. Yet Lottie, who owed him nothing, had gone out into the storm to bring him a hot meal.

How could Patrick have been so callous? Anger at his cousin's heedless life rose in his throat like bile. He loved Patrick like a brother, but if ever he found his cousin, he would knock his teeth in for what he'd done to Lottie.

"There's bread in the pantry," Lottie broke into his black thoughts, "and butter and jam. Please, help yourself."

"Later," he said, studying her face, noting the black circles of pain beneath her eyes. "We need to talk first."

He moved to the fireplace and set a match to the logs already laid. For a long time he watched the flame, debating within himself the wisdom of confessing his relationship to Patrick. There was no question he would spend the winter at Pine Creek Farm, if for no other reason than that Patrick's son needed him. But how was he to convince Lottie? Just because he was Patrick's cousin wouldn't make him welcome in her house.

He used the poker to set a blazing log back into place, then came to kneel beside her couch. Choosing his words carefully, he laid out his argument before her. "Your hands will take weeks to heal, Lottie," he said slowly. "You're going to need help."

He saw the quick rejection flare in her eyes. "Michael can help."

"Michael is only a boy," he interrupted. "Running a farm alone is too much for him."

"I can . . ."

"No, you can't." His voice was gentle, but his words were firm as he watched her struggle against the inevitable. "You can use your hands for small things. It'll be like you're wearing a very thick mitten, but it will be weeks before you can do hard labor again." His heart wrung with pity, he pressed on, forcing her to accept the unacceptable. "You won't be able to handle a hay fork to feed your cattle when the snow covers the pastures. You can't tighten a cinch on a saddle or hitch up a team."

He held up a finger to her lips, stilling the denial that trembled there. "You know I'm right, Lottie," he said. "The truth is, you need me . . . and I need you."

He smiled a little, coaxing her to surrender, wishing he had Patrick's gift for cajolery. "How be we strike a bargain?" he said. "I'll spend the winter at Pine Creek Farm. I'll look after you and Michael, tend your stock, see that grain gets threshed, do everything that's needed until your hands are healed. Then, in the spring, you'll grubstake me for a trip to the gold fields at Big Bend."

He sat back on his heels, waiting for her response. In her eyes, he could see the struggle she waged between his logic and her own desires. She wanted to turn him away, no question. She would rather toil and suffer with her burns than accept his help.

"For Michael's sake," he urged, knowing that for Michael she would make any sacrifice.

He'd won. He could see surrender in her eyes even before she spoke. "There is one condition," she said, and he could tell from the stony set of her mouth there would be no compromise. "You will never speak to Michael about gold or prospecting."

Relieved to have won his point without the necessity of telling her he was Patrick's cousin, he readily consented. "Agreed," he said, holding out his hand to her; then, remembering, he drew it back and sketched a cross over his heart. "Cross my heart." He called up the childhood ritual and was rewarded with a faint lightening of her expression.

He debated telling her who he was but in the end decided to let it wait until morning. She'd had enough shocks for one day. He added another log to the fire and came to stand by her couch once more. "That should keep you warm."

She looked so fragile, he had to repress the urge to gather her into his arms like a child and rock her to sleep and promise her that everything would be all right in the morning. Instead, he brushed a strand of hair off her face and tucked the blanket more snugly about her shoulders.

"We'll talk more tomorrow," he promised and strode out of the room before he could make a fool of himself.

Before returning to the barn, he availed himself of her offer of food, cutting a thick slice of bread from the loaf on the pantry shelf and spooning up a bowl of stew from the pot that still simmered on the black woodstove in the large kitchen. Even if he hadn't been half starved he'd have appreciated the flavors of her cooking. Hungry as he was, the food tasted like manna from heaven.

When he stepped out into the darkness, the rain had stopped and a sliver of moon peeked from behind a cloud. The world smelled new and fresh and exciting. He straightened his shoulders and swung out briskly toward the barn. In the morning, he thought, feeling a stirring of anticipation, they would talk. Lottie could tell him about her farm. He would tell her about Patrick Malone and Sean O'Connor.

Chapter 3

Lottie heard the door close behind the stranger who was so suddenly an essential part of her life, and closed her eyes, seeking the oblivion of sleep. Yet, despite her exhaustion, she stayed wakeful, a host of conflicting emotions sweeping through her as powerful as the storm that had swept through the valley, and just as frightening.

She opened her eyes, hoping to banish the seductive sound of Sean's voice and the gentle touch of his hand. She fixed her gaze on the fire dancing in the hearth, but it set her thoughts turning again to the man who had set the match. The man who seemed to have set a match to her heart as well.

He had come into her life a stranger, and in less than a day he had invaded her home, captivated her son, and set her thoughts to wandering down forbidden paths. He was a foreigner, yet the touch of his hand, the beguiling lilt of his voice, and the firm tread of his feet all seemed familiar, as though she had known him forever.

Dismayed by the direction of her thoughts, she

closed her eyes again, determined to sleep. Tomorrow would be a hard day. She had to rest. Once she had regained her health and her spirit she could deal with Sean O'Connor. But darkness only heightened her senses. Behind her closed eyelids, she recalled the rough tenderness of his fingers as they brushed lightly over her face, lifting her tangled hair. For one heart-stopping moment, she had thought he would kiss her.

In her shocked state of mind, she had readied herself for the touch of his lips on hers, longing for the tender embrace. When he had straightened and walked away, she had felt bereft.

Now, she told herself, she was glad—glad and relieved. She felt unnaturally close to him because they had fought the fire together. Didn't soldiers in battle form instant bonds like that? What's more, his bandaging her hands had forced them into a strange sort of intimacy. Her reaction to him was nothing more than overwrought nerves.

She sighed and opened her eyes. No matter how firmly she tried to banish him from her thoughts, she could not. The fire burned brightly, warming the room, sending shadows flickering over the walls. She shivered and drew the blanket tighter. The flame that brought light and cheer to her hearth could just as quickly bring terror and destruction in her barn. Love could be like that, she thought, warm and nurturing, or wild and destructive. She shuddered and turned her head to look toward the kitchen. She wished Sean had stayed.

Despite the pain of her hands and the turmoil of her thoughts, as she lay on her couch considering the morrow, a strange peace stole over her soul. In the years since Patrick's disappearance, she had battled alone, held her head high, and made a life for herself and her son. She would do it all again in an instant.

All the same, since Sean O'Connor was here and determined to stay, she admitted to a secret relief. Another adult about the place—a man, with a man's strength and a man's toughness—would lighten her burdens. For one brief winter she would enjoy a respite. In the spring he would be gone, and her life and Michael's would continue, unchanged. And one day, Patrick would come home.

The fire died down and still sleep would not come. The room grew chill and her body became stiff and cramped on the narrow sofa. Perhaps if she were in her own bed. It was only the strangeness of her surroundings that disturbed her, calling up passions long buried under a mantle of self-control and grief.

The grandfather clock, abandoned by the remittance man who had built this house, struck three. The darkest hour of the night. Had that first owner, the younger son of an English peer, listened to the clock ticking away his hours in exile? Had he walked the floors at Pine Creek Farm in the middle of the night waiting for the message that would send him fleeing from this place she loved, eager to return home?

She sat up, irritated with herself for indulging in fanciful musings, and threw off the blanket Sean had tucked about her. Silently, she left her couch, lit a candle from the dying fire, and glided soundlessly up the stairs. She passed the door to Michael's room, then paused before a second, empty bedroom. In the morning she would prepare this one for Sean. For one winter a man with the look of Patrick would sleep in the room next to hers.

A small shudder shook her shoulders, and she

escaped gratefully into her own room at the end of the hall, the master bedroom she'd meant to share with Patrick.

Closing the door behind her, she lit her bedside candle and looked at her familiar surroundings with new eyes. Richly textured paper of roses, rioting in a mass of deep red and gold, offset by orderly dark stripes, covered the walls. The brilliant colors, once so vibrant, were now faded and dull. Worn patches showed through the paper even in the candlelight.

Like everything else at Pine Creek Farm, she had kept this room just as it had been when Patrick first brought her here, steadfastly refusing to make any changes, holding everything in trust for his return. But in the darkest hour of night, she realized, she had done them all a disservice. She had not been able to stop the march of time. Despite her efforts, change had come, and the house she had kept so carefully was now only a faded replica of a once opulent dwelling. *Like my life.*

Appalled at the unbidden thought, she set down the candle and hurried to open the door of a bedside cupboard containing a decorated box. Gently, she took out the box, cradling it in her arms because her bandaged hands were so clumsy. She sat down on the side of the bed, lifted the hinged lid and gazed hungrily at her store of memories.

The box was filled with her love letters to Patrick—ten years' worth, tied in ribbon, a bundle for every year of his absence. The first packet—thick with page after page of her love, poured out in anguished longing for the man who had captured her heart—was already yellowed, the ribbon faded and frayed. She knew each letter began with *My darling Patrick* and ended with *Your loving Lottie.* Each was a testament to her love and devotion to the only man to hold her heart.

She had begun the letters to share them with him when he came home so that he would not miss a single moment of those early days of her pregnancy and Michael's birth. As the years passed, she had continued to write, whether as a record for Patrick or as a solace to herself she could never be sure.

Succeeding bundles had grown smaller as the demands of a farm and a baby overtook her. The later letters became a kind of diary, detailing life at Pine Creek Farm, recording Michael's growing up, commenting on the changes in the town. The passionate, anguished love revealed in the early writings had been tempered by time, but she still ended each one with a prayer for Patrick's safe return.

The bundle for this year, 1886, was the thinnest. Looking at it, she felt guilty. She no longer wrote every night, spending the last minutes of her waking day with Patrick in her mind. This summer she had written only once, telling him that the hay crop was heavy and the barn floor groaned beneath its weight. Now it was harvest time and she hadn't written again.

A fierce longing gripped her heart. A longing for strong arms about her, for laughter, for shared passion, for the comfort of another. "I've not forgotten," she whispered savagely, touching her bandaged hands to the papers. "I'll never forget you, my darling."

The words were almost desperate. Her memory of the man she had loved and waited for all these years was growing dim. If she closed her eyes she could recall the essence of Patrick, his big, open heart, his lilting voice, his hearty laughter, even the smell of fresh air and excitement that always accompanied him. But she had no picture to wear in a locket about her neck, no fine painting to hang above the mantel to remind her of the exact shape of his lips, or the cast of his chin. She had lost those details somewhere in the hardships and sorrows of the past ten years.

Until today, she had even begun to forget the sparkling, irresistible blue of his eyes. Today she had seen those same eyes once more and for one breathless, heart-stopping moment she had thought her long vigil over.

It had been a fleeting moment. Almost at once she had recognized the differences. The sorrow and bitterness on Sean's face were unknown to Patrick. The blue of Sean's eyes held secrets instead of laughter. The timbre of his voice was darker, his speech more measured.

Who was he? she wondered as she replaced the letters in their box. Who was this man who had come to her rescue three times in one day? Who had challenged her and touched her and set her thoughts on paths long since forgotten?

In the morning, he had promised. In the morning they would talk. She shrugged out of the man's shirt and trousers she habitually wore, thankful not to struggle with the tiny buttons of a lady's dress. After pulling a loose nightgown over her head, she got into bed, blew out the candle, and burrowed into the pillows.

In the morning. She had no doubt Sean O'Connor would keep his promise.

"Ma?" Michael's tentative question roused her from sleep, penetrating the swirling confusion of her mind, bringing her to painful awareness. "Ma? Sean sent me to bring you breakfast."

Sean? Her sleep-drugged mind struggled with the name. *Sean!* A storm of emotion whirled through her as she came fully awake, the events of yesterday crowding her conscience. Had she really promised Sean O'Connor, a prospector, that he could winter at Pine Creek Farm?

She struggled to sit up without putting pressure on her hands. Sleep had restored the tenor of her mind. In the stern light of day, the fanciful longings and musings of the darkness scattered.

"Sean says you're staying in bed today. What's wrong?"

"Nothing," she snapped, her helplessness and Sean's presumption setting her temper on the rise. What right had he to order her to keep to her bed, make free of her kitchen, and give instruction to her son?

"I had a little accident with the lantern last night," she admitted. "I've hurt my hands, but it's nothing we can't handle." She held up her bandaged, awkward limbs. "You'll have to help me with some things for a while."

"Sean and me cooked you an egg and made toast," Michael said, presenting a carefully laden tray for her inspection. "Sean told me about your hands. He says he's going to stay and help us for a while. He said I was in charge of cooking until you're better."

In sharp contrast to his mother, Michael seemed pleased and proud to have Sean O'Connor in the house. "Are the eggs all right?" he asked anxiously as his mother made no move to eat her breakfast. "I tried to do them like you do but the yolks broke. Sean says scrambled is good, too."

"Scrambled is fine." With an effort, she took a fork into her bandaged hands and made a clumsy attempt to eat. For Michael's sake, she did her best to appear calm, to reassure him. No need frightening the boy.

She could have saved her effort. Michael was already so enthralled with their uninvited guest that he hadn't a thought to spare for the near disaster that had befallen them. Instead, he rattled on endlessly with "Sean says . . ."

She listened with only half an ear, her mind busy devising ways to manage despite her hampered hands. Much as she hated to admit it, Sean had been right when he'd declared her unfit for heavy work. She would have to struggle just to take care of her personal needs. The realization did nothing to improve her mood.

"Is Mr. O'Connor still in the house?" she finally interrupted Michael's excited chatter.

"He says to call him Sean," Michael said, glancing out the window as though searching for his new hero. "He's gone to the barn. He said he wanted to get at the chores."

"Then you can help me get dressed before you go to school."

"But Ma, Sean says . . ."

"I don't care what Sean says." Michael's chatter had exhausted what little patience she had left. "I'm getting up and I'll go downstairs and tend my own kitchen. You will go to school. Now take this tray away and go fetch my scissors."

Setting his jaw at an aggressive angle, Michael did as he was bid, returning in mulish silence clutching her sharp dressmaker's scissors.

She'd managed to get out of bed and was seated on the little stool in front of her dressing table.

She spared a brief glance at the mirror and saw herself with dark circles under her eyes, her skin so pale she looked ill, and her hair a dull, knotted mass about her face. She looked away from the mirror. "I want you to cut my hair," she said, brusquely, brushing at the tangled braid that lay over her shoulder.

In an instant, Michael's stony expression changed to shock. "You can't cut your hair off!" he exclaimed. "What if Pa comes home?"

At her son's words, pain pierced her heart. She had told Michael every detail of her time with Patrick—every look, every word—including his admiration of her glossy hair. For ten years she had lived every day of her life in anticipation of Patrick's return, and she had taught Michael to do the same. "When Patrick comes home" had become the foundation that underlay every thought and every action of their lives.

Had she been wrong? She had thought only to teach Michael to love the man who had fathered him. Now she wondered if she had robbed him of his childhood instead, destroying his joy in the present by always looking toward tomorrow.

"If he does," she said shortly, refusing to dwell on her unhappy thoughts, "he'll have to understand. Until my hands are healed, I can't brush and braid my hair, Michael. It will be easier if it's cut short." With a great effort, she controlled the tremble in her voice. "Now, go ahead."

She clamped her lips together hard when she felt Michael lift her hair. For a long moment he didn't move, but then he took a deep breath. The scissors snipped shut. The heavy braid fell into her lap. The thick tresses Patrick had loved to twine between his fingers, telling her they bound his heart to hers, were gone. She swallowed hard. She wanted to cry, for Patrick and for the girl she once had been.

"Ma?"

Gathering her resolve, she blinked her welling tears away. For Michael's sake she had to be strong. Tears were useless and nonsensical. Hair would grow back.

"Here," she said, thrusting the braid into his hands, "throw it in the stove."

She saw the storm of rebellion gathering in Michael's eyes, but he reluctantly obeyed, clumping down the stairs with heavy feet.

While he was gone, she struggled to pull on shirt and trousers despite her bandaged hands. She wriggled socks onto her toes and thrust her feet into her boots. When Michael returned, he tied the laces for her and pulled a brush through her shorn locks. Deliberately she kept her eyes averted from the mirror.

"I'll tell Sean you're up," Michael announced, whisking past her as she walked to the stairs. He dashed outside, ignoring her shouted protest.

Resigning herself to the inevitable, she went to the kitchen and filled the kettle from the pump. The action hurt her hands but she persisted, using her wrists and elbows to accomplish the task. Sliding her arm through the high hooped handle, she carried the kettle to the stove, setting it over the hottest part.

She would have her promised talk with Sean O'Connor over a cup of tea. There was much she had to tell him, particularly where Michael was concerned.

When the boy burst back into the house with Sean behind him, she was attempting to measure tea leaves into a fat, brown teapot, mistress of her domain.

"Are you wanting to martyr yourself, girl? You should be in bed still."

Even though she was prepared for him, the lilting rise and fall of Sean's cadences caught at her heart, stirring her memories. *Patrick.*

She kept her back to him, fumbling with the teapot, seeking self-control.

"Let me," he said, brusquely taking the tea caddy from her hands and measuring the leaves briskly into the pot. She stepped back, keeping a safe distance between them. Even so, she was acutely aware of his vibrant presence filling her kitchen with an unaccustomed energy. She had almost convinced herself she had imagined his tenderness of the previous night. In the light of day, she had assured herself, he would be just one more misguided miner, his heart and his head filled with nothing but a fool's dreams of gold.

She had been wrong. His eyes on hers were gentle and full of compassion. The strong, sinewy hands that guided her into a chair, close to the warmth of the kitchen stove, touched her as though she were fragile and precious.

"It's only my hands that are hurt," she protested, sinking into the chair. "There's nothing wrong with the rest of me."

"Probably not, but you've had a shock. It won't hurt you to rest a bit."

He poured the boiling water over the tea leaves and set the pot on the table to steep. "Michael and I have it all worked out," he explained casually, as though she had nothing to say in the matter. "He'll do kitchen chores and I'll do barn chores. You can supervise." He poured out a cup of tea, adding milk and sugar without asking, and set it in front of her.

"Michael goes to school," she said coldly, emphasizing each word so there could be no mistaking her meaning. She would brook no arguments on that point. Michael was *her* son. She would allow no one, however well intentioned, to interfere with her decisions where he was concerned.

"Aw, Ma, Sean says . . ."

"No." She felt the tension tightening her stomach, saw Michael's mouth set in mulish stubbornness, saw him glance at Sean for guidance.

"If your mother can do without you, you'd better go." Sean poured a second mug of tea for himself. "School is important."

Much to Lottie's chagrin, Michael stopped arguing, although his scowl remained firmly in place. Muttering under his breath, he picked up his schoolbooks, put on his coat, and went out, giving the door a resounding slam as he went.

"You'd best ease off on the rein there," Sean remarked, eyeing her over the rim of his cup, "or he'll bolt for sure."

"I can handle my own son, Mr. O'Connor, and I'll thank you not to interfere."

She saw the dull red creep up his thin cheeks, saw the glint of injured pride in his blue eyes, but she refused to back down.

"Drink your tea," was all he said. She could hear the thread of steel in his voice. "We've some talking to do."

"Yes, we do." She held herself very straight. "To begin, you'd better tell me something of yourself. Do you know anything about farming?"

"Yes," he replied, his voice carefully neutral as he put down his empty cup and refilled it, never once looking at her. "I've worked a field or two in Ireland. Not mine, of course. Belonged to some rich Englishman who never set foot on the place. My aunt's family were only tenants. It's a pity you never knew my Aunt Bridget."

"Why would I want to know your aunt?" she asked impatiently, building her resentment against him, guarding her heart from danger. "I have one hundred and sixty acres, more than a field or two. I haven't time to waste the morning listening to family reminiscences over a cup of tea."

"My aunt, God rest her soul," he continued as though she hadn't spoken, "took me in when I was orphaned. She was a hard woman but she knew her duty. Her name was Bridget Malone." At last he looked up, his eyes boring into hers, his words slow and deliberate. "Patrick Malone's mother."

For the second time in two days, Lottie's world went spinning out of control. She felt giddy and light-headed. How fortunate that she was seated and didn't need to rely on her trembling knees to keep her upright. It would have been too undignified to have collapsed onto the floor.

"It's no wonder you nearly swooned the first time you saw me," he continued as though unaware that she had nearly fainted on him a second time. "Patrick and I are very much alike."

"Yes," she murmured, staring at him like a mesmerized rabbit, unable to move, unable to think, helpless and hopeless. *Patrick's cousin. Could he take Michael away from me?*

"I'm sorry," he said.

"What?" She was so dazed she couldn't understand a simple sentence. She had to collect her scattered thoughts, had to sharpen her wits to meet this new peril.

"I'm sorry for what Patrick did to you," Sean explained slowly. "He was always heedless of others."

"Don't!" Her chin came up, and she glared at him with all the hauteur of an outraged monarch.

"Don't what?" he asked, rising and taking her cooled tea away. "Don't speak the truth? Don't admit that Patrick was charming and blithe and carefree? That he broke hearts from here to Ireland?" Bitterness tinged his voice, hardened the line of his jaw. Bitterness and anger.

She couldn't allow him to speak so of her beloved. "Patrick loved me!" she cried, clinging to the one constant in her life.

"Of course he did," Sean replied, more gently this time, his eyes on hers, full of pity. "Drink your tea, Lottie," he said, placing a fresh cup before her. "You need its strength." He waited, matching his will to hers.

At last, unable to withstand his determined gaze, she grasped the cup with both her bandaged hands and raised it to her lips. She would give in on the small things. On the big things there would be no surrender.

"I don't doubt Patrick loved you, girl," he said, sitting down opposite her again, the rigid line of his lips softening with understanding, "but he was wrong to promise to wed you and then leave you."

"He promised he would come back." Even in her own ears, her excuses sounded weak, the unreasoning complaint of a petulant child insisting on a treat. Not the image of the strong, competent, solitary woman she wished to portray.

"He made other promises," Sean said, his voice hardening. "He said gold would fill his pockets and flow home to Ireland. Enough gold to buy food and shoes and decent clothes. Gold to bring his mother and sisters and brothers and even me to this new country. If only I would stay behind a little while. Your precious Patrick promised he would make us all rich." He banged his fist on the table in frustrated rage. "His mother died waiting for him to keep that promise."

"Don't," she said again, shaking her head helplessly. She couldn't bear to hear cruel words about Patrick.

For herself, she could withstand any sorrow, any hardship, but Patrick's memory must be kept pure. She'd built her life on the strength of their few brief weeks together. The memory of his love had sustained her. If she once allowed herself to doubt, to condemn, then she would have to admit she had wasted ten years of her life. For Michael's sake, for Patrick's, and even for her own, she couldn't let that happen.

"Patrick would not betray me," she said, a thread of steel underlying her words. "I am sorry his mother could not wait for him. I'm sorry if you think he's done you harm, but I know Patrick would not betray me. Something has happened to delay his return, that's all. He will come back."

She glared at him, defiant, refusing to cringe before the disbelief and pity and, finally, resignation that she saw in Sean O'Connor's eyes. Her gaze, holding his, remained defiant, proud, resolute and undaunted.

For one long, tense moment she thought he would argue with her, try to persuade her, add more hateful words about her beloved Patrick. In the end he merely shrugged and turned his eyes to gaze out the window.

"Then I'd best be getting back to work." He rose and headed for the door. "The horse stalls need cleaning. We'd better send word with Michael tomorrow to delay the threshing crew for another few weeks, until you're strong enough to handle the cooking."

She nodded her assent, holding herself stiff and unyielding in her chair. When the door slammed behind him she slumped forward, exhausted by the effort of confrontation. By no means was the war over yet, she knew. Sean may have conceded this one battle to her, but even on such short acquaintance she felt certain he was not a man to be turned from his purpose. If he meant to challenge her for Michael's affection and loyalty, he would not be turned aside.

She wished she had the courage to order him off the place, to send him out of her life and Michael's before it was too late. Instinctively she knew that he posed a danger. She would never know peace of mind so long as Sean O'Connor lived at Pine Creek Farm. But much as she hated to admit her weakness, she knew that, until her hands were healed, she needed him.

Sean stabbed the pitchfork into the pile of horse manure, leaned down on the handle, and lifted. With a grunt he loaded the stinking pile onto Lottie's old wheelbarrow.

Shoveling horse shit. Was this where all his fine dreams had led him? God, he hated dirt. All his life he'd grubbed and sweated in the dirt of his native soil, and what had it got him? Nothing. When at last he had escaped the bondage of family and obligation, all that his years of labor had afforded him was a steerage class ticket on a ship bound for Canada.

For fifteen miserable days he had been confined to the dark, stinking hold of a ship, surrounded by sick and suffering and filthy humanity. Crowded in like cattle with a hundred other miserable, desperate souls, he had endured, maintaining his sanity with the dream of the gold fields and riches.

He had thought he would go mad when one poor woman gave birth in that hellhole and still the crew would not allow her on deck to breathe clean air. The wee, sickly mite she bore died before he was two days old, the body slipped into the sea by an indifferent priest and a harried sailor.

The young mother, weak and sorrowing, had been detained at Gros Isle, her pitiful bundle of clothing and bedding spread out on the grass and rocks, exposing her poverty and vulnerability to the prying, callous view of Canadian health inspectors. She had probably died there, he thought, confined in a wooden quarantine shed, lumped in with cholera and smallpox victims.

Well, Sean O'Connor was through with filth and poverty. He was bound for the gold fields. Let Patrick shoulder his own responsibilities this time. He needn't feel an obligation to poor, deluded Lottie Graham, content to work her life away on a farm with nothing but toil and fear and an empty promise to keep her company. Besides, she'd made it clear she didn't want his help.

He pictured her sitting there all defiant and regal despite having her hair chopped off like a scarecrow, her hands blistered and burned, her son pulling at the apron strings she'd wrapped so snugly about him. Despite all that, she had refused to hear ill of Patrick. He kicked viciously at a pile of dirty straw. What had his cousin ever done to deserve such loyalty, such love?

Patrick looked on life as an adventure. Nothing was serious to him. He would smile and beguile a woman, then abandon her for another without an instant's compunction. Sean had seen it often enough. Patrick would clasp a pretty colleen about the waist, whisper in her ear, dance her around the room. Of course, she hoped to be his forever, pining after his handsome face while he passed on to the next who took his fancy.

He, Sean, hadn't that gift. His words were slower, his laughter buried beneath the burden of responsibility that weighed upon his shoulders. For him, life was no laughing escapade, but a serious undertaking to be carefully considered and attacked with resolution and determination. His handsome face attracted the girls as easily as Patrick's, but they didn't fall in love with the serious cousin.

He lifted the fork again and used the weight of its load to work off his irritation. If any woman had loved him with such unswerving devotion, he'd have done better by her than Patrick had by Lottie.

He finished loading the wheelbarrow, dropped his fork, and hoisted the handles, trundling the load out to the pile behind the barn. Tipping the barrow over, he added its malodorous contents to the pile, which was steaming in the cold morning air. He lifted his hat, dragged an arm across his sweating brow, and replaced the broad-brimmed hat firmly on his hair.

His eyes lifted to scan the line of mountains serrating the horizon, gathering dull, metal-gray clouds along their peaks. There was winter in those clouds.

He looked out over the fertile fields of Pine Creek Farm and felt a rush of satisfaction, knowing the harvest was safely stored in the barn. When the snow came, they would be ready. Lottie would have an easy season this year; he would see to that.

But come spring, he vowed, he would be on his

way. Lottie and Michael were Patrick's responsibility, not his. He'd sacrificed his dreams to take up
Patrick's duties once. He wouldn't do it again. He
ignored the twinge of his conscience. Lottie had
made it abundantly clear that the sooner he was
gone, off her farm and out of her life, the happier
she'd be. If the woman hadn't the sense to appre-
ciate his help, he wasn't about to argue.

He looked toward the house, his eyes ranging
over the empty verandah and along the garden
until they found what he sought. Lottie, sitting on
a worn wooden bench beneath a bare-branched
apple tree, her face turned toward the western
horizon. *Waiting,* he thought, *wasting her life away
waiting instead of living.* He turned away, a peculiar
ache in his heart. He vented his frustration with a
stream of invective, but whether he cursed Patrick
for abandoning her, or Lottie for her stubborn
pride, or himself for caring, he couldn't be sure.

"I'll be able to do more work soon," Lottie said a
week later as they sat at the kitchen table, the two of
them enclosed in the pool of light from the oil lamp.
"You don't need to make the bandages so thick."

"You want to risk an infection?" His head was bent
over her hands, intent, concentrated, and shockingly
intimate. She turned her eyes away, unwilling to acknowledge his nearness, staring hard at the ging-
ham curtains in the window and trying to remember
what her life had been like before Sean O'Connor
had come, uninvited, onto the scene.

Had it only been seven days? Seven days in which
all her old ways were turned upside down and a new
life was thrust upon her? It seemed as though he
had been part of her life forever.

Each evening since the fire, he had removed the bandages from her burned hands, cleaned the weeping skin, applied fresh ointment, and rewrapped her hands in fresh linen. It was a rite that bound them together in a unique way, alone with each other, touching, the everyday world shut out. If it weren't for the pain, she could almost see their nightly ritual as a lovers' dance, exclusive to the two of them. She bit her lip as he washed the deepest of her burns.

"You're running low on this salve," Sean said.

"I'll ask Michael to call on Sadie Gardener tomorrow on his way home from school," she said, her voice trembling and breathy.

He glanced up sharply from his task, his eyes dark with sympathy. "I'm sorry," he said gruffly.

She nodded briefly, gritting her teeth against the need to cry out. He returned to the tedious work of swabbing the raw, blistered skin of her palms. The backs of her hands had escaped with only light burns and were healing well but her palms had been badly damaged. Despite her brave words, it would be some time yet before she could do hard work. The enforced idleness chafed at her almost as much as her burns.

She scowled at Sean's dark head bent over her hands and was surprised by an onslaught of breathlessness that had nothing to do with the pain of her burns and everything to do with the gentleness of his touch. Averting her eyes, she assured herself that her reaction was caused only by his resemblance to Patrick. She couldn't possibly be attracted to Sean O'Connor, or any other man for that matter. Patrick had been her one true love. She wouldn't risk her heart or her independence again.

Her gaze wandered back to Sean, studying him,

trying to fathom what drove him. "Why did you stay behind when Patrick came to Canada?" She blurted out the question that had teased her this past week.

"I was needed at home." His voice was gravelly. He didn't raise his eyes from his task.

"To work that field for your Aunt Bridget? I thought you said you had ambition." She couldn't resist goading him, building her defenses against the attraction she felt for him.

This time he did look at her, his eyes like chips of blue ice. "Duty trumps ambition," was all he said, making her feel ashamed.

"If I offered you a grubstake now, would you go?" She couldn't stop probing the wound.

He sat very still for a long moment. She saw the longing in his eyes and held her breath, but his answer was unequivocal. "No." He bent his head and applied ointment to her hand.

"But you want to go."

"Yes." He didn't look up at her again.

While he wrapped the bandage over her palm, she acknowledged a grudging gratitude that loyalty and duty bound him to Pine Creek Farm, at least for now. Would he ever know contentment, she wondered, or would he always be torn between duty and longing, between the going and the staying?

In the short time she had known him she'd learned that, physically, Sean's resemblance to Patrick was uncanny. The way his blue-black hair curled onto his collar was identical. Watching him cross the barnyard with long, purposeful strides was like watching Patrick returned from the wilderness. But the resemblance was superficial. There was a depth to Sean, compounded of sorrow and hardship and determination that Patrick had never had.

Patrick was light and laughter, a brook burbling

and sparkling clear as it raced over polished stones, rushing headlong toward the future. Sean was deep and dark, a river flowing relentlessly along its chosen course, hiding secret, powerful currents beneath its calm surface. A part of her wanted to know those secrets; another part shied away, fearing what she might discover.

"Tell me about Pine Creek Farm." The question interrupted her reverie.

"It's the best farm in the district," she said, sitting up a little taller, holding her head proudly.

"The best?" She could hear the teasing lilt in his voice, but rose to his bait anyway.

"The best," she said unequivocally. "That big, flat field down by the creek"—she jerked her chin to indicate the direction—"produces more hay per acre than any other around. I get top price for my cattle because they're bigger and heavier than the competition."

"Michael says your friend, Sadie Gardener, makes better strawberry jam?" He slanted her a slow smile.

"The strawberries grow wild. It has nothing to do with the fertility of the land. Besides, I'm the only one in the valley who can grow russet apples."

"And what's so special about russets?"

"They were in that pie you ate two helpings of at supper."

"Well now, that was a mighty fine pie." She felt a tiny glow of pleasure at his compliment. "I'll concede russet apples are worth boasting about."

"Next year, I'm going to try growing that Red Fife wheat they're using on the Prairies now. There was a report in the *New Farmer Magazine* that it doesn't rust. Can you imagine what that means? Our harvest could double. Pine Creek is the best farm in the Kootenays now and it's going to get better."

She tossed her head slightly, daring him to contradict her, ready to defend her land as fiercely as she defended her love for Patrick.

But her battle readiness was wasted because he only gazed at her in astonishment. "You speak of the land the way a mother speaks of her child," he said, shaking his head slowly, "with love and pride and gentleness and hope all mixed together." He shrugged as though unable to fathom such emotions. "Your heart is too bound up in this place, Lottie girl."

"What do you mean by that?" She heard the implied criticism.

"Nothing"—he met her angry gaze steadily—"if you don't mind being tied down."

"Tied down, in your terms, maybe," she said, squaring her shoulders and sitting as straight as the lady she'd been schooled to be. "In my terms, Pine Creek Farm feeds and protects both me and mine. That's a blessing, not a burden."

"It's all in the way you look at it then," he said quietly, unrolling a length of bandage and snipping it off with the scissors. "Still, I get the feeling there's something special to you about Pine Creek Farm, apart from its excellent crops."

A small gasp escaped her. How had this man, this stranger, seen into her heart so easily?

"I'm right, aren't I?" he pressed her, beginning the tedious task of wrapping the gauze about her hand from wrist to fingertips.

"Yes," she admitted softly, her eyes stinging with tears. "It's more than just a farm. It was Patrick's gift to me."

"A gift that ties you to drudgery?" His eyes challenged her even as his hands continued to comfort.

"A gift of freedom," she flashed. "Here, in the

wilderness, I'm mistress of my own domain in a way I never could be in the city. I can walk or run or ride on my own acres anytime I please. The work is hard, yes, but the reward is abundance." She threw up her chin, defying him to contradict her. "I'll grow richer on Pine Creek Farm than many a poor miner grubbing along the banks of the gold creeks."

"Give it up, my girl." Sean put the gauze and ointment back into their box, before looking her full in the face. "You'll not persuade me to give up prospecting. I plan to strike it rich. Then I'll move to New York City and live the life of Reilly. You'll not catch me working my life away on a farm."

"You'd rather lose it falling into a river or freezing to death on a mountainside?"

"Is that what you think happened to Patrick?"

A dreadful silence filled the room, heavy and dark with menace, crowding in from the corners, diminishing the puddle of light from the oil lamp. They sat facing each other, perfectly still, her bandaged hand clasped in both of his. Stormy brown eyes challenged blue, hers sharp with defiance, his dark with compassion, the only sound a spatter of rain hitting the windows.

For one awful, long moment she didn't answer. Couldn't answer. Grief filled her mouth. She couldn't bear to live if Patrick were dead. She hated Sean O'Connor for tricking her into confessing her doubts. Anger flickered in her heart and she fanned the flames, encouraging it to grow, allowing it to replace the grief. Whatever others believed, she could not accept that Patrick was dead. Perhaps he was hurt or lost, but she had clung to his promise to return for so long that she didn't know any other way.

She pulled her hand away. "No!" she cried. She would not allow Sean to lead her into disloyalty. What was he but another poor immigrant dreaming of gold at the end of the rainbow? He was wrong about the gold and he was wrong about Patrick.

Sean shrugged slightly and she saw the disbelief in his face, but he allowed the matter to drop. "What happened to the farm's previous owner?" he asked instead.

"He went home to England," she explained, relieved to turn the conversation in a new direction. Her lip curled with scorn. "He was one of those impoverished younger sons who came out to Canada thinking he could live here like an English lord without doing a scrap of work himself."

A bark of derisive laughter greeted this piece of information, and she knew Sean shared her contempt for laziness.

"You saw all that finery in there"—she waved her free hand toward the sitting room—"the Axminster carpet and plush furnishings. The cupboards are filled with Spode china and Irish linens, the trappings of a rich man. You might not have noticed that first night, but there's even a pump organ."

"Never!" Sean exclaimed, pausing in his ministrations to raise disbelieving eyes. "You're pulling my leg, girl."

"Word of honor." She smiled slightly, holding up her hand as though taking an oath. "When there's time, I like to play it." She dropped her bantering tone and continued. "The Canadian West is no place for an idler, no matter how blue his blood, and our fine young gentleman didn't like hard work. When news came that his older brother had been killed and he was now the heir, he couldn't wait to shake the dust of the Rockies from his shoes and hightail it out of here like a scared jackrabbit.

"Patrick spent an entire season's findings to purchase the place as it stood. That's why he wanted to make one more trek up to the Big Bend. With the gold from one more summer, he said, we would make Pine Creek Farm the envy of the Kootenays. There was no need. We could have managed on what we had until the first crops came in, but he wouldn't listen."

She blinked rapidly at the sudden tears stinging her eyes. "He put my name on the deed as a pledge he would return." She swallowed hard. "I gave him a locket as my troth to him."

She fell silent, overcome with loneliness. It was all so long ago. Sometimes she wondered if she had dreamed that whole wonderful winter when she had been the envy of every female in Prospect. Patrick Malone had escorted her to dances at the Kootenay Club, had taken her on a sleigh ride on a moonlit winter's night, had courted and wooed her with unflagging ardor, until finally, in the spring, he had brought her here, walked with her through the neglected garden, waltzed her through the fine rooms of the house, and asked her to marry him.

Her heart had been his long since. That day she had given him her hand, and her virtue as well. Under the fragrant boughs of the Sweetheart Tree they had made love and she had thought life could hold no greater sweetness. She sighed deeply. It all seemed like an improbable dream now.

"How did you manage on your own," Sean asked, his voice deep with pity, "especially when Michael was a baby?"

"I managed," she said crisply, rejecting his sym-

pathy, shutting the door on her memories. "A farm
needs a man, so I became a man." She indicated
the men's clothing she wore, the men's boots on her
feet. "Patrick had taught me to shoot so I could hunt
and protect my herd. My hands . . ." She smiled with
sad irony. "Patrick used to say I had 'lady's hands,'
white and soft." She paused, fighting back her sorrow before saying in a hard voice, "I grew calluses
on my hands."

"Myself, I much prefer a woman to a lady." Sean
looked up suddenly. "There's character in the calluses."

For a long moment she held his gaze, unable to
look away, drowning in its swirling depths, feeling
the power go out of herself as his gaze dragged her
under.

At last she broke the contact between them, looking past him, concentrating on the shiny chrome
handles on her cookstove. "I did what was necessary," she said tonelessly. Her gaze flicked to his
for an instant and then away.

"Sean!" Michael came bounding down the stairs
and joined them at the table with his schoolbooks.
The intimate moment shattered and she was glad.

"Could you tell me about where you grew up in
Ireland? I've got to write something for a geography lesson. The teacher said we should interview
someone who'd come to Prospect from far away."

"I could tell you about Toronto," Lottie offered,
nettled that Sean had so quickly replaced her in
her son's esteem.

"Naw." Michael dismissed her suggestion without
even considering it. "I want to know about Ireland
and my pa."

"Don't say *naw*," she scolded. "Does your teacher
let you talk like that?"

"Nope," Michael said with a wide grin, his eyes dancing with mischief. *So like Patrick.*

"Mind your manners or I won't tell you anything," Sean said, reaching out to ruffle the boy's hair.

"Yes, sir." Michael sat up very straight and attempted a sober mien, but the teasing lurked just below the surface. "Please, sir, could you tell me about Ireland, sir?"

"Brat!" Sean laughed, but he relented enough to embark on a long description of the Emerald Isle. Michael listened with rapt attention; Lottie with sadness and envy.

It hurt her to see Michael so hungry for information about his father, information she could not give him. She had recounted for him every minute of the time she and Patrick had spent together, but how could those few months compete with the memories of a shared boyhood?

"Of course you'll be knowing about the 'little people,' " Sean said.

"You mean dwarfs?"

"No, lad, I mean the leprechauns." Sean dropped his voice to a mysterious whisper. "They've magical powers, you know, and if you can catch one, he'll have to give you his pot of gold. Patrick and I used to hunt for them, at the end of the rainbow or in a fairy glade."

"And you still do," Lottie said, getting up abruptly from the table. She walked away before he could reply, snatching a coat from the peg by the door and going out into the night. The brief rain had ended, and clouds scudded across the sky, carried on a sharp wind, revealing myriad twinkling stars.

By instinct her steps led her to the Sweetheart Tree and the bench beneath its spreading boughs, bare of their leaves now, but dressed with memories. She took her accustomed seat and looked toward the horizon.

The wind whistled down the mountainside. There would be snow by morning. She could see it in the clouds, feel it in the air, and sense it in the silence that lay over the land. Thank goodness the grain crop was inside the barn.

"Michael said I'd find you here." Sean's voice made her jump. His approach had been so silent in the darkness she hadn't been aware of him until he joined her on the worn old bench. She started to rise, resenting his intrusion.

"No, wait a minute." He placed a hand on her arm, pulling her back. "I'm sorry, Lottie," he said gently. "I'm sorry you've been so hurt, especially by my cousin. I'm sorry if I've upset you, but most of all, I'm sorry that Patrick has never known his son."

"That's not my fault," she flared, ready to do battle.

"No, it's not"—he soothed her ruffled feathers—"and it's not my fault either. I'm not your enemy, Lottie. I'm not trying to steal Michael from you, but he is of my blood. I care about the boy." His voice grew harsh. "It's bad enough he's never met his father, but I won't let him be scarred by your bitterness as well."

This time she did jump to her feet, rounding on him like a tigress. "What right have you to question me?" she demanded. "You come here with your pockets to let and your head stuffed full of daydreams and tell me how to raise my son? I'm his mother. I bore him and fed him and sacrificed for him. You've no right to question me."

Sean, too, stood—taller than she and more powerful. "Hush, girl," he scolded, placing his hands on her shoulders, holding her lightly, face-to-face.

In the moonlight, his expression was unreadable, but his voice held a steely purpose beneath the velvet glove of compassion. "I'm not denying all you've done, all you've accomplished here, work that no woman should be asked to do. You are magnificent, girl, but if you won't allow the boy to dream, it'll all be wasted."

She shook her head, trying to clear her thoughts, but the touch of his hands, the warm whisper of his breath on her cheek, held her in thrall. She could only stand there, helplessly, as his words seared her soul.

"Think," he said, placing his arm about her shoulders and turning her to gaze out over the moonlit fields of Pine Creek Farm. "How would you have managed alone if it hadn't been for your dream of making this place a haven for Patrick to come home to? Why do you come here, to this spot"—he touched his foot to the abandoned bench—"if not to dream? Would you deny Michael the comfort of a dream, a hope for tomorrow?"

"Of course not." She sank onto the bench again, her knees trembling, whether from anger or from the touch of Sean's arm holding her close, she couldn't say. "But he needs real dreams, not fairy dust."

"Ah, but that's where you're wrong, my girl." He settled onto the bench beside her, leaning his back against the tree trunk. "What would the world be without a little magic?"

"I won't have him mooning about the place, dreaming of a pot of gold when he should be doing chores."

"I've agreed to that," he said. "I won't tell him

tales of Bill Barker's strike in the Cariboo, or of the thousands of dollars already taken from Wild Horse Creek. But I will tell him of whimsy and magic and beauty. There's no harm in that and a great deal of good, as you well know if you think about it."

"I don't know what you mean," she said, holding herself stiffly away from the lure of his comforting arm.

"Michael says you call this the Sweetheart Tree," he said, rapping his fingers against the gnarled trunk behind them. "Why?"

"Patrick called it so," she said. "It's from an old legend. . . ." Her voice trailed off and she felt her cheeks growing hot. She was grateful for the darkness.

"An old legend?" Sean prompted.

"If you kiss your sweetheart," she explained on a sigh, "the one you're meant for, beneath the Sweetheart Tree, the story is, it will burst into bloom and your love will be true forever." She forced the words past the sudden hoarseness in her throat. "When Patrick brought me here, this tree was covered in blossom, so it became our Sweetheart Tree."

She didn't tell him that the tree had been barren of blossom and fruit ever since.

"Ah, you've a fey soul beneath your toughness, Lottie girl. No wonder Patrick loved you."

"That was a long time ago," she said harshly, rising from the bench and turning back to the house.

Chapter 4

Lottie stood in the barn watching the golden stream of grain pour from Jack Williams's threshing machine. The noise of the machinery deafened her ears, the dust from a whirlwind of straw choked her throat, and the hot smell of a coal-fired steam engine clogged her nostrils. She loved it. The blood sang in her veins as quickly as the oats streamed from the thresher. She watched the fruits of her labor pour richly into the granary and lifted her head with pride. She had done well.

"It's a good crop, Lottie," one of the men shouted over the noise.

She waved her hand in acknowledgment. The bandages were finally gone. She should be in the kitchen helping to prepare an enormous meal for the threshing gang, but she couldn't pull herself away from the sight of her harvest.

Besides, Sean had arranged with Rose, one of the Kootenay Indians who frequently crossed Pine Creek Farm, to prepare and serve the food. Rose had cooked at least ten pounds of potatoes and there were a dozen apple pies standing on the shelf in the larder. Lottie herself had placed a huge roast of her own beef in the oven early this morning. At noon the threshing crew would gather around the long table in the kitchen and eat every scrap. Every housewife in the countryside fed the threshers like heroes, but they always ate like starving rangers anyway.

She smiled to herself. Pine Creek Farm would do itself proud when the men came in today. She prided herself on the sumptuousness of her table, and she knew from the faces that appeared year after year that her bounty had not gone unnoticed.

Inevitably her eyes were drawn to Sean, forking sheaves into the great maw of the threshing machine. Despite the dusting of snow on the ground outside, he had stripped off his shirt. Sweat gleamed on his shoulders and back, making tiny rivulets in the dust that clung to his skin; muscles rippled over a well-developed chest and along sinewy arms.

It had been a mere three weeks since he had arrived in a thunderstorm, hungry, tense, and unknown. Pine Creek Farm had healed him. Now he walked with an air of confidence. Other men accepted his direction without question and Michael followed him about like an adoring puppy.

As though aware of her gaze, he looked up and caught her eye. A wide grin creased his face and he gave her a slow, deliberate wink. She felt herself blush and turned away, suddenly aware that she was a woman intruding into a man's world. She fled the dust-filled shelter of the barn and hurried back to the house. Even though her hands were not healed enough for heavy work, she could ensure the table was set, the teapots filled and the washing-up basin well supplied with towels.

Sean watched her go and his grin grew wider. He liked her blushes. Once the bandages had come off her hands, she'd trimmed her hair, shaping it so it curled softly about her face instead of sticking out all over like a broom. The result drew attention to her luminous eyes and sculpted the fine line of her jaw. Even dressed in overlarge men's clothes, Lottie was a beautiful woman. She shouldn't be hanging about with a gang of men in the barn, even if it was her own.

"A bit scrawny for my taste," sounded a leering voice at his ear, interrupting his thoughts, "but I wouldn't mind getting a leg over her just the same. All women look alike in the dark, eh?" The lewd comment was accompanied by a cackle of hoarse laughter as a thin, dark-faced man jabbed his elbow into Sean's ribs.

White-hot fury jolted through him like lightning, eclipsing his good mood. His fist shot out like a piston, connecting with bone-jarring accuracy against the man's bewhiskered jaw. The fellow sank into the straw with a faint moan, and lay still, out cold.

"What'd you do that for?" Jack Williams complained as the threshing crew stopped their work to watch. The flow of sheaves to the thresher dried up.

His face set in anger, Sean brushed through the tight circle of men who'd gathered about the two combatants. He strode to the horse trough, scooped out a bucket of icy water and tossed it over the prostrate form in the straw. His opponent awoke, spluttering and shouting. Scrambling to his feet, he lunged at Sean, only to be felled again with a sharp jab to the chin. A roar of approval went up from the bystanders and shouts of "Fight! Fight!" competed with the noise of the steam engine.

"Get out!" Sean roared, standing menacingly over the dark-faced man who, this time, had enough sense to remain on his knees. "Get off this farm and don't ever speak ill of Miss Graham again, if you know what's good for you."

The man rubbed his face, whining that Sean had broken his nose. "You're as crazy as—" he broke off and bolted for the door as Sean lunged toward him, fists at the ready.

"Anyone else?" he challenged, rounding on the group of men still standing idle by the straw stack.

"Now, now, then," Jack Williams intervened. "There's no harm done, and we've got a lot of grain to get through if we're to finish by tonight. Here, Tom." He picked up a dropped pitchfork and handed it to one of the younger men who'd been eagerly calling for a fight. "I want that stack over there all through the machine before we break for dinner."

The men drifted back to work and soon the threshing mill was running at full steam. Sean forked sheaves with a speed born of frustration and anger. How could he leave Lottie alone out here, with no man to protect her? *Damn Patrick. Damn him to hell.*

"Hey! Sean!" Michael came bounding into the granary, his face glowing with cold and excitement. "Ma says to come in and eat and then I can come and work with you."

Sean paused and mopped his face with a handkerchief. "You finish all those chores I gave you this morning?"

"Yep." Michael threw out his chest with pride. "I

fed the chickens, watered the horses, gathered the eggs, and peeled a hundred potatoes."

"Only a hundred?" Sean's tension dissipated in the face of Michael's enthusiasm.

"At least," the boy grumbled, "and I helped Rose with the beets, too. Look." He held up his hands to show the deep red stains.

"You'll live." He grinned and ruffled the boy's hair fondly before signaling to Jack Williams to shut down the threshing mill.

Under his watchful eye, the threshers trooped inside for their meal, took their places at the table, and treated Lottie with utmost respect, one young man even addressing her as "Miss Graham" as she served him his third piece of pie. The tightness eased from Sean's shoulders, and he felt a rush of pride as he looked at the homey room, the well-laden table, and Lottie presiding like a grand hostess. She was doing women's work again, her fingers plying a needle instead of a pitchfork. He felt a burst of pride and protectiveness. Before he left Pine Creek Farm, he vowed to himself, Lottie would be treated like a respectable woman.

"Did you hear about them two miners was shot up on the Wild Horse?"

The question was like setting a cat among the pigeons.

"It's them Indians," grumbled a grizzled older man. "That Chief Isadore feller, he don't know his place. I say hang any one of them that comes onto a white man's land." He banged his fist on the table, making the cutlery rattle.

A chorus of loud approval greeted his comment, shattering the peaceful mood of the dinner table. Lottie saw Rose flush darkly and her hand shook as she poured out mugs of hot tea.

"I'll do it." She took the teapot and watched as the Indian woman escaped to the shelter of the pantry. "You don't know if the Indians are responsible for the killings," she said quietly, a steely rebuke underlying her well-bred tone. "And they were here first." She moved around the table, filling mugs of tea. "The trouble only started when Judge Parker forced them off Norton's Flats. They haven't enough land to graze their cattle now."

"I heard Judge Parker lost a half dozen head last week. He's talking about sending to Fort MacLeod for a division of the Northwest Mounted Police. They'd soon teach them redskins a lesson."

She'd reached Sean at the head of the table. Her hand brushed his shoulder as she offered him more tea. He glanced up and read the message in her eyes. "Time," he said to the steam boss sitting beside him, and got to his feet.

"Time's up, boys," the threshing boss announced, taking his cue. "Thanks for the dinner, Lottie." He nodded courteously to his hostess. "We'll be finished by supper time."

"Then I'll expect you in for the evening meal before you go home."

The rest of the men took their cue and pushed back from the table. Still muttering about the troublesome Indian situation, they trooped out of the house and headed back to the barn. Michael went with them. She was tempted to call him back but, in the end, made no protest. She didn't like the wild talk about posses and hangings, but at least it would keep their minds off tales of big strikes on the gold creeks.

"You can come out now, Rose," she called as she began collecting the dirty dishes.

There was no reply. She opened the pantry door

and discovered it empty. Cold wind whistled through a small open window. She sighed and crossed the little room to close the window. She couldn't blame the girl for taking flight, she supposed, but her absence couldn't have been more inconvenient. Her hands were still too raw to subject them to hot water, and she needed clean dishes for the evening meal. Reluctantly, she drew on her coat and headed out to the barn. Michael would have to do the washing up.

Inside, the barn was dim except for one ray of sunlight, dancing with dust motes that pierced through the chinks in the rough boards. She raised a hand to shield her eyes from its bright shaft and searched for Michael. She found him, not far from Sean.

She beckoned him over to her side. She saw him speak to Sean, saw his hero nod and give him a slight push before he reluctantly came to join her. She knew she was in for an argument before she spoke.

"Aw, Ma," Michael protested hotly when she'd explained her need. "I already did all my chores. You promised I could help Sean this afternoon. I've already missed the fight."

"Fight! What fight?"

"I wasn't supposed to tell you," Michael admitted, shamefaced.

"What fight?" she persisted, enunciating each word clearly and staring hard into her son's eyes.

"Sean and one of the threshers. Sean knocked him down and told him to get out. He didn't lay a finger on Sean, though, so there's nothing to worry about."

"Why were they fighting?"

"I don't know." Michael suddenly looked guilty, brushing his toe back and forth along the floor-

boards and watching the action with intense con-
centration.

"Michael . . ." Lottie felt her patience running
out.

"Is there a problem?" Sean asked, joining them
where they stood at a little distance from the
threshing mill.

"Yeah." Michael seized on the interruption to
change the subject. "Ma says I've got to go wash dishes
since Rose took off and left them. It's not fair."

"Rose left?" He raised his eyebrows at Lottie.

"We can't blame her, I suppose, after all that
talk at dinner."

"Dumb Indian." Michael shoved his hands in his
pockets and banged a toe repeatedly against the
floorboards.

"Michael! Don't let me hear you speak like that.
I thought I'd taught you to respect the Indians in
this territory."

"It's not fair." Her son's face reddened, but he
didn't back down.

"Life's never fair." Sean lifted his hat and wiped
sweat off his forehead with the back of one hand
before replacing the battered hat. "You've just got
to make the best of it. Now, go help your mother.
The sooner you get started, the sooner you'll be
finished."

Michael opened his mouth to protest further
but Sean forestalled him. "Could be I've something
interesting to show you this evening," he said, rolling his eyes upward while a mysterious half-smile
tugged at the corner of his mouth.

"What?" Michael demanded, instantly forgetting his grievance.

"Later." Sean cast a conspiratorial glance at
Lottie. "Chores first."

Reluctantly, Michael let the matter drop and went back to the house with his mother, Duke, his dog, plodding faithfully beside him. Lottie longed to press Michael on the subject of the fight. There was certainly more to the story than he had told her but she held her tongue. He wouldn't tell her the truth anyway and would resent her questions. Her son was beginning to grow up. He desperately needed a father. She should be grateful to Sean, but she wasn't.

While Michael washed, Lottie dried. The dog stretched out in front of the stove, head on his paws, watching his young master with soulful eyes.

"I sure am glad Sean found us," Michael said, splashing soapy water onto the floor.

"I thought we did all right on our own."

"Yeah, but things are a lot better since he showed up."

"Why do you think so?" She wiped a handful of plates and set them around the table again.

"We laugh more," her son explained unexpectedly, "and I've heard you singing, even though your hands are hurt."

She was startled by his perceptiveness. "You don't resent him telling you what to do?"

"Naw." Michael drew out the word the way he'd heard the older men do. "He's shown me lots of good stuff when I'm helping him too, like how to tie a better knot and how to judge a good horse. Even Duke likes him, don't you, boy?" He raised his voice to the dog, which responded with a quick thump of his tail against the wooden floor. "Besides"—his face darkened—"it'll be good to have him around if the Indians make trouble."

Lottie could make no reply. For the first time in his life she had to acknowledge that she could not keep her son safe. For ten years she had guarded and defended her family and her property, but this year the unrest among the Indians was more manifest. Despite her brave face, she was worried. Tales of terrible massacres in the American West had drifted north across the border, filling her with foreboding.

"We've never had trouble with Indians," she said finally, wiping off the last plate, schooling herself to sound unconcerned. "If we treat them fairly, they'll not bother us." Yet in her heart she silently agreed with her son. She, too, would be glad of Sean's presence this winter.

By nightfall the threshers had finished their work. The grain crop for Pine Creek Farm was threshed and stored in the granary bins. The work crew had eaten another enormous meal and departed. The tidying up was done and Lottie felt a deep sense of peace as she settled into her rocker beside the stove with a piece of mending in her hands.

Michael and Sean sat at the table, Michael's schoolbooks spread over its surface. Usually Michael chattered like a whiskey jack while Sean listened, but tonight Michael was engrossed in something Sean was telling him.

"Right here." She looked up in time to see Sean pointing to a squiggly outline in Michael's atlas. "That's County Clare, where your pa and I grew up."

"What was it like?" Michael asked.

"Green," Sean replied, "and always the smell of peat smoke in the air."

"Do you think you'll ever go back?" She couldn't help asking.

"Never." His reply was swift and certain. "It was beautiful to look at, but a poor place to live. Nothing but sheep grazing. Patrick and I vowed to get away as soon as we could."

"How come you didn't come out together?" Michael asked, looking up from the atlas.

"Oh, there were reasons." Sean turned his head toward Lottie, his gaze locking with hers. "Duty, loyalty, responsibility."

She tossed her head and met his look with a hard stare of her own. "Sounds very virtuous and dull." She bent her head to her stitches. "I'd much rather a man had passion and a sense of adventure and humor." She jabbed her needle viciously through the heavy woolen coat and stabbed her finger as well.

"Is that what you taught the children in school?"

Heat raced to her cheeks but she refused to back down. "I taught them to love learning and to think for themselves," she said before putting her injured finger to her mouth and sucking the pain away.

"You taught arithmetic, and history, and geography too, Ma." Michael recalled her to the matter at hand. "You taught me how to read a map. Look." He dragged a creased and folded paper from under the atlas. "Bet you don't know what this is."

Reluctantly, under Sean's watchful eye, she crossed the room to gaze at the page Michael held out for her inspection. The blood drained from her face as she gazed at the crooked line denoting a creek, a pick and gold pan crudely drawn beside it. "Where did you get that?" she demanded.

"Sean gave it to me. It's a map my pa drew. See, it shows Prospect right here on the Kootenay River, and there's the Moyie. This"—he tapped his finger on the pick-and-gold pan sketch—"this is where Pa prospected on the Big Bend."

Furious, she reached out and snatched the map from under Michael's hand, ready to crush it and toss it into the hottest part of the fire.

"Ma, don't!" Michael shouted. "It's mine. Give it back." He held out his hand.

Love for her son and the painful knowledge that he had never known his father stilled her hand. With a great effort, she controlled herself. "Go and bring in some more firewood, Michael."

"Aw, Ma!"

"Now, Michael. Sean and I have something to discuss."

Heaving an exaggerated sigh, the boy closed his schoolbooks, letting each one drop with a heavy thud. The eagerness she had glimpsed in his eyes when he had shown her the map was replaced with a sullen glower. "Can I have the map back?" he asked as he pushed back his chair, making its legs shudder and scream against the bare wooden floor.

"No," she replied sharply. "Now pick up your chair and put it under the table properly."

Without another word, Michael spun on his heel and slouched from the room, leaving the chair askew in the center of the kitchen.

Sean, who had watched the spectacle without comment, rose and picked up the chair, setting it carefully and quietly in its place at the table. "I'm telling you, Lottie girl"—he resumed his seat—"you'd best ease up there or you'll have real trouble with that boy."

She rounded on him, all her pent-up feelings bursting forth in a raging torrent of words. "I'll raise my son as I see fit," she said angrily. "What right have you to come strutting into my life and telling me how to live? You've not watched as other mothers turned their backs on me, or seen Michael come home from school with a black eye and a bloody nose because some other youngster made rude remarks. How dare you question my judgment? You don't know anything."

Sean rose to his feet, towering over her, his face suffused with a rage as black as her own, yet his voice was calm. A stark contrast to her own shrill squalling.

"Perhaps it's because I don't know," he said, his hands clenched tightly across the back of the chair. "I'm an outsider, Lottie, as you've made very clear, but sometimes an outsider can see more clearly. I warn you, girl, you'll lose that boy at the rate you're going."

"We were fine until you came along." She made a valiant effort to lower her voice.

"Are you sure?"

She opened her mouth for a quick retort, then closed it again as she recollected Michael's growing petulance over the past few months. She could tell by the quick flicker of light in Sean's eyes that he had seen her hesitation.

"That is none of your business." She held out the map in a hand that shook. "We had an agreement," she said. "No talk of prospecting in front of Michael. You broke your word."

A dull flush stained his cheeks but his gaze held steady. "Turn the page over," he said, his voice cold.

She did as he bid and discovered that the map was only an afterthought; the real treasure was a letter from Patrick. The ink had faded with time but the sloping flourish of the writing still echoed her lover's dashing style. The paper had creased through years of use, yet the brightness of his personality showed clear and strong in the strokes of his pen. Tears gathered along her lashes. She blinked them back. She had cried enough.

She read the signature, *Patrick,* and felt a crippling wave of jealousy. During their courting days there had been no need for notes or letters. Patrick had filled her life with his physical presence, waiting to walk her home after school, arriving at her door with a pony saddled and ready on a Saturday morning, filling her mind and heart with the joy of first love. Now she wished desperately that she'd had a love letter from him, a love letter to prove she hadn't dreamed that whole magical time.

"I was showing the boy his father's letter." Sean stressed the last word. "He found the map on his own. And he'll find prospecting on his own if that's what he wants, no matter how hard you fight it. Gold fever's in the air he breathes, girl. You can no more keep him from it than you can bring Patrick home."

They were interrupted by a gust of cold air as Michael threw open the kitchen door, his arms full of firewood. Lottie rushed to open the lid on the woodbox and he dropped the wood inside with a clatter.

"Can I have the letter back now?" he asked, still with a belligerent scowl.

"It's my letter," Sean said harshly, taking it from Lottie's stiff fingers, folding it and stuffing it into his pocket. "Have you finished your homework?"

"Course not," Michael grumbled. "It's Friday. I've got two whole days before I have to do it."

"It wouldn't hurt you to finish your assignments ahead of time." The schoolteacher in Lottie winced at Michael's offhand attitude.

"Aw, Ma, you're such a killjoy."

"Michael!"

"None of that, now," Sean interposed. "Your ma's right. Finish your homework tonight and you can have the next two days completely free. I was thinking," he added with a conspiratorial wink at Lottie, "that now the hay's all in, the threshing's done, and the snow's not too deep, tomorrow might be a good day to do a little fishing. O' course, I'm new around here, don't know the best spots. I could do with a guide."

"I can show you." Michael's bad temper evaporated. "The best place is across the lower field, where the creek goes into the forest. About two minutes in there's this really big pine tree, and the creek has to bend, and there's a deep pool. If you want the biggest trout in the Kootenays, you'll find him in that spot."

"Would I be right in thinking you want to come, too?" Sean teased. His eyes, meeting Lottie's over the top of the boy's head, held both affection and conciliation. But even though he hadn't spoken the words aloud, she heard "I told you so" hanging in the air between them.

"You bet. We'll need bait. . . ." Michael jumped up from the table.

"Just a minute." Sean held up his hand. "What about that homework?"

"I can do it on Sunday."

"Or you could do it now and keep the Lord's Day as you ought."

"Oh, all right." Michael dropped into a chair and made a great show of spreading out his texts and notebooks and sharpening a pencil.

Lottie watched the both of them—Sean lounging back in his chair, feet stretched out toward the stove, totally at ease; Michael hunched over his books, chewing the end of his pencil—perfectly content in each other's company. With a twist of her heart she turned away, leaving the mending undone.

Slipping on a coat, she stole out of the quiet house. Solitude in the midst of trouble had been her choice for so many years, she now sought it automatically. For a moment she leaned on the verandah railing, breathing in the night, filling her lungs with clear, cold air, waiting for the peace of the mountains to fill her soul. Then she turned her steps toward the barn.

A skiff of snow covered the ground, muffling her footsteps. Frost, on tree limbs and fence posts, sparkled in the light of a crescent moon. An owl hooted faintly in the woods behind the house. Close in, she could make out the dark shapes of her cattle corralled in the barnyard, as safe from marauding wolves and Indian raiding parties as she could make them.

Once inside the now silent barn, she first checked on the horses, running a hand down their enormous withers and patting their velvety noses, murmuring soft words as she checked that their feed troughs were full and their stalls lined with clean bedding. A barn cat rubbed against her ankles and she stooped to brush a hand along its back, enjoying the sensual pleasure of soft fur and a throaty purr as the puss twisted and bumped its head against her hand. Giving the cat a final pat, she turned at last to the full granary, the real purpose of her visit.

She hung the lantern from a nail, leaned her folded arms on the high wall of the bin, and feasted her eyes on the bounteous mounds of ripe grain within. Enclosed in the small circle of light cast by the lantern, she scooped the kernels into her hands, letting them run through her fingers, as rich as liquid gold.

Better than gold, she thought, as she greedily cupped more grain into her hands. Midas, with his golden touch, had starved amid his riches, but Pine Creek Farm with its golden harvest could feed a multitude. She scooped up another handful of oats and held it aloft, letting the grains trickle through her fingers, then tossed it in the air like rice at a wedding.

"It's a good harvest." The deep voice behind her made her jump and bump her elbow against the bin wall.

She whirled to face him, embarrassed that he had caught her indulging in childish play. The memory of the angry words spoken earlier still hung between them. "What are you doing here?" She hugged her bruised elbow against her chest, shielding herself.

"Maybe the same as you." He came to stand beside her, resting his elbows on the bin, gazing at the heaped grain within. "To admire the harvest, or"—he turned his head, his face close to hers— "maybe I came to admire the farmer."

He was too close. She could feel the warmth of his body, smell the soap on his skin, see the place where he had nicked his chin with his razor. Small, intimate details she'd sought to ignore, but couldn't. Whatever her resentments, she couldn't control her response to this man. She could feel her bones melting, her resentment dissolving like a cloud of breath on a frosty morning.

His power drew her. Without her consent, her body swayed toward him, wanting to lean into him, slip her arms around his waist, feel his arm drop about her shoulders, rest her head against his broad chest. Her eyelids felt heavy as she imagined the touch of his fingers in her hair, or the light brush of his kiss across her brow.

High in the rafters a rush of wings signaled the return of a barn owl. The noise jarred her aware, breaking the spell of the lamplight and the night. She jerked herself upright, as though stung by a bee. How had she become so enthralled that she'd let this feckless prospector share her harvest ritual? This moment belonged to her alone, a time she treasured and hugged to herself. Even Michael was excluded.

Yet tonight she could not summon the resolve to turn away from Sean O'Connor. Much as she tried to whip up her resentment against him, honesty compelled her to acknowledge her debt. It was his strength and labor that had saved her harvest, his gentleness that had ministered to her burned hands, and his generosity of spirit that had accepted Michael's hero worship and provided a good example for him. This was his harvest as much as hers.

She edged slightly away, concentrating on the bins of grain. "It's a good harvest," she said stiffly, moving out of the glow of the lantern and hiding in the shadows, her heart thudding in her chest. "I have to thank you for it. Michael and I alone could not have saved all of it from the hailstorm." She sounded just as prim and stiff as a maiden schoolmarm, she thought with satisfaction. Her voice held neither warmth nor affection. They had agreed in the beginning that they were necessary to each other for one winter—that was all.

"Maybe. Maybe not." He shrugged, looking at the floor, brushing a few stray kernels of grain back and forth with his foot. "Then again, if I hadn't been here, you wouldn't have burned your hands." He shuffled his feet, staring hard at the toes of his boots. "I'm sorry, Lottie," he said at last. "I didn't mean to show the boy a gold map. It was Patrick's words I was sharing. I'm sorry if I've made trouble between you and the lad." He looked up at last, his eyes dark and unreadable in the lantern light.

All her cool reserve melted away in the face of his distress. "No." She stretched out her hand to touch his arm, her heart turning over in response to the world-weary sadness in his voice. "No," she repeated more firmly. "I won't deny I've resented you"—she took her turn at studying the floorboards—"your strength, your way with Michael. He needs a man in his life. Patrick—" she broke off, swallowing past the sudden lump in her throat.

Sean's hand came up to cover hers where it still rested on his sleeve. "Hush, girl," he murmured, stroking his thumb along her fingers. "Don't fret yourself."

"I've tried so hard," she murmured, entranced by the touch of his hand on hers, the sense of otherworldliness evoked by the nighttime hour. "I'd do anything for Michael, but I couldn't make his father real to him. You did that."

"Then I'm glad I came." His eyes locked on hers, his hand tightening on her fingers, drawing her closer.

She moved a step nearer, powerless to resist the magnetic pull of their attraction. His arms closed about her, urging her still closer, until her arms went around his neck. She arched her back, pressing her body tightly against him. She was not surprised by the hardness of his muscled body. What caught her unawares was the softness of her own.

She had done a man's work for so long, she had thought her femininity a thing of the past, yet of its own volition her body yielded to his, bending, accepting, comforting.

"Ah, darlin' girl," he whispered, his lips descending on hers, robbing her of her last rational thought.

There was such sweet tenderness in his kiss she felt tears gathering in her eyes. Yet there was an edge of mastery as well, a combination of power and hunger that left her breathless.

At last he broke the kiss but he held her still, his face buried in her hair, her cheek against his chest. She could feel his heart thudding like a hammer under her ear. "Patrick was a fool," he whispered, angling her chin up for another kiss.

She jerked away, appalled that she had let down her guard and admitted to her loneliness. For long moments they stared at each other. He with his hands stretched out to her, she with her body tense, poised on her toes like a wild animal at bay. Finally, without a word, she swung away, snatched the lantern from its hook, and ran from the barn, fleeing as if the hounds of hell were snapping at her heels.

As she went, she rubbed at her lips with the back of her hand, in a vain attempt to erase the taste of Sean's lips on hers.

Sean watched her go. It was just as well. When the time came for him to make his own foray into the gold fields, he wanted no fetters of love or duty to hold him back.

Freedom, he reminded himself, turning away from the open door and wandering back into the haymow. He had come to this wild, new country seeking riches and freedom. He was through with family ties. He admired Lottie, her courage and spunk, even her temper; die-away misses had no appeal for him. But Lottie with her outlandish clothes and even more outlandish lifestyle brought a smile to his face and a song to his heart. Kissing her had been like tasting fine wine, but he wouldn't lose sight of his goal, even for Lottie's kisses.

Chapter 5

Fleeing into the house, Lottie hurtled up the stairs and into her bedroom, slamming the door hard, as though wood and brass could lock out her demons. Leaning her back against the door, her hands behind her still grasping the handle, she drew in great, heaving breaths, trying to calm her racing heart. Her mouth burned from Sean's kiss, and she felt as though she had run miles through the mountains rather than the short, straight path between the farmhouse and the barnyard.

On trembling legs she crossed the room to her washstand, poured cold water from the ewer into the basin, bent over and splashed her face. Still the heat from Sean's kiss burned her skin. She scrubbed her mouth with her fingers, trying to erase the memory. She didn't want to love again. It hurt too much.

Desperately she whispered Patrick's name over and over, trying to bring his face before her mind's eye, using his memory as a shield against the longings stirring in her heart. But Patrick was lost in time. Sean was here and now and it was his face that filled her mind.

She took a rough towel and wiped her face again and again, leaving her lips throbbing and raw. Still she could taste Sean's mouth on hers. She threw down the towel and hurried to her bedside table, yanking open the doors and plucking the box of letters from the shelf. Feverishly she dumped them onto her bed, touching them, untying the ribbons and reading again the frenzied words of love she had poured onto the pages over the past ten years.

My darling Patrick, she read, opening the first letter.

Where are you? I miss you so. I'm writing these letters to you so that when you come home we can read them together and it will be as though we had never been apart.

There is to be a child, Patrick. Your child. I love him already and imagine him with your laughing eyes and merry spirit. Every evening I sit on that little bench, under the Sweetheart Tree—do you remember carving our names in its bark? I talk to our child there, promising him you'll be here before his birth. Make my promise come true. Let the river keep its gold, my darling. You are riches enough for me.

With tears running down her cheeks, she folded the letter, tenderly placing it aside, and picked up another. *We have a son,* she read.

Out of our love, Patrick, has come this miracle of life. A boy. He will grow tall and strong and merry like his father. Already I can see your black hair fuzzing his head.

His birth was hard, Patrick. I needed you. Why weren't you here when I was so desperately alone? I'm a disgrace, you know. None of the women in town will speak to me. But we have a son, my darling, and all else

*pales. He is beautiful and healthy and lusty. He will be a
joy to us, my love. I can't wait for you to meet him. I have
named him Michael.*

A tear dropped onto the page, blurring the ink.
Gently she blotted the stain and refolded the letter, tucking it away carefully with the others.

When she had retied all the ribbons and stowed
the box away safely in the cupboard once more, she
crossed the room to where a small desk sat against
the wall. Sitting down, she opened a drawer and
took out a sheet of writing paper. She took up her
pen and wrote *My darling Patrick,* across the page
in a flowing copperplate script, the penmanship that
had helped to earn her her place as Prospect's
schoolmistress all those years ago. She stopped
writing and lifted her head to gaze at the burgundy
striped wallpaper behind the desk, counting the
tiny flowers that marched in pairs along each gold-
edged stripe. For the first time since they had met,
she didn't know what to say to Patrick.

My darling Patrick. She read the words again, then
touched her pen to the paper and wrote from her
mind instead of from her heart.

*I am so frightened. The Indian raids have grown
more frequent, and Chief Isadore has chased away our
only constable.*

She stopped writing and lifted her head, listening to the sound of the kitchen door. Sean had
come in. She could hear his footsteps on the stairs.
Her pen faltered, but she pressed on.

*The harvest is in, Patrick, the granaries full to over-
flowing, the floors groaning under the weight of the hay.*

She paused, resting her chin in her hand. Would
she tell him that his cousin, Sean, had arrived at Pine
Creek Farm? Did she want to confide how much
Michael admired Sean? Would she tell him that as

she lay in her big, lonely bed at night with her eyes closed that it was not his face she saw in her dreams but Sean's?

She clenched her fingers around the pen so tightly that her knuckles hurt. *No!* she cried in her heart. She would not forget her first love. He had given her Michael; he had given her Pine Creek Farm. It was enough.

"Patrick," she whispered, touching her fingers to his name. "Oh, Patrick, I'm frightened."

Her only reply was the crackle of frost on the shingles and the gentle rustle of a tree branch blowing against the windowpane. With unutterable weariness, she dipped her pen in the ink and added a brief prayer for his safe return, then signed it *Your loving Lottie*. She blotted the ink and carefully folded the page, adding it to the sad little bundle for this year. Guilt piled on guilt and she crept into bed with a heavy heart.

Breakfast the next morning was a strained affair. Michael, full of excitement, forgot his manners, gobbled his food, and talked constantly with his mouth full. Lottie's reprimands went unheeded, but Sean's slightest suggestion was treated as God's own word. Lottie skirted around Sean like a shy colt, and she noticed he treated her with exaggerated politeness, taking care never to meet her eyes or carelessly allow their fingers to touch. After the easy camaraderie of the past few days, the strain was palpable. All in all, she thought, it would be a relief when she was finally left alone.

Yet, when Sean and Michael had departed, fishing rods in hand and a gargantuan lunch stowed in their packs, she found herself wandering listlessly about the house, picking up and then setting down a variety of small tasks, unable to settle, unable to quiet the thoughts that churned through her mind. It wasn't being alone that bothered her. She was used to solitude. But today she felt abandoned, left behind. Her son was entering the robust world of men and she was excluded.

She wandered into the parlor and sat down at the organ, pumping the foot pedals, playing a few notes, experimenting with stops, but her heart wasn't in the music. The sounds she made were disjointed and jangled her nerves. She gave up and closed the instrument, trailing about the room, running her hand over tables and along the bookshelves, looking for dust and finding it.

She wiped her fingers against the leg of her trousers, but instead of getting a cloth and giving the room a thorough dusting, she wandered over to the long, west-facing windows and gazed out toward the lower field. Without meaning to, she realized, she was watching for a glimpse of Sean where the creek entered the forest.

She wheeled away from the window and marched back to the kitchen. What a hopeless case she had become, waiting for a man, always waiting. She had better things to do on a fine morning than moon about, wishing for Sean O'Connor.

Setting her shoulders, she pulled on a warm coat, collected the egg basket, and went out to the henhouse. When she had scattered chicken feed she checked the nests, quickly gathering a half-dozen eggs and tucking them carefully into the padded basket. She would send a couple of dozen into Prospect with Michael on Monday morning. He could drop them by Jed Barclay's Mercantile when he rode in to school.

Unbidden, the image of the yellow silk resting on the yard goods shelves of Jed's store popped into her mind, setting off a chain of memories and a yearning for pretty things she had forgotten all about. Perhaps she would go into Prospect herself one day soon. Not to buy anything as frivolous as yellow silk, of course, but it would do no harm to look at it.

She walked through the stable, checking that the horses had water and hay, then came back to the house and made herself a solitary lunch, eating it with a book of poetry propped open on the table before her. But not even Tennyson could hold her attention today and she was soon gazing into the distance, her mind a jumble of half-formed intentions and incomplete plans.

At last she left the kitchen, leaving her used dishes on the table, and went up to her bedroom. From under the bed she hauled out a big cedar-lined trunk, hauling it into the center of the room. For a long time she simply knelt on the floor, staring at its big, brass studded handles and hinges. She had brought this trunk with her from Toronto, filled with clothes and fripperies.

After she met Patrick, she had made the trunk a hope chest, filled with items for her trousseau and fine linens for her bridal bed. When he'd failed to return, she had pushed the trunk away, out of sight, and never opened it again. She couldn't bear to see all her bright dreams reduced to a forlorn jumble of colored cloth.

She touched her fingers to the leather covering of the trunk, remembering how she used to love the feel and smell of it. The metal clasps were cold to the touch, their brass dull and darkened from neglect. She pulled the tail of her shirt from her waistband and used it to polish a circle on the clasp, bringing light and a dull glow to one small spot amid the dust and dreariness of the rest.

Like Sean, she thought, and was appalled at the direction of her musings. Yet there was no denying that Patrick's cousin had brought a gleam of light into a darkened house and her own shadowed life. No wonder Michael idolized him.

She had thought she gave the boy everything he needed, but she could see now how much he had been missing. Her narrow life with its obligation to work and duty and survival had cheated her son of play and friends. Sean had come into their strait-jacketed world and, overnight, loosened its bounds, enriching it with light and vigor. Despite her efforts to hold it still, life moved on.

Taking a deep breath, she unclipped the hasps on the trunk but didn't raise the lid. Would she find the seeds to a new life in the old chest, or merely open a Pandora's box? For long moments she knelt on the floor, her hands resting against the closed cover of the cedar chest, trying to summon the courage to look inside.

Let the past rest, safely locked away in a deep chest, hidden beneath the coverings of her bed, she argued with herself. The calluses on her hands and heart had served her well. Why tear them off now?

And yet . . . The feel of the yellow silk beneath her rough fingers had stirred such an ache of desire, a yearning for gentleness and softness and pretty things. Not that she would trade her freedom and independence for all the silk in China, but could she not have both? Could she not don her work boots and trousers, saddle her horse and ride with wild abandon across her own fields in the morning, and in the evening sit by the fire in soft skirts and dainty slippers?

She could make men's heads turn in admiration instead of ridicule.

She snatched her hands off the trunk and clasped them behind her back. She did not need or desire the attentions of men. Just because she longed to feel pretty and feminine did not mean she was setting a snare for a man, least of all Sean O'Connor.

She stood up and crossed the room to gaze at herself in the mirror on her dressing table. Her hair was growing longer. She caught it in her fingers and pulled it back, fastening it with a comb. Short tendrils escaped and curled in soft wisps along her brow and in front of her ears, giving her a wistful, gamine appearance. She pinched her cheeks, raising a soft, pink flush under the suntanned skin. She turned her head, preening and admiring herself. With a flush of pleasure and surprise, she realized she was still pretty.

Sean insisted on calling her "girl" even though she considered herself long past the age of girlhood, but as she smiled shyly at herself in the mirror she caught a glimpse of that girl. Abruptly she spun away from the mirror and flew across the room to her trunk. Without giving herself time to consider, she threw open the lid and laid her hands on a lacy blouse that lay on the surface. It was a high-necked affair that she had worn as a schoolteacher, coupled with a gray worsted skirt that fitted snugly at the waist, straight in the front and gathered in soft folds over a ruffled petticoat at the back.

She laid aside the blouse and began lifting garments from the chest with eager hands. Dresses, jackets, more blouses, nightdresses, petticoats and corsets, ribbons and gloves—all swirled from the chest in a glorious array of color and texture. They scattered on the bed, the floor, and the dresser, or hung gaily from the door hooks.

She twirled about the room, giddy with excitement, reveling in the finery she'd denied herself. She snuck a peek through the window to assure herself that the sun was still high in the sky. Sean and Michael would not be back for hours yet. Then, throwing aside years of discipline, she abandoned all thought of the work that awaited her and gave herself over to indulgence.

She hurried downstairs and dragged a tin bath from the back of the larder and set it up beside the stove, then raced upstairs again to collect soap and towels. Back in the kitchen she filled the tub with hot water from the reservoir on the stove. Then she locked the doors and pulled off her heavy plaid shirt, vest, trousers, long johns, and thick socks.

She looked down at herself, studying her naked body in the full light of day, something she'd not done in a very long time. Her breasts were well formed and firm. Her stomach was flat, her legs lean and strong from the years of hard work. A vee of darker skin at her throat showed where the summer sun had touched her, but the rest of her skin was pale as cream. She wasn't eighteen anymore and she'd borne a child, yet she wasn't ashamed of her woman's body. She could please a man if she'd a mind to. The thought made her blush. She stepped hastily into the bath, pulling her knees up and sliding down as far as she could, hiding herself beneath the water.

She scrubbed herself thoroughly and washed her

hair. Then she stepped out of the tub, wrapped herself in towels and fetched a jar of vinegar from the pantry. Before emptying the tub she gave her hair a vinegar rinse to bring out its shine.

Back in her bedroom she searched the deep recesses of the cedar chest until she unearthed a tin of talcum powder and a puff. She fluffed herself all over with the sweet smelling powder. Then she pulled on drawers, stockings, a chemise and, finally, a boned corset.

Grasping the ties in both hands she pulled hard, lacing her figure into the fashionable shape of a tiny waist, high breasts, and curving hips. She grimaced slightly as the garment pinched her ribs and constricted her breathing. No wonder she'd given them up. She could never have forked hay or walked hour after hour behind the horses in such restrictive garments, but when she caught sight of herself in the mirror, all such mundane concerns faded away. She gazed at herself in astonished pleasure.

She looked like a woman, a pretty woman, with enticing curves and sensuous movements. Her breasts rose in creamy mounds above the tight lacings of the corset. Her neck looked graceful and vulnerable under the curling tendrils of her hair. She twisted about, looking at herself over her shoulder, and blushed bright red at the wanton woman who fluttered her lashes and cast a shy invitation over an exposed shoulder.

Quickly she turned away from the mirror, her hands fumbling with the strings of her corset, but her fingers stilled as she caught sight of a silk evening gown in French blue, tossed like a froth of bachelor's buttons across the foot of her bed. She reached for it, touching the lacy flounce at its hem. Before she could stop herself she had scooped it up, dropped the full skirt over her head, and settled the bodice firmly on her hips.

She felt as though a fairy godmother had waved a magic wand, turning her from Cinderella into a princess. She straightened her back, holding her head proudly. Slowly, with small steps, she glided across the room, her hips swaying ever so slightly, setting her skirts to swinging with a soft rustle.

Color flamed in her cheeks as she caught sight of herself in the mirror again. Her shoulders rose, smooth and creamy, above the folds of the blue gown. The low-cut neckline displayed so much of her bosom she felt like a wanton. *If the fine ladies of Prospect could see me now,* she thought with a grim smile, imagining the harsh whispers. She had heard them all when Michael was a baby, the very proper ladies murmuring about decency. Then she'd been wearing men's clothes, big and dark and voluminous, hiding her body from view. If she dared to show herself in Prospect dressed like this, Thelma Black and Mary Jane Lewis would want her arrested as a threat to the common morality.

She turned away from the mirror, tearing at the gown's fastenings, stripping it off so quickly she could hear threads breaking. Angrily she tossed it onto the bed, then yanked off the corset and petticoats as well, jumbling them into a heap beside the dress. She pulled on her shirt and trousers with shaking hands, bundling herself into the bulky garments, berating herself for her foolishness. She had better spend her time cleaning the chicken house than playing dress-up in front of a mirror.

Hastily she gathered up the scattered clothes and bent to stuff them into the trunk, not even taking the time to fold them properly, when her eye was caught by an old photograph resting in the bottom of the chest. The dresses and corsets fell from suddenly limp arms, and she reached for the faded picture. It had been taken when she was about sixteen and showed her and her older sister, Louisa, standing on the wide front steps of the parsonage in Toronto.

Both girls had been dressed in their Easter finery, ready for church, but it wasn't the puffed sleeves or the beribboned hats that brought a lump to her throat. It was the look of expectancy on the face of the young Lottie. The face that looked out at the world from that picture had known that adventure lay just past the dawn and life was full of color and music and laughter.

She sank to her knees amid the jumble of lace and silk and fine cotton, holding the picture with both hands, overcome with longing for her family. Louisa had been her best friend as well as her sister. She'd helped the young Lottie to put up her hair and taught her to walk with the graceful swaying hips of a lady. Against their father's orders she had even taught her to waltz.

"Just in case," Louisa had whispered as the two girls circled the manse sitting room, humming softly to keep the time.

Lottie had giggled and trod on her sister's toes. Louisa had yelped, then clapped a hand over her mouth and hopped about on one foot, holding her injured toes in the air. Then the two of them had collapsed on the sofa in gales of suppressed laughter.

How she missed her sister. How she missed the laughing and the teasing and the security of family. Where was Louisa now, she wondered, a sharp pang of guilt searing her heart. Only once had she written home, a letter to her mother, filled with the joy and fear of her pregnancy. Patrick would be back before the baby was born, she had assured her parents. Everything would be all right. They would be married right away.

The reply had come from her father, berating her for her "carnal sin" and informing her that her name would not be spoken in his household until she had become an "honest woman."

She touched her fingertips to Louisa's pictured face and felt the ice about her heart crack, just a little. Had Louisa rejected her too, or did her sister sometimes remember little Lottie and yearn for news of her?

Carefully, almost reverently, she placed the photograph on her dressing table, shielded from the sunlight so it would not fade, but turned so that she could see it when first she woke in the morning.

Slowly she refolded the clothes and returned them to the trunk, taking care to smooth out the wrinkles and tuck any stray edges inside before closing the lid. She hid them all away, those foolish, feminine fribbles, except for the lacy blouse and the gray worsted skirt and one modest petticoat. These she hung in the wardrobe.

It was growing late, the light fading as the sun slipped behind a mountain peak. She put a hand to her hair, yanking out the pins that held it, letting it fall in a disheveled tangle about her ears. It was still too short to confine in a proper braid, but she pulled it back tightly from her face and bound it at her neck with a length of brown yarn, the same wool she had used to knit socks for herself and Michael last winter.

Then she went down the back stairs to the

kitchen. She stoked the cookstove and peeled potatoes and set the table, all the while her mind busy weighing all the conflicting emotions of the past twenty-four hours. Picking up each memory, she turned it over, examining it as carefully as a miner examines the sand in his pan, seeking to separate the dross from the gold.

While she would not concede that she'd clung to the hope of Patrick's return for too long, she admitted that she was ready to make some changes in her life. It was time to open the windows of her soul, allow the light and warmth of the sun to penetrate the chill recesses of her heart. She would show Michael the goodness of life, not just the work and the duty. She would start tomorrow.

A commotion at the kitchen door signaled the return of her menfolk. "Ma!" Michael burst into the kitchen, his face glowing with cold and excitement, the quarrels of yesterday forgotten. "I caught him, Ma. I caught that big trout. I've been after him all summer but he wouldn't bite. Sean showed me a new fly and I got him. Look!" He held up a six-teen-inch rainbow trout. "Can we have it for supper?"

"Had a good day, did you?" She grinned at her son before taking the fish from him. "Yes, we can have it for supper. I was counting on you bringing something back. Otherwise we'd have had to settle for biscuits and gravy."

"I cleaned it myself, Ma. Sean says it's not fair to make you do it, since you didn't get to come."

"That was very thoughtful of you." She cast a grateful glance toward Sean, then turned her head quickly when she surprised an appreciative gleam in his eye. She laid the trout on a cutting board and took up a sharp knife, cutting it into steaks, then dipping them in flour and seasonings before dropping them into a fry pan already sizzling with melted butter. "Wash up, now. Supper will be ready before you are."

For the rest of the evening, she listened to Michael's enthusiastic retelling of every cast, every fishy nibble, and every detail of Sean's prowess with a fishing pole, a campfire, and a cleaning knife. Oddly, she didn't mind too much. She was learning to accept that the camaraderie between her son and Sean was unique to man and boy. She could observe but not share. It didn't mean they'd forgotten her.

Besides, she was preoccupied by the decisions she had reached in her long afternoon alone with the open trunk. Life at Pine Creek Farm was changing, and had been for several months, but it had taken the advent of Sean into their lives to force the realization. Michael was growing up, and after ten years of waiting—existing in a kind of animated suspension—she was ready to embrace life again.

Lottie was up before Sean on Sunday morning. She hurried outside to feed the chickens and collect the eggs, then back to the kitchen to stoke the stove and prepare breakfast.

"Morning, Lottie. You're up early." Sean met her at the door, his hair still mussed from sleep, his face unshaven, but as handsome as a peacock nonetheless.

"Good morning, Sean." Her stomach did a strange little flip, combined of excitement and dread. This morning marked the beginning of a new era at

Pine Creek Farm. She hoped it would be a happier one. "It's a fine morning."

"Sure and it is." He smiled broadly as his eyes deliberately skimmed over her face, lingering a second longer on her mouth.

She bit her lip, and then wished she hadn't. She didn't mean to be provocative. "I . . . uh . . . I'm just getting fresh eggs for breakfast." She held up the basket, holding it between them.

"It'll be a treat." He didn't look at the eggs, nor did he move out of the doorway. She'd have to sidle past him, much too close, if she wished to go inside.

She stepped back onto the verandah and moved aside. "I'll see you after you've finished in the barn, then."

"Right." At last he moved away, swinging down the steps with easy grace, whistling as he sauntered down the path to the barn.

She scuttled through the open door and set the eggs on the table, then removed her coat and hat, smoothing her hair and taking deep breaths. As she set the table and got bacon frying in the skillet, she rehearsed what she wanted to say to Sean and Michael.

"Morning, Ma." Michael hurtled past her and out the door, pelting after Sean.

"Your coat," she called after his fleeing figure, but he paid her no mind. "If the lad catches pneumonia, I'll make Sean do the nursing," she muttered to herself.

Finally, with a sense of burning her bridges, she set the coffeepot to burbling over the hottest part of the stove, flipped the bacon onto a plate, and set it in the warming oven. Then she scurried up the stairs to her room, scolding herself for feeling like a fugitive in her own house.

Without giving herself time for second thoughts, she stripped off her shirt and trousers, scrambled into her petticoat and corset, and pulled the lacy blouse and worsted skirt over her head. With shaking fingers she fastened the hooks of the skirt and the tiny buttons of the blouse. Then she whisked herself back downstairs to be ready in the kitchen when Michael and Sean came in for their breakfasts.

She had her back to the door and was slicing bread to toast on a wire rack over an opened cover on the stove when she heard the sounds of their arrival. Michael, chattering away, pushed the door open, making it bang against the wall.

There was a moment of stunned silence followed by a disbelieving "Ma?" Astonishment sent his voice high into the soprano range so that the single syllable sounded more like a squeak than a question. He cleared his throat and tried again. "Ma?" This time he managed to sound somewhat like a bullfrog.

If she hadn't been so nervous she would have laughed. As it was, she took a deep breath to calm herself, smoothed her hands over the apron she wore and turned to face her bewildered son. "Breakfast's ready. Wash up and come to the table."

"Ma, you're wearing a dress!" He might as well have said she had sprouted wings.

"I know that," she snapped. "Don't stand there gawking. Go and wash up."

Her son stared at her open-mouthed for another moment, shrugged, and went to the sink to pump water over his hands, all the while casting bewildered, round-eyed looks over his shoulder.

Behind him Sean said not a word but his eyes, as they rested on the lace at her throat and the shiny curls of hair caught low on her neck, filled with admiration and speculation. She turned her back and studiously broke eggs into the frypan. The fire from the stove added to the heat in her cheeks.

When the three of them were seated with plates of steaming food before them, she at last tried to explain the changes she intended to make in the routine of Pine Creek Farm.

"I've decided," she informed them tersely, "that we should observe Sunday, 'the Lord's Day,' as you reminded us yesterday, Sean. I grew up in a parsonage where Sundays were marked by church services and long, solemn afternoons. Music and laughter were forbidden. I didn't want that for you, Michael, but perhaps I've thrown out the baby with the bathwater, as they say."

She glanced down at herself and gave a self-deprecating smile as she smoothed her skirt over her knees. "I never minded putting on Sunday best," she said. "It was just the dreariness of the day I hated. But Sundays should be special. From now on, we'll make it a day of rest, as much as we can. And we'll put on our best clothes, and we'll thank God for all His blessings." She let her eyes flit briefly toward Sean's thoughtful face and then away. "Of course, I cannot dictate to you in matters of religion, Sean."

"I've no objection to clean clothes and a day off," he replied, lazily reaching for his third slice of toast and slathering it generously with the strawberry jam she had put up last summer. He bit into it with relish, his eyes never leaving hers. She swallowed hard, her mouth suddenly dry.

"How come you want us to dress up?" Michael

asked. "We've read the Bible in our everyday clothes before."

Explaining *what* she intended was simple. Explaining the *why* behind her changes was harder, especially with Sean lounging in his chair, cradling a cup of strong coffee between his hands and regarding her with open admiration.

"I know"—she squirmed a little—"and we still will. God doesn't care what we wear so long as we listen to His word. But Sundays should be special, a day apart. You don't want every day to be just like every other, do you? Besides, even farmers need a day off. Now go upstairs and clean yourself up. I'll do the dishes and then we can go into the parlor and have a prayer and sing a hymn."

Michael looked puzzled, but when Sean rose from his seat and announced his intention of having a wash and a shave, the lad left the table and went bounding up the stairs.

Lottie rose and began to gather the used dishes, making very sure not to meet Sean's eyes. "Thank you," she said stiffly. "Michael sets great store by your opinion."

"Glad to help." She heard the smile in his voice and felt her ears turning red.

She stood awkwardly beside the table, her hands full of dishes, waiting for him to leave. Somehow she couldn't force herself to cross the kitchen in front of him. She was far too conscious of the way her skirt and blouse emphasized her figure, far too aware of herself as a woman and Sean as a man. She wished she had never started this, but now that she had, it would be too embarrassing to run up to her room and discard her finery in favor of shirt and pants. She was stuck with her choices and apparently she was stuck behind the table indefinitely as Sean seemed in no hurry for his shave.

"You're in the right, Lottie girl," he said, stepping closer, causing her to scurry around the table, keeping well out of his reach. He stopped and looked at her with raised brows, making her feel ridiculous. The man had been living in her house for six weeks and until two days ago, there had never been an improper moment between them.

But that kiss by the granary had changed everything, thrown her off balance, awakened old dreams, stirred up forgotten feelings, and sent her rummaging through an old trunk. Now Sean's steady regard made her blush like a maiden and sent the air whooshing from her lungs.

The matrons in the town would have considered her trousers far more immodest than what she wore now. But with Sean's knowing eyes upon her, she felt almost indecently exposed in a high-necked, long-sleeved blouse and a skirt that touched the floor.

"I . . . uh . . ." She looked desperately about the room, seeking some safe topic of conversation, something to divert his attention away from her. But the room yielded nothing out of the ordinary. The kettle on the cookstove steamed gently. Duke lay sprawled in a patch of sunshine streaming in through the window. The table, chairs, cupboards, rag rug, the bootjack by the back door, even the stack of mending sitting beside her rocking chair had not changed. "I'm glad you approve," she said finally.

"Oh, I approve," he said, grinning at her with all the roguish charm of Patrick and an added sparkle

of his own. He allowed his eyes to run over her
from the top of her head to the toes of her high
buttoned boots before returning to her pink cheeks.
"Indeed, I do approve, my girl." And at last he left
her. She could hear him whistling on his way up
the back stairs.

She let her breath out in a great puff of air and
set the dishes down on the table again, pressing
her hands to her hot cheeks. Her thoughts were
not concentrated on the holiness of Sunday morning, and the tight feeling in her chest was not en-
tirely due to the unfamiliar corset.

Duke whined and brushed against her skirt, reminding her that she still had tasks to accomplish
before the "day of rest" began. She scraped the remains of their breakfast off the plates and into the
dog's dish, added a bone from last night's soup,
and set it on the floor. Duke wagged his tail in appreciation and devoured the lot in two minutes,
with much gulping and guzzling and slurping of his
tongue. At least the dog didn't care what she wore.
She gave herself a shake, picked up the dishes again,
and finally carried them to the basin, then filled it
with hot water from the kettle and got down to the
job at hand.

She had dried the last plate, removed her apron,
rolled down her sleeves and fastened the buttons
at her wrists when Michael breezed into the kitchen
with Sean in tow. "Ma, look!" he shouted, thrusting
out his arms and showing the sleeves of his best shirt
to be at least two inches too short. "I've grown again."

"Well, I can't let the cuffs down any more," she
sighed. "I'll have to go into Prospect next week
and get you a new one. I've eggs for Jed Barclay
anyway." A vision of the yellow silk danced into her

mind, and she firmly pushed it away. She hadn't
set aside the Lord's Day to indulge in vanity.

"Let's go into the parlor now. You can do the
Bible lesson." Michael rolled his eyes but refrained
from arguing when Sean asked him which passage
he intended to read.

"The story of David and Goliath, I guess. I like
the part where David cuts off the giant's head."

"Michael! That story is about faith in God, not
blood and gore." This time it was Lottie who rolled
her eyes.

"Maybe we should hear the battle story and then
a psalm," Sean suggested, winning Lottie's gratitude
and Michael's grudging acceptance.

When Michael had finished the reading, Lottie
seated herself at the organ and played over one of
her favorite hymns, crooning the words softly at
first, but singing with more confidence when Sean
joined in. By the time they'd reached the last verse
he'd added a harmony line, his deep baritone
blending with her clear soprano. She turned her
face to him, beaming with pleasure. "I didn't know
you could sing."

"There's a lot you don't know about me, Lottie
girl."

She turned away from his intent gaze, keeping
her eyes on her fingers. Aimlessly she pressed the
keys, seeking a new melody, covering the sudden
silence between them. He was right. He was a mystery to her, a mystery she feared to explore.

"Are we done? I want to go outside and play
with Duke."

"Go ahead." She seized on Michael's interruption
to break the tension between herself and Sean, but
when her son had left and Sean still stood beside

her at the organ, turning the pages of her hymn-book, she felt even more vulnerable.

"Let's try this one." He opened the page to "By Cool Siloam's Shady Rill." "It reminds me of Pine Creek."

She opened her eyes wide, surprised to find that Sean O'Connor's tough exterior harbored the soul of a poet. She concentrated on finding the right stops to portray the gentle music, keeping her eyes glued to the notes on the page, hiding the warm glow his words brought to her heart.

"Did you never want to return home?" he asked, after they'd sung a couple more songs.

"No." She left the organ stool and crossed to the window, looking out at Michael and Duke wrestling in the yard.

"Books and music seem important to you, and there's not much of that in Prospect, as far as I can tell. What made you come West?"

"The adventure." She crossed to a small uphol-stered chair with a deep seat that accommodated her skirts. "I found love." She smiled gently and glanced again to the window.

"And when Patrick disappeared?"

"My father was a stern man." She kept her face turned away from his searching gaze. "I had com-mitted a sin that he couldn't forgive." She paused a moment, then tilted her chin at a defiant angle and turned her head to look directly at him. "I don't regret my choices."

"Michael's a fine boy." She saw his jaw tighten and remembered that he knew what it meant to be unwanted. "His grandfather made a grave mis-take."

Her shoulders sagged as some of the tension left her. She couldn't remember when she'd last heard

words of praise for herself. Other farmers com-
mended her crops and her livestock, but no one
gave her or Michael their personal approval.

A tentative smile curved her mouth. "Thank
you," she whispered.

"Reckon I'll go see if the lad wants to build a hay
fort." With a last nod for her, Sean left the room.
In a moment she could see him outside with her
son. She couldn't hear what they said. Michael
began jumping up and down with enthusiasm.

She smiled again. It would be a good winter. She
wouldn't think about the spring just yet.

By evening she was certain her experiment had
been a success. After her initial shyness, she had
grown comfortable in her skirts, and the quiet
rhythm of Sunday, long buried in her mind, had
emerged as familiar and dear as an old friend.

She went to bed content, slept the sleep of the
innocent, and woke to pandemonium and confusion on Monday morning.

Chapter 6

A great squawking and screeching from the henhouse, followed by the thud of feet pounding down the stairs and the slam of the kitchen door, wakened her in the wee hours of the morning.

Fox, she thought, scrambling into her shirt and trousers. No feminine finery today. She seized her rifle from the wall and raced after Sean. Marauding Indians she would have to live with, but a marauding fox she could dispatch.

As she had expected, Sean had reached the chicken coop ahead of her, but the scene that greeted her made her blood run cold. A half dozen hens lay scattered about the henhouse floor, bloody feathers telling their own story. Backed into a corner of the coop stood Sean, holding the lantern with one hand and a pitchfork with the other. Before him, teeth bared, hackles raised, stood a timber wolf.

The animal was easily six feet long from his nose to the tip of his tail, standing about thirty inches high at the shoulder. Even in the half-light of the henhouse, Lottie could see blood and foam flecking his face and neck and dripping from his snarling mouth. *Rabid.* She raised the rifle to her shoulder.

"Don't move." Her voice was level but carried an intensity that easily cut through the growling of the wolf and the squawking and flapping of the hens. Sean gave an imperceptible nod, his eyes never moving from the wolf's snarling jaws.

She shifted her feet, sidling around the animal, trying to draw a bead on him that would keep Sean out of the line of fire. With slow stealth she circled the wolf. The kill had to be clean and instant. If she only wounded him, the enraged animal could charge. One cut from his tooth, no matter how superficial, would mean an agonizing death for Sean O'Connor and a burden of sorrow for Lottie Graham that she could not bear.

Her mind registered these facts in a kind of dispassionate trance, while another part of her brain remained calm and acutely aware of every stirring of breath, every bristle of hair on the animal's back, every beat of her own heart. She kept her rifle trained on the beast, her finger on the trigger, hands steady. Just another foot, she thought; only one more step and she could safely pull the trigger.

"Ma!"

She'd been so focused on the wolf she hadn't heard Michael open the henhouse door, or seen Duke by the boy's side.

The wolf swung around, ready to attack this new foe. Duke growled, his lips curling, teeth bared, hunched low to the ground, ready to spring forward.

"Hold him, Michael!" she shouted, and swung

the rifle barrel, following the wolf's course. Just as the great beast gathered himself onto his haunches, ready to spring, she squeezed the trigger. Inside the small confines of the henhouse, the report was deafening. The wolf shuddered once and dropped to the floor.

"Get Duke away!" she yelled, pumping a new cartridge into the chamber, all the while keeping her gun trained on the stricken animal. "He mustn't touch the wolf. It's rabid."

Young as he was, Michael knew the awful import of those words. Clutching his dog by the scruff of his neck, he hauled him, snarling and yelping, backward out of the henhouse and slammed the door. She could hear the dog barking in protest as Michael pulled him toward the house and safety.

"One bullet, right between the eyes." Sean used the pitchfork to nudge the wolf, turning its body over, exposing the single, killing hole in its head. "Quite a shot, my girl."

"At this range, even an amateur would have a hard time missing." She tried to dismiss his admiration with a toss of her head, but the action made her dizzy, so she stood very straight and very still instead. Her hands gripped tight to the rifle.

"An amateur wouldn't have stayed calm and steady and gone for a clean kill. Pity, though"—he stared at the dead wolf—"he was a magnificent animal."

"Yes," she whispered, fighting to steady her knees.

"Here now." He leaped to catch the rifle as it slipped from her trembling hands. "Easy, girl," he crooned, holding the gun in one hand and slipping his other around her waist. "It's all over now, darlin'. It's all over."

"That's my problem," she whispered, her voice

shaking. "I can manage a crisis, but I fall apart when it's over."

"Come on." He urged her toward the door. "Come outside. Some fresh air will see you right again. Let me tell you"—he kept talking, his words pouring over her like balm—"I'm a man that's thankful you can handle the crisis. That great beast would've killed me, for sure. Where did you learn to shoot like that?"

They were outside now in the cold morning. Sunup was still an hour away at least, but the sky was beginning to lighten over the peaks of the mountains. The stars had disappeared and the moon was a pale, ghostly orb in the western sky.

"Sit down." Sean overturned a feed bucket, making a seat.

Her knees gave way and she sank gratefully onto the makeshift chair, breathing in great gulps of air. She put her elbows on her knees and dropped her head into her hands, trying to stop the shivering that held her in its grip.

Sean knelt beside her and rubbed his hand up and down her back until her trembling ceased. "Better now?"

"Better," she agreed, taking one last deep breath. She raised her head and looked toward the mountain peaks, then got shakily to her feet. She stood a moment, making sure her knees would hold her. Feeling stronger, she took another breath of cold air, using its bite to dispel the last of her shock. "Thanks." She reached for the rifle. There was work to do. Shocked or not, she still had to face the day. "I'll be all right now. I'd better go and help Michael with Duke. The dog must be kept away from that carcass."

"I'll go with you." He released the rifle into her hand, but stayed close beside her.

"I told you, I'm fine." Reaction made her short-tempered. "I can do for myself. I always have." She plunged toward the house with rapid strides.

"I know that"—Sean easily kept pace with her—"but you don't have to. Not while I'm here."

"And what about when you're not here?" She rounded on him with blazing eyes.

The question left them both stunned. They halted, staring at each other, the silence widening between them. She had never meant to care if Sean stayed or went, yet here she was screaming at him because she feared being abandoned yet again. The stricken look on his face betrayed his inner struggle. Her words had taken him unawares, but it was a fair question.

Surely he hadn't forgotten his intention to leave in the spring. But had he ever considered what it would mean to her? Or to Michael? He'd become part of their lives. She had come to depend on him. She had come to lo—

Her mind snapped closed on the word. She would not love Sean O'Connor. He was a prospector. They faced each other, as frozen as the landscape about them, their breath hanging in little white puffs between them. The sky had lightened, so she could see the glint of his eyes, clear and cold as ice. She wished she'd held her tongue. She wished she had never basked in the gentle warmth of his approval. She knew better than to trust a man. She could depend on herself, and herself alone.

"I'll go and start a fire," Sean said, his voice devoid of any emotion. Her unanswered question hung between them, as thick and cold as the air they breathed.

Squaring her shoulders, Lottie marched back to her house, her head high, glad of the work that awaited her. A shaft of sunlight emerged from behind the mountains, striking harshly against her eyes. She turned her face up, shielding her eyes with her hand. A hawk, already on the hunt, circled above the meadow. As she watched, it folded its wings and plummeted toward the ground, swooping in on its kill. She turned her head away. For all its beauty and bounty, this was a cruel land, culling without mercy the feeble and helpless. She hefted the rifle over her shoulder, glad of the strength in her muscles. She must not grow weak. Sean would be gone in the spring.

"Michael," she called, pushing open the kitchen door, stepping inside, and stamping her feet to warm them. "Go and help Sean. He's burning the wolf carcass. Leave Duke in the house."

"Are we still going to take the wagon into Prospect this morning?" Michael seemed more excited than upset by the morning's events. "I want Sean to show me how to drive a team."

She threw up her hands in exasperation as the door slammed behind him. She was perfectly capable of driving a team, had done so for the past ten years, and had even shown Michael the proper way to thread the reins through his fingers. Yet her ungrateful offspring acted as though it had never happened.

Had Sean thought what it would mean to Michael when he packed up his gold pan and his saddlebags and left them? Roughly, she emptied the chamber of her rifle and slung the gun onto its rack. She flung off her coat with an angry shrug. Her tread was heavy as she set about preparing breakfast, stirring the porridge pot with a quick hand and slapping the bowls willy-nilly onto the table.

Duke whined at the back door. "Go lie down!" she shouted.

The dog turned sad, brown eyes on her and slunk back to his mat by the stove. She felt like a murderer. "Sorry, boy." She squatted down on her heels and patted his soft coat. Tears welled in her eyes and she put her face against the dog's smooth head, wishing life hadn't made her so hard. Duke rewarded her affection with a wet doggy kiss and she drew back, smiling and wiping her face on her sleeve. "Good old Duke." She kissed the brown spot between his eyes. "You never bear a grudge, do you boy?"

By the time Michael and Sean came in, breakfast was on the table and she had her emotions under control.

"Guess what, Ma?" Michael shouted before he was barely through the door. "Sean says he's ready to come into town too. Can I ride beside him? He's going to show me how to use the whip. He says he can take a fly off a horse's ear without touching the horse."

She rolled her eyes. "In case you haven't noticed," she said dryly, "it's winter and there are no flies."

She saw Sean's mouth twitch and longed to join him in laughter, but she had been schooled too long in loneliness and self-denial to indulge in camaraderie with a man who was destined for the gold fields. She turned abruptly away. "Eat your breakfast," she said. "You don't want to be late for school."

Over breakfast they agreed that Michael and Sean would drive the wagon into Prospect with Cloud tied to the back. Michael would need him for the homeward journey. "I'll take Titian and stop at the farms along the way to warn them about the wolf," she said. "I'll meet you at the Mercantile."

"Can we go now?" Michael pushed away his empty porridge bowl and jumped up from the table.

"In a minute, boyo. Don't you have some dishes to wash first?"

"Aw, Sean."

"Never mind." She took pity on him. "I'll do the dishes and Michael can deliver the eggs to Jed Barclay."

"Yippee." He leaped up from the breakfast table, gave his mother a hard hug and shot out the door with the egg basket in his hand. "Come on, Sean."

"Sure you'll be all right?" The man followed the boy but at a slower pace and he didn't hug her.

"Don't worry about me. Titian's a trusty mount."

"See you at the Mercantile, then." He touched a finger to the brim of his hat and followed in Michael's footsteps.

With the menfolk out of the way, she quickly cleaned up the kitchen, gave Duke a last consoling pat, and went down to the stable, ready to saddle up and be on her way. But as she entered Titian's stall, she was hauled up short by surprise. Her horse stood saddled and ready with a blanket tied to the back of the saddle. *Just in case.* She could almost hear Sean's voice. "Oh, laddie." She slipped an arm around Titian's neck and pressed her cheek against his face. "What are we going to do without him?" She led the horse outside and swung up onto his back with practiced ease. "We're going to do just fine, aren't we?" She gathered the reins into her hands, kicked her heels against his flanks, and trotted briskly out of the yard.

Despite the troubling thoughts that nagged her, she enjoyed the ride through the early winter morning. A few inches of snow covered the ground, not enough to impede a horse and rider, but enough to transform the landscape into a sparkling fairyland. At the farms and ranches the men greeted her cordially enough and thanked her for her effort in bringing them the news. None of the women appeared to invite her inside, but she was inured to their coolness. However, when she reached the Gardener place, she was welcomed by plump, comfortable Sadie.

"Come away in, Charlotte." Sadie stood bareheaded on the front porch. "It's been too long since I've had company. Abner"—she raised her voice to call to her husband—"take Charlotte's horse to the stable for a little bit." While a silent Abner led Titian away, Sadie ushered her visitor inside. "Tell me, how's that boy of yours?"

"Growing like a bad weed." Lottie sat down at the scrubbed wooden table in the center of the kitchen and felt some of the tightness ease from her shoulders. "That's one of the reasons I'm heading into Prospect this morning. His arms are sticking out of his sleeves like matchsticks." She watched the woman who'd befriended her when others turned their back pour boiling water over the tea leaves in a brown, earthenware teapot.

"I hear you've got a man helping you this winter." Sadie bustled about, setting mugs and milk and sugar on the table.

"Yes." Lottie paused for a moment, debating whether to tell Sadie Sean's story. In the end her

need for a sympathetic ear overruled her usual reserve. "You've been my friend, Sadie," she said at
last, drawing a deep breath, "my only true friend
in Prospect. I have to tell you that Sean O'Connor
is Patrick's cousin. He's almost an uncle to Michael."

"Well, blow me down." Her hostess plopped into
a chair and let out a gasp of surprise. "However
did he end up at Pine Creek Farm?"

Over a cup of strong, sweet tea Lottie told how
Sean had blown in with the storm, and how he had
captivated Michael's young heart, and how worried she was about what would happen to her son
when his hero packed up his things and left them
in the spring. "As soon as the ice goes out of the
creeks, he'll be gone," she said. "I should never have
let him stay. I should have managed somehow."

"With your burned hands? Don't be daft,
Charlotte. Just you thank the good Lord for sending you help when you needed it and let the future
take care of itself. Michael's a smart lad. He'll understand." She stopped talking and leaned across
the table, resting her plump arms on its scarred
surface. "Or is it really Michael we're talking about
here?" Her gaze rested kindly but knowingly on
Lottie. "Is it you, Charlotte, who can't bear another
loss? Have you given your heart away, dearie?"

"I gave it to Patrick long since," Lottie whispered, staring at the pattern of tea leaves in the
bottom of her cup. "Even though a preacher never
blessed our union, I believe we are truly wed. For
Michael's sake . . ." A sob rose in her throat, forcing itself past her tightly clamped lips. "Oh, Sadie"—
she covered her face with her hands—"what am I
going to do?"

"Ah, Charlotte, you poor girl." Sadie patted and
soothed her as though she were no more than ten

years old herself. "Patrick's been gone a long time, Charlotte. It's no sin to give him up for lost. You're still a young woman with a life to live. Now dry your eyes. You've grieved long enough, child."

Lottie sniffed and dug in her pants pocket for a handkerchief. "You know, Sadie, you're the only one who calls me Charlotte, the only one who remembers who I once was. To everyone else I'm 'Crazy Lottie.'" Her voice broke and she buried her face in her handkerchief.

"I never did understand that 'crazy' stuff." Sadie poured another cup of tea and pushed it across the table to Lottie. "You're not the only woman who's got a little ahead of the preacher."

"But I'm the only one who turned down the men who'd have 'made an honest woman out of me.'" She tried to joke but failed. "They made me feel dirty, Sadie." She shuddered. "My love for Patrick was so perfect and they made me feel ashamed." She sipped the tea, and then added with a hint of spunk, "I guess it was easier on their pride to call me 'crazy' than to admit I'd turned them down. I didn't mind, really. It kept people away." She sighed and stared into the teacup. "I truly believed I could only love like that but once. But now . . ."

Sadie gave a loud and very unladylike snort, slapping her hands against the table in disgust.

"Now you listen to me, Charlotte. Things change, life goes on. No matter how much you loved Patrick, you can't stay stuck in the past. Now you just forget this 'Crazy Lottie' nonsense. You're tough, Charlotte, a survivor, the kind of woman who's needed on the frontier. If some no-account tries to make you feel bad, you just look 'em in the eye and hold your head high. And if you find love again, rejoice in your good fortune and damn the gossips."

Despite herself, Lottie gave a watery chuckle. "Such language, Sadie," she protested. "Be careful, or Thelma Black and her ilk will turn on you, as well." She dabbed her eyes.

"Just what has that girl got against you?" Sadie scowled. "She and Mary Jane Lewis have kept that old gossip alive when everyone else would have forgotten."

"I think those two were just born nasty." She turned the teacup around and around in her hands. "They were no end of trouble in school. I tried being nice, I tried being stern, but I could not make them behave. Finally I resorted to ridicule. One day, when Thelma was particularly insolent I made her put on a dunce cap and stand in front of the class while I heaped scorn on her stupidity. I shouldn't have done it, but I was too young to know better."

"Surely she's not carried a schoolgirl grudge all these years?"

She shrugged her shoulders in resignation. "It's made her feel important, I suppose. You may have noticed that even with men outnumbering women ten to one in the district, Thelma hasn't managed to attract a beau."

"Small wonder. Sour-faced bit of spite that she is."

"Well, she had an enormous crush on Patrick back then, so she was already jealous of me. To make matters worse, he came by that day and saw her. We laughed about it afterward, but Thelma was mortified. From that day on she hated me. She was positively gleeful when the school board dismissed me. Her father was one of the trustees, so no doubt she heard all the details."

"She's never going to change, then, but you can, Charlotte." Sadie fixed her with a stern eye. "If a man you can care for has come into your life, then grab hold of your happiness with both hands and hang on tight."

"I can't, Sadie," she whispered. "Sean is leaving in the spring." She fought against her emotion. She wouldn't cry any more. "He's bound for the Big Bend."

"Ah, Charlotte, you poor dear." Sadie used the hem of her apron to dab a spot of moisture from her own eye before going on in a brusque tone, "There's lots of time between now and then. None of us knows what the future holds. You just make the most of the time you've got."

"You're such a tonic, Sadie." Lottie gave one last defiant sniffle, wiped her nose, and put her handkerchief in her pocket. "Thank you." She touched the older woman's hand. "Thank you for being my friend." She got to her feet, reluctant to leave the cozy warmth of the kitchen but drawn by duty and necessity back into the cold of the winter's day.

As she waved good-bye, fresh flakes of snow floated down from a steel-gray sky. She dug in her heels and put the horse to a trot.

Her first stop in town was the bank. Her agreement with Sean had been for a grubstake in the spring, but she couldn't allow the man to work all winter without payment. She drew out a sum of money to pay him a fair wage plus some extra for herself. Michael would need more than a new shirt at the rate he was growing.

Folding the money and stuffing it deep into her pocket, she left the bank building and proceeded along the boardwalk to Barclay's Mercantile. As they had arranged, Sean was waiting for her there, seated with a group of men around the potbellied stove, exchanging stories about the harshness of winter, the price of beef, and, inevitably, the wealth of various claims along the gold creeks.

"Hello, Lottie," Jed greeted her. The loiterers about the stove fell silent, curious eyes turned upon her.

"Jed," she replied, trying not to flinch under the stares.

"Hear you shot a wolf in your henhouse this morning."

"Yes." She moved closer to the counter, grateful for an excuse to avoid the company. "Those eggs Michael brought in will be the last I have for you for a while. I'll let one of the biddies set in the spring to bring the flock up to strength. Problem is, the wolf killed my rooster too. You know of anyone with a cockerel they'd be willing to sell?"

"You could try the Widow Jones over by the ferry landing. I hear roosters crowing over there all the time." He jerked a thumb over his shoulder at the storeroom behind. "I got in those nails you was asking for. You still want 'em?"

Sean joined her, standing close beside her, leaning his hip against the counter, a bulwark between her and the group toasting their feet by Jed's stove. She flashed him a grateful look before ordering five pounds of nails.

"Anything else I can do for you today?" Jed weighed out the nails and dropped them into a sack.

"Michael needs new shirts." She cast a longing look at the yard goods section of the store. The bolt of yellow silk still nestled on the shelves, lovely and bold and incongruous amid the dark worsteds and sturdy ginghams.

"I got some ready-made over here." Jed lumbered out from behind his counter and led her toward the back of the store, out of sight of the loungers. "That boy's growing like tansy. Seen him on his way to school t'other day and blamed near didn't know him. What you feeding him, Lottie? Oh, sorry," he broke off as the bell over the doorway signaled the entrance of another customer. "I'll just leave you here to look for a moment and I'll be right back." He shambled back to the counter with the ambling gait of a big black bear. She could hear him greeting his newest customer.

Sean had followed her into the dry goods section. With Jed busy at the front of the store, they were alone. "Here," she whispered, digging into her pocket and pulling out the roll of money she'd collected at the bank. She glanced about to be sure no one was watching, peeled off several notes and held them out to him.

"And what's all this then?" He frowned at the money in her hand, but made no move to take it.

"Your wages. I didn't want to give it to you in front of . . ." She jerked her head toward the clutch of men.

"You think they might rob me?" He still made no attempt to take her money.

"I thought you might feel embarrassed," she hissed at him, stuffing the money into his shirt pocket and backing swiftly away.

"Now, why would I feel that?" He took the bills out of his shirt, smoothed them out and counted them. Then he folded them neatly, placing them back in his pocket. "It's honest money, isn't it?"

"I just thought . . . my being a woman and all . . ."

He cocked his head and slanted her a sideways glance. A twinkle gleamed in his eye, and a slow smile spread across his face. "Oh, yes"—he nodded—"beneath all your prickles, you are indeed a woman."

"Oh, don't be ridiculous." She spun away from him and dove into the pile of shirts laid out on display. As fast as she could, she selected two that would be a little overlarge for Michael. At the rate he was growing, they could be too small by next week.

She gathered them into her arms and plunged toward the front of the store. As she passed the yellow silk, she couldn't resist reaching out a hand to touch its shimmery surface. She saw Sean watching her and snatched her fingers away, stuffing her hand deep into her pants pocket.

"I'll take these," she said to Jed, dropping the two shirts—one for Sunday, and one for school—on the counter.

By the time Jed had wrapped the shirts, totaled up her account, and helped Sean load it all into the wagon, she was as jittery as a cat and twice as bad tempered. She could feel the eyes of the men who gossiped around the stove following her every move, could practically hear the wheels turning in their heads as they watched her with Sean. A spate of lewd stories would be circulating the minute she mounted her horse and rode away. She didn't mind so much for herself, but her heart ached for Michael.

"I'll see you later at the farm," she said to Sean as he held her mount's head. She slipped her foot into the stirrup and swung lightly into the saddle. In her agitation, she jerked the reins, causing her horse to whinny and rear. "Sorry, laddie," she muttered, patting the gelding's neck to settle him down. Without a backward glance she set off at a trot down Prospect's wide main street, her face set for home, away from the prying eyes and clacking tongues.

Sean turned back into the store. There were a couple of details he needed to see to before returning to Pine Creek Farm. For starters, he pointed out the bolt of yellow silk to Jed and asked for enough to make a lady a fine gown. His request was greeted with a loud burst of laughter from the cronies still basking by the warmth of the stove.

He turned and confronted them, his face set in hard lines, his fists clenched, ready for battle. "Something funny?" he asked in a steely voice.

"You calling Crazy Lottie a lady?" asked a be-whiskered old-timer. "Better buy her a new pair of pants than that fancy stuff."

More laughter greeted this sally. Another man took up the line. "I'll bet she sleeps in her trousers and with a pitchfork by the bed."

"I wouldn't know." His voice was icy calm despite the rage that rose in his throat. His first instinct was to pick up each of the loiterers in turn, shake him by the scruff of his neck and toss him into the street, but for once he held on to his temper. A dust-up in Jed's store wouldn't help Lottie's reputation any.

"In my book," he said, "she's a lady. She has courage and determination. She's not afraid of hard work"—he let his eyes scan the lounging men with scorn—"and she has a dignity that goes way beyond clothes. If ever I needed help, I'd take Lottie Graham over a dozen of the likes of you any day of the week."

One of the younger miners half rose from his chair. "You calling me yellow?"

"I thought I was calling you lazy," Sean replied, "but if you prefer coward . . ."

"Stop it." Jed interposed his impressive bulk between the combatants. "No need to get riled up. You boys must be gettin' too warm, sittin' by the stove all this time. Could be you got other things to do for a while?" He surged forward, rather like a slow moving avalanche sweeping all before him, somehow clearing the store without lifting a finger.

"Now, then," he said, closing the door behind the last of the morning's lingerers and dusting off his hands. "I'll just wrap this up for you before any more wiseacres come by." He took a large sheet of brown paper from a shelf by the cash box, secured it with string about the neatly folded silk and pushed it across the counter to Sean. "Anything else?" He held his stubby pencil poised over his order pad.

"No." Sean shook his head, amused by the ease with which Jed had dispatched his rivals and suspecting he would receive the same treatment if he hung about too much longer. He pulled out the wad of bills Lottie had shoved into his pocket, counting off enough to pay for the silk. He gave them to Jed. "Don't put that on Lottie's account. I'm paying."

"Thought you was saving up for a grubstake?" Jed counted the cash into a money drawer. "Change your mind about prospecting?"

"Oh no," he shook his head emphatically. "Come spring, I'll be on the trail to Big Bend, no mistake about that. But Lottie's paying me fair wages. I can afford to give her something."

He picked up the parcel, tucked it under one arm, and took his leave. He still had a couple of other matters to attend to before heading home to Pine Creek Farm.

His first stop was the post office, where he mailed a short letter to his young cousins informing them of his whereabouts and giving Prospect as a return address. When he had left Ireland, he had thought to simply disappear, but seeing Lottie's pain over Patrick's unexplained absence had changed him. It wasn't fair to leave those who loved you without a word.

His next stop was the schoolhouse. Lottie might scold him for taking Michael out early, but the ominous sky and the steadily falling snow was a perfect excuse, and he had a notion the lad could do with a little moral support. It couldn't be easy being ten years old and never having known your father. If the louts he'd met at the store were anything to go by, Michael took a lot more chaffing than the other kids. It wouldn't hurt to show them the boy had a man on his side.

He walked up the shallow steps of the schoolhouse and entered through the single door. Before him sixteen students of various ages were bent over their desks, apparently deeply absorbed by their lessons while the doyenne of the schoolhouse paced slowly about the perimeter of the room. She was a young woman, soberly clad in a brown dress, and with a severely primmed mouth.

Lottie must have been about her age when she first came here from Toronto, he thought, but he couldn't believe his Lottie had ever scowled so fiercely at her pupils or slapped the pointer so relentlessly into her hand as she trod between the rows of desks.

He cleared his throat, drawing her attention. She wheeled about, piercing him with sharp eyes. "The hotel is down the street." She pulled her lips into an even tighter line.

"Oh, I don't need the hotel." He walked boldly into the center of the room. "I'm here for Michael Graham. Come on, lad." He smiled encouragingly at the boy as Michael dropped his pencil and stared in wide-eyed astonishment at his hero. "There's a big snow coming. You'd best come home with me in the wagon."

"Now just a minute." The schoolteacher held up her hand, halting Michael's eager scramble to put away his books. "Who are you and by what right are you taking Michael out of school?"

"I'd be his cousin Sean then, wouldn't I." He let his eyes scan the other pupils, lingering a moment over the bigger boys, letting the information sink in. "I'm staying with him and his mother for a bit."

"*You're* Sean O'Connor?"

He saw understanding dawning in her eyes. "Michael may have mentioned me."

"With every breath," she replied dryly, but her eyes softened just a shade.

"I'm sorry if he's been tiresome."

"Has he told you about the Christmas party?" she asked, nodding toward a large poster tacked to the wall next to the blackboards. "I don't think Miss Graham has ever attended one. Perhaps this year?" She left the question hanging and turned to urge Michael to hurry. "Don't keep your cousin waiting." He followed her gaze to the window. The snow seemed to be even thicker than when he'd entered. "Attention, class." She clapped her hands. "Put your books away. We'll dismiss early today."

As Michael approached with his hat and coat on, and his schoolbooks bundled under his arm, she held out her hand to Sean. "It's been a pleasure meeting you, Mr. O'Connor. Do think about the Christmas party. It would mean a lot to Michael."

"I'll certainly bear it in mind." He shook her hand, rapidly revising his opinion of Michael's teacher. Beneath the grim exterior, he suspected, lay a deep compassion for the students entrusted to her care. Prospect had been uncommonly lucky in its schoolmarms.

When they stepped outside the snow was falling more thickly than ever. The road back to the farm would be nearly impassable if they didn't hurry. "Come on, lad!" he shouted, as Michael tied Cloud to the back of the wagon and scrambled up onto the seat. "Show me where the Widow Jones lives, then we'll head for home."

Chapter 7

Snowflakes were falling thick and fast by the time Sean and Michael reached Pine Creek Farm. The horses labored as the wheels stuck in the deepening drifts; the outlines of the rough road nearly invisible. Relief flooded over him when he finally sighted the farm's outbuildings looming in the twilight.

"Run and open the doors," he said to Michael as he urged the team toward the shed where Lottie kept her wagons and farm implements. "As soon as you've stabled Cloud, go into the house and tell your mother we're home. She'll be worried."

The boy scrambled to get the double doors open, and Sean drove the team straight in, grateful to have reached home without mishap on the road. He jumped down from the wagon seat and moved to the horses' heads, murmuring praise and encouragement as he patted their necks and unhitched the traces. He remembered the first day he had come here, how Lottie had treated her horses with such affection. "And no wonder, hey laddie?" he crooned to the big bay. "You've earned your keep and more besides."

He led them out of the shed and into the stable, giving them time to drink from the horse trough along the way, then rubbed them down and filled their mangers with hay. When the team was properly cared for, he checked on Cloud and Titian and his own little mare, then turned his steps toward the house.

Before heading indoors, he made a quick detour back to the wagon shed and retrieved the package of yellow silk and the rooster he'd collected from the Widow Jones. On his way to the chicken house he noted the acrid tang of burned fur still hanging over the farmyard, and shuddered at how close they'd all come to disaster.

"There you go, young son." He carried the bird into the henhouse and opened its wooden cage. "See what you think of these biddies." He paused a moment while the young cock strutted out of his cage and into his new harem, blinking warily. The hens clucked sleepily from their roosts, all terror of the morning forgotten. He shook his head over the stupidity of hens, and left them to get acquainted with their rooster.

At last he mounted the steps of the verandah, the parcel of yellow silk safely stowed under his jacket, protected from the wet. Smoke rose in a lazy curl from the chimney and he could see the glimmer of lamplight through the curtains. Inside, he knew, Lottie would have a hearty meal awaiting him, a juicy roast, maybe, with lots of mashed potatoes and vegetables from the root cellar and pie for dessert. Or maybe she had made her famous beef stew, the first meal he had tasted from her hand. His stomach rumbled in anticipation and he quickened his steps.

It was good to be home, to have a comfortable house and a hot meal to welcome him in from the storm. Better still, it was good to have Lottie, by turns prickly as a thistle or gentle as a summer breeze, waiting for him, ready to challenge him and care for him. He felt a smile curve his mouth. Any woman who could keep her head when faced with a rabid wolf deserved a present, and he'd seen her eyeing the silk with longing in her eyes. He was mightily pleased with his purchase.

He stepped inside, took off his coat, shook the snow from it, and hung it on a hook beside the door. The tantalizing aroma of onions and carrots wafted from the kitchen. Beef stew. Perfect for a stormy winter's night. He hurried into the warmth, eager to see her face.

She was standing by the stove, stirring something in a skillet. Her hair had come loose from the small knot at the nape of her neck and curled softly about her face, making her look like a young girl. The heat from the stove had brought a sheen to her brow and a flush to her cheeks. Her figure was completely obscured in heavy pants but her flannel shirt was open at the neck, showing the graceful column of her throat. She was scowling at something Michael had said.

Sean's smile grew broader. He loved Lottie in a temper. It added a tang to their days the way onions added spice to a stew.

"What's all this about a dance?" she said, abandoning the frypan and turning to face him, hands on her hips, fire in her eyes.

"Ah," he sighed, as understanding dawned. "So young Michael has told you about the party at the schoolhouse then."

"He told me you'd promised we would go, and

I've told him we'll do no such thing. Whatever possessed you?"

"Well now," he said, seating himself easily in the rocking chair and tipping his head to one side, the better to assess her reaction. "Although I'm not averse to a bit of music and dancing, I didn't make any promises, so you can stop glaring like an outraged shrew." He repressed a chuckle as temper flashed in her eyes. "On the other hand, I do think it's worth considering." He got up and lifted the lid on a big pot simmering on the stove. "Mmm." He sniffed the aroma appreciatively. "Do you suppose we could eat first and argue later? My stomach's shaking hands with my backbone."

"I'm not arguing," she said loftily, before turning her back. "I'm just not going."

"But, Ma—" Michael began, then broke off and took his seat at the table when Sean shot him a quick wink and a shake of his head.

Lottie glared at the two of them, suspicion writ large on her face, but her two men sat meekly waiting while she dished up heaping bowls of potatoes and beef and carrots and turnips. Finding no antagonist, she had no choice but to sit down and make pleasant conversation. Sean talked of the new rooster and the snowy condition of the roads and the need to exchange the wagon for the cutter for the rest of the winter and ate two helpings of stew.

Finally, when the dishes were done and put away and Michael was gone to bed, Lottie and Sean were left alone. "What have you been grinning about all evening?" she demanded, free at last to vent her displeasure.

Sean felt the grin spreading even farther across his face as he pictured Lottie's delight in the gift he had hidden for her under his coat in the hall. "Be right back," he said, and went to retrieve it. He returned in a trice and, with a flourish set the package on the table in front of her. "It's for you," he said. "Go ahead and open it."

She didn't move, staring at the plain brown package as though it might be a viper poised to strike. "What is it?" she said at last.

"It's a gift," he said softly, placing his hand in the small of her back and gently urging her forward. "Have you forgotten how to receive a present, Lottie girl? You're supposed to open the wrappings and say thank you."

Still looking dubious, Lottie at last touched the string about the package, loosening the knot and pulling away the brown paper, revealing the glowing fabric within.

He hadn't been certain how she would react, but he had never expected the great, heaving sob that rose from her throat or her sudden collapse into the nearest chair, her head buried on her arms folded atop the table.

"Here, now, Lottie darlin'." He knelt beside her chair and gathered her sobbing form into his embrace. "Hush, my girl, hush," he crooned, rocking her gently back and forth.

It was a measure of her distress that she made no attempt to pull away but allowed him to hold her, leaning her head against his shoulder while sobs that seemed to come from the deepest recesses of her soul shook her body.

He held her, soothing her with stroking hands and murmuring voice, letting her cry, letting all her pent-up grief wash over them both. While his heart ached for her sorrow, it also sang for joy that she accepted his comfort. Patrick had wounded her beyond bearing, but he, Sean, had brought her healing. Lottie's tears would wash out the poison and bitterness from her heart, cleansing, renewing, setting her free.

When her sobs grew quieter, he pushed her a little away so he could see her face. The tears were drying on her cheeks and the tip of her nose was red but her eyes were glowing. Their brown depths were as clear and luminous as the best brandy, warmed by a candle. Her lips were soft and pink, quivering and irresistible.

"Ah, darlin'," he groaned, dragging her back into his arms, tipping her head back and kissing those beguiling lips. All thought of comfort and solace fled as he felt her mouth yield to his, felt her body soften, becoming pliant in his arms. His kiss deepened, seeking and demanding, giving and returning. He rose from his knees, pulling her up with him, the better to hold her close, shocking himself by the strength of his desire for this maddening, temperamental, bewitching creature.

His fingers tangled in her hair, pulling out the rest of her loose bun, letting her hair fall wild and free. He threaded his fingers through her thick tresses, cupping the back of her head with his hand, bending her backward over his arm, straining to hold her even closer. His lips released her mouth and traced a line of kisses down her neck, finding the hollow in her throat beneath her open collar. He could feel her pulse beating there, could feel the heat of her skin.

She stiffened in his arms, her hands pushing at his shoulders. "No," she whispered, while the pulse in her throat beat even more wildly.

He stilled, holding her close a moment longer; then with a deep sigh he raised his head, looked into her face and saw the glow of passion tinged with fear in her eyes. Slowly he relaxed his embrace, allowing her to stand upright, away from him. He could feel her trembling like a little brown wren caught in a fowler's snare. He would have to go very slowly if he wanted to win the trust of this most enticing woman.

"Was that your way of saying thank you?" he teased, running his hands across her shoulders and down her arms until he held her fingers in his. "If so, it was my pleasure."

"Don't be a fool." She blushed wildly and pulled her hands free. She took a step away from him, turning her back and attempting to smooth her hair.

He chuckled, relieved to hear the bite in her voice. For a moment, while she had sobbed in his arms, he had been afraid for her. Afraid that an act of kindness had accomplished what years of travail could not, pushing her beyond her limits of endurance.

"Do I take it that you like this yellow stuff?" He poked a finger into the folds of the silk.

"It's beautiful," she said softly, touching the fabric and then withdrawing her hand, "too beautiful for me." She backed away from the table. "You've wasted your money, Sean O'Connor. I can't wear this."

"And why not?"

"Because I'm Cra—" He put a finger to her lips to stop the ugly word. "Because I'm a farmer," she said at last, holding out her work roughened hands. "Silk is for a fine lady."

"You're as fine a lady as I've ever seen." He caught her chin between his fingers, forcing her to meet his eyes. "It's not that, though, is it?" As usual, he could see through her deception. "You're afraid, afraid to be the real Lottie Graham, afraid you might be hurt again."

"I've a right," she said, lowering her lashes, hiding her thoughts from him. "Besides, they laugh at me in town."

"Only because you let them. You've let that old scandal rule your life. If you'd give people half a chance I think you'd find they're a lot more accepting than you think. You make life hard for yourself, girl, and even harder for Michael."

"Don't you dare to lecture me," she flared, high spots of color on her cheeks, fire flashing in her eyes.

"It's high time someone did." He stuffed his hands into his pockets to stop himself from taking her by the shoulders and shaking her until she saw sense. Or until *he* did. What was he doing kissing her? He didn't want a wife and family. He wanted freedom and gold. He took a few quick, impatient steps about the room. "I'm going to check on the cattle." He snatched his coat off a hook and headed out into the night, slamming the door behind him.

Lottie paced restlessly about the kitchen, fanning the flames of her temper, assuring herself that Sean O'Connor was an interfering outsider who knew absolutely nothing about a woman's life on the frontier, especially an unmarried woman with a child. Parties and dresses—She halted her mad pacing and glanced toward the parcel on the table. The yellow silk spilled from its confines like molten sunshine and all her indignation melted away.

She had yearned for this pretty fabric, dreamed of the life it represented, touched her fingers to it in secret pleasure, assured herself that wishes were harmless. Yet Sean had discovered her hidden longings and used his wages, money he needed for himself, to buy her a present.

Sadie would tell her to take the silk and enjoy it, to take what Sean offered and let Thelma and her friends stew in their own spite. She picked up the silk and held it against her cheek, reveling in its smooth, cool texture. It felt like spring and youth and hope. She stood up and held the fabric against herself, looking down as it swirled in a puddle at her feet. The fragile material snagged on the coarse wool of her pants.

Carefully she set it aside. She wasn't ready yet. She couldn't wear a yellow silk dress in Prospect. She would explain it to Sean tomorrow, when they were both calm and the fires of passion, which had burst so suddenly into flame between them, were well tamped down.

In the meantime, she carefully folded the brown paper wrappings over the silk, smoothing the edges and retying the string with a perfect knot. She left a lamp burning for Sean, took the package and went upstairs. Safe in her own room, she opened the cedar trunk and laid the silk inside. She would never wear it, of course, but on dark days she could open the trunk and touch it, remembering for a brief time that she had once been young and pretty and loved.

Loved by *Patrick*, she reminded herself sharply, slamming down the lid on the trunk and hurrying to open the cupboard that held her letters. Gathering them into her hands, pressing them to her face, she breathed in the scent of the rose petals and apple blossoms she had scattered among them.

She dropped them onto the bed, hurried to her

desk, and took up her pen. *My darling Patrick.* She used the old ritual like a charm to conjure up her lover. She touched her fingers to his name, trying desperately to bring him to mind. But tonight the formula failed her. Tonight Sean's face danced between her and the page, Sean's voice sounded in her ears, and Sean's touch still lingered on her skin.

"Patrick," she whispered aloud, closing her eyes and willing her heart to respond. She didn't want to love Sean. She wouldn't risk her heart again. "Patrick, I need you so." She waited. The house was still, the falling snow muffling the sounds of the outside world. She opened her heart, seeking the comfort of her memories. But there was no answering peace for her this night. Her tears dropped onto the paper, blurring the ink, washing Patrick's name from the page.

Much later, having walked off his temper, Sean returned to the house. The kitchen was empty but a lamp burned on the table. *Lottie's version of an apology,* he thought, a wry smile pulling at his mouth. Nevertheless, his spirit lifted. He picked up the lamp and ran lightly up the stairs.

Her door was ajar, and as he passed, he could see her bent over her desk, a bundle of letters, tied in a ribbon, on her lap. As he watched, a tear slipped down her cheek and she whispered, "Patrick." It was like being doused with ice water. While he'd been mooning about under the stars, coming to terms with the fact he'd fallen in love with a sharp-tongued, pigheaded, beautiful, and courageous woman, she'd been pining after his rascal cousin. His jaw hardened. If she wanted to waste her life, it was her own business.

Take A Trip Into A Timeless World of Passion and Adventure with Kensington Choice Historical Romances!
—Absolutely FREE!

Enjoy the passion and adventure of another time with Kensington Choice Historical Romances. They are the finest novels of their kind, written by today's best-selling romance authors. Each Kensington Choice Historical Romance transports you to distant lands in a bygone age. Experience the adventure and share the delight as proud men and spirited women discover the wonder and passion of true love.

4 BOOKS WORTH UP TO $24.96— Absolutely FREE!

Get 4 FREE Books!

We created our convenient Home Subscription Service so you'll be sure to have the hottest new romances delivered each month right to your doorstep—usually before they are available in book stores. Just to show you how convenient the Zebra Home Subscription Service is, we would like to send you 4 FREE Kensington Choice Historical Romances. The books are worth up to $24.96, but you only pay $1.99 for shipping and handling. There's no obligation to buy additional books—ever!

Save Up To 30% With Home Delivery!

Accept your FREE books and each month we'll deliver 4 brand new titles as soon as they are published. They'll be yours to examine FREE for 10 days. Then if you decide to keep the books, you'll pay the preferred subscriber's price (up to 30% off the cover price!), plus shipping and handling. Remember, you are under no obligation to buy any of these books at any time! If you are not delighted with them, simply return them and owe nothing. But if you enjoy Kensington Choice Historical Romances as much as we think you will, pay the special preferred subscriber rate and save over $8.00 off the cover price!

He started to swing away, leaving her to wallow in her own useless grief. His movement must have caught her attention for, while he still watched, she raised wet eyes to his, all her loneliness and all her confusion gathered in their peaty depths.

"Ah, darlin'." He crossed the room in two swift strides and gathered her into his arms, his resolve melting away in an instant.

"I can't remember," she whispered, her voice full of despair. "I can't remember Patrick."

"Is that such a bad thing?" He brushed a lock of hair from her cheek, letting him see her face. "Would you spend your life a widow without ever being a wife? Let him go, Lottie. Let him go."

"That's what Sadie said. But I can't, Sean. For Michael's sake, at least, I mustn't forget."

"Ah, love." He stroked her back, marveling at how slim she felt in his arms. "Don't be so hard on yourself. Patrick wouldn't want it. You remember, he was laughter and adventure and devil-may-care. He wouldn't want you to grieve forever."

"But Michael . . ."

"Hush," he crooned, rocking her like a child. "Hush, my darlin' girl. Michael knows all he needs. Haven't you told him over and over that he looks just like his handsome, dashing father? Haven't I spent hours regaling him with stories of our youth? You're a free woman, Lottie. Let Patrick go."

"I can't," she whispered, pushing him away.

He rose to his feet and stood looking down at her, gripped with a fierce desire to haul her into his arms, cover her mouth with kisses, tear away the clumsy clothes that masked her graceful body, and force her to forget Patrick in a storm of his own love.

For one long, pain-filled moment they stared at

each other, glances locked, challenging, warring with each other. But Lottie's eyes, tear-drenched as they were, never wavered. He drew a long breath and turned away. "Then there's nothing more to say." The door closed behind him.

"Hey, Ma. Come quick." Michael burst into the kitchen on Saturday morning, scattering the gloom that had enveloped her since Sean had walked away. "I've something to show you in the barn."

"Calm down," she protested as he snatched the scrub brush from her hand. "What's so important that I have to come now?"

"Wait and see." He grabbed her hand and hauled her along with him to the door. She barely had time to snatch up a warm coat before he dragged her outside.

The snow had fallen for two whole days, loading the tree branches with white, shrouding every stump and tussock with soft mounds of pearly fluff, smoothing out harsh lines, covering over muddy ruts and gouges. The landscape was clean and pure as Creation. The sun shone clear and brilliant from a deep-blue heaven. The air was crisp and invigorating, but not so cold as to snatch the breath. A perfect winter's day. Her spirit lifted. She couldn't stay downcast in the face of such beauty.

"Slow down, Michael," she laughed, as he dragged her toward the barn. "Let me enjoy the sunshine. Whatever it is can wait a minute."

"Aw, Ma, Sean's waiting for us. You can look at the sunshine later."

"All right," she capitulated, quickening her steps. "Race you," she called when she was sure she had a head start.

"No fair!" Michael shouted. She was two strides short of the barn door when he sped past her. "Home free!" He touched the finish line.

"You must have taken a shortcut." She collapsed against the wall, laughing and breathing hard.

"Hah!" Her son made a rude face. "Come on. You've got to see."

They entered the barn together, pausing a moment until their eyes adjusted from the brilliant sunshine to the dim light of the haymow.

She saw Sean then, leaning on a hay fork, watching her. Her smile faded. For the past two days he had treated her with formal politeness and courtesy, keeping her at a distance. She knew he was right. They must not allow the passion that sparked and sizzled between them to burst into flame again. But she missed his friendship.

Sean thrust the pitchfork into a mound of hay and came to meet them. "Now, what's all this about?"

The question was directed at Michael, but she answered anyway. "Your guess is as good as mine."

"Well, young 'un?" He ruffled the boy's hair. "What's the big mystery?"

"Over here." Michael ran ahead of them toward the hayloft. As quick as a monkey he scrambled up the ladder leading to the top of the mow, then hung over the edge to peer down at them. "Come on up!" he shouted, his face flushed with excitement.

Rolling her eyes in exaggerated resignation, Lottie set her foot on the bottom rung of the ladder. "Come on, Sean," she tossed over her shoulder. "We'll never have a moment's peace until we see what he wants."

Quickly she climbed the ladder, straight up between the beams of the barn, up into the dusty, mote-laden air at the top of the mow. No skirts for her today, she thought, grateful for the freedom of her pants and boots. She loved coming to the top of the barn, feeling as though she left all her troubles on the ground and floated, light as gossamer, in the sweet-smelling hay that billowed around her like waves in the ocean. She gave a quick bounce and dropped onto the hay, letting her legs fly out from under her.

Then she leaned over the side of the mow to call to Sean, to urge him to join her in a moment of innocent play. But the words died on her lips as she saw him, only three rungs up the ladder, his face white and sweating, his fingers curled like claws about the upper rungs, his body pressed tightly against the stringers.

"Sean?" She lay flat on her stomach, her arms hanging down toward him. "Sean, what's wrong?"

"Can't do it," he said between gritted teeth. "Sorry."

"Ma?" Michael called from the far end of the mow. "What are you waiting for?"

"Just a minute, Michael. We'll be right there." Quickly she slipped back down the ladder until her feet rested on the rung above Sean's hands. "Hang on, I'm going to climb over you."

He nodded, but didn't relax his paralyzed grip. Squeezing herself onto the outside edge of the ladder, Lottie managed to scramble down the hay with her feet while maintaining a handhold on the rungs. Once her feet were below his, she eased herself back onto the ladder with her body on the outside, preventing him from falling if he should let go.

"All right now," she said, "you can't fall. I'm here. Do you want to go up or down?"

"Down." He released his hold on the crosspiece long enough to shift his hands down to the next rung. In only a minute they were both standing on the floor between the haymows. Lottie, blushing hotly because the maneuver had brought them into embarrassingly close contact, kept her back turned to Sean and made a great fuss over dusting off the bits of hay and chaff that clung to her trousers.

"Sorry," Sean mumbled. "I guess I've made a right fool of myself this time."

"I take it you've no head for heights." She risked a quick glance at his set face.

"You've the right of that, my girl. Never have. Patrick used to laugh at me for it but I can't help it."

"Then why didn't you say so instead of starting up that ladder?"

"The boy." Sean cocked his head in the direction Michael had taken. "Didn't want to disappoint him. I thought—hoped—that close in to the mow like that, I could manage."

"Didn't want to disappoint him, or didn't want him to know his hero has an Achilles' heel?"

"Well, maybe that too." He had the grace to look shamefaced and her heart melted. She half reached out her hand to comfort him, then snatched it back.

"Never mind," she said gruffly, mounting the ladder once more. "Your secret's safe with me."

Before he could protest or Michael had time to come looking for them, she went swiftly up the ladder again and joined her son in the far corner of the mow. "Now, what's so important?" She dropped onto her knees beside him.

"Where's Sean?"

"He couldn't waste time playing games in the haymow," she said tartly, and felt like a murderer as she watched her son's face fall. "The cattle were kicking up a ruckus outside." She tried to soften his disappointment, taking the blame on herself. "I told Sean he'd better check on them. Now show me what's so all-fired important that you dragged me away from my scrubbing and up to the peak of the barn in the middle of the morning."

"It's Tiger," Michael explained, his excitement returning. "Look." He pulled aside a wisp of straw to reveal the striped tabby barn cat. "She's got kittens."

Sure enough, huddled against their mother's belly lay four tiny creatures. Blind and helpless, they found her teats by touch and suckled hungrily. The tabby watched with worried eyes and bared teeth as Lottie and Michael gazed at them entranced. No matter how often she saw it, the miracle of new life still thrilled and humbled her. "Oh, kitty, you little marvel," she breathed softly and wished Sean could have been with her to share the magic.

"I like that one." Michael pointed to a black kitten with tiny white paws. "Which one do you want?"

"They're all beautiful and they'll grow into great mousers." She patted Tiger's head. "We'll give her an extra helping of cream for the next few days."

"I'm calling that one Boots." Michael touched a gentle finger to the kitten with the white paws. "You can name that one." He pointed to a pure black.

"Well, let's see." She cocked her head to one side and watched the nursing kittens. "How about Bear?"

"Boots and Bear." Michael nodded. "I think we should let Sean name one, too."

"Fine, but don't pester him to come up here. When the kittens have opened their eyes you can bring them into the house. That will be time enough for naming."

"I hope he calls that one Jack." Michael pointed to an orange kitten. "He looks like a jack-o'-lantern."

"Then why not Pumpkin?"

"Ma"—he dragged out the single syllable in disgust—"that's a sissy name."

"Or Marmalade, or Rosebud?" She grinned as Michael groaned.

"I'm asking Sean." He replaced the wisp of hay that shielded the little family from hostile eyes, and scrambled to his feet.

She returned to the house in a thoughtful mood. Sean had been truly terrified. This man who had crossed an ocean and a continent without a qualm, who had faced down a bully and a rabid wolf without turning a hair, had been petrified with fear the minute he was five feet off the ground in the haymow.

She picked up her scrub brush and renewed her attack on the grease spots staining the floorboards beside the stove, all the while turning over in her mind this new insight into the man who had come to hold such an important place in her life.

She felt a new sense of tenderness toward him. He had seemed so strong. She smiled at his reluctance to disappoint Michael. He wasn't immune from hero worship either.

She dropped the scrub brush in her bucket and carried it outside to empty beside the house, taking care not to spill water on the steps. No need risking broken legs from an icy stair. She shielded her eyes with her hand and looked toward the barn. Sean was forking hay into the corral while the cattle milled about, pushing and shoving each other to be the first to the fresh feed.

After ten years of living alone with only a child

for company, it still shocked her to see a man on the place. It shocked her even more to find herself admiring the set of his shoulders and the easy way he swung the heavy forks of hay. Her chores awaited her inside but she spent another moment enjoying the tableau by the corral.

Michael hovered by the tall man's side, talking a blue streak, as far as she could tell from where she stood. Sean turned and said something to the boy that had them both laughing. Her heart lurched. When Sean had first come to Pine Creek Farm he had never smiled, let alone laughed. Now he was sometimes as lighthearted as Patrick.

She picked up her bucket and went inside, away from the sight of the man who was not Patrick, laughing with Patrick's son. And what of the spring, she wondered, when Sean packed up his belongings, saddled his horse and shook the dust of Pine Creek Farm from his boots. What then?

She shook her fist at the distant mountain ranges. Michael would lose this man to the gold fever too and the pain would be even greater than it was for a father he'd never known.

She sighed heavily and made her way back inside, the empty pail bumping against her legs. She went to the pantry and mixed up a piecrust, rolled out the dough and set it into the pie plate. She peeled and sliced apples for the filling, then, before setting it to bake, added a trim of braided dough to seal the edges. Sean wouldn't find a better pie anywhere in Prospect.

Chapter 8

Two weeks later, Lottie gazed out the kitchen window to a pristine world, with only Sean's footsteps leading from the house to the barn to mar its purity. It had been snowing almost constantly from the day she'd learned of Sean's fear of heights. The farmstead was knee-deep in the stuff. Sean was taking feed to the cattle twice a day and keeping a close eye on the calves. They could easily get stuck in a snowdrift.

"Wow, new snow." Michael tore past her and out the kitchen door, calling for Duke as he went.

"Your coat," she called, but the door had already slammed behind him.

She clicked her tongue and turned to stir the porridge on the stove. He'd be back in a minute. It was too cold to stay out long in only a sweater. She set a pot of water over a cooking lid, ready to boil eggs, and listened for him to come pounding back inside. When the water came to a boil and he still hadn't come in, she collected his coat and mitts from the hook by the door and went out to find him.

She needn't have worried. Michael was smothered in Sean's outer coat, his head wrapped up in Sean's muffler, and he was too busy tramping out a grid in the snow to notice that his hero was blowing on his hands to keep warm.

"What in the world?" She stared at the maze of paths covering her garden.

"Ma." Michael looked up, his eyes brimming with glee. "We're playing fox and goose."

"Well, leave that and come get your coat." She held it out to him and he bounded down a zigzag path to meet her. "Sean showed me," her son babbled as he shucked off Sean's coat and muffler and scrambled into his own coat and mitts. It's a game. Come on." He tugged her hand, and she followed him into the crisscrossing tracks. "We're the geese"—he laughed—"and Sean's the fox. If he catches us alone, we're dinner. If we box him in, he's a fur hat." He dashed away down one of the paths.

"What about breakfast?" She dodged as Sean came toward her, a determined glint in his eye.

"It'll keep, girl, but a fine morning like this will flee away."

"Michael!" she shrieked as Sean backed her down one of the paths. It was only a silly game but her competitive spirit wouldn't let her be calmly tagged and sent back to the house.

"This way," her son called. "He can't get us if we stay together." Just in time she reached a crossing path and darted down it, out of reach of Sean's long arms.

"Hah!" She flung the challenge over her shoulder, only to realize too late that she'd taken another wrong turn. Michael had skipped down a connecting path, but she'd started down a dead end.

"I've got you now." Sean ran through the maze toward her. "Give up."

"Never!" She raced back to the crossing, making a valiant attempt to dodge past him, but she was too late. He caught her foot and the both of them went down in a cloud of soft snow.

She was laughing hard and panting, her mouth open in a wide smile as she sucked air into her lungs and tried to wriggle her way out of Sean's grasp.

"No, you don't, my fine goose." He hauled on her ankle, dragging her back to him. He leaned over her, his eyes full of laughter, his teeth gleaming against his early morning beard. "Now you must pay a forfeit."

"What sort of forfeit?" She gazed up at him, and slowly her smile faded. Their glances met and locked. His mouth was only inches from hers. The dancing blue of his eyes stilled and grew dark. She held her breath. He could kiss her if he wished. His face was only inches from hers. She'd forgotten the heart-stopping anticipation that happened just before a kiss. She moistened her lips with the tip of her tongue and waited.

"Snow angels!" Michael shouted and threw himself into the snow beside her, his arms and legs working like windmills.

"Watch out!" Lottie gasped as she received a face full of snow. She pulled away from Sean, glad when he let her go without a struggle, glad and disappointed. Burying the thought, she threw herself on her son, tussling with him in the powdery snow, sharing his delight in the yearly miracle, glad to share a moment of play with no cross words between them.

"Sean, help me!" Michael shrieked as she grabbed a handful of snow and threatened to push it down his collar. He rolled away from her and scrambled to his feet, dancing just out of reach. "Can't catch me, can't catch me."

"I can." Sean caught him by surprise, throwing him up over his shoulder and marching off toward the barn with him.

"Ma!" Michael squealed with laughter and pounded uselessly against Sean's broad back.

"Serves you right," she called after him. "Breakfast's ready as soon as you are."

She watched as the man and boy disappeared inside the barn, then turned and entered her house, enjoying the sense of well-being that flowed over her.

When her menfolk entered the kitchen a few minutes later, Michael carried a box containing Tiger and her kittens. She rolled her eyes at Sean but made no other protest.

"Their eyes are open now," Michael said, carefully setting the hay-filled box into the space behind the stove. "You said I could bring them in then."

"So I did." She set a saucer of cream on the floor for the mother. "If you look in my mending basket you'll find a bit of an old sweater. You can use that to line the box on top of the hay."

"Good idea." Michael scrambled to his feet and hurried to retrieve her mending basket from its place beside her rocking chair. "There you go, Tiger." He talked softly to the mother cat as he tucked the soft wool around her and her kittens.

Watching him, Lottie felt her heart swell with pride. He was a good boy, strong and healthy, full of mischief and energy, yet with a gentleness for the fragile beings of this earth. She raised her eyes and met Sean's gaze, his warm look and slight nod sending a silent approval. It was ridiculous to feel so happy, she told herself, but she couldn't help the bubbly feeling.

"Have you named them all?" she asked Michael, seeking a diversion from thoughts of Sean.

"We've all named one. That's Boots and Bear"— he pointed to the kittens they had named earlier—"and Sean named the orange one Brandy. But this one"—he picked up a little tiger-striped one, the image of its mother—"this one hasn't got a name yet. We should all name it together."

"How about Nuisance," Lottie said as the kitten wriggled free and landed in the cream. She picked up a cloth to wipe up the spill, but Tiger had licked up the treat before she could get to it.

"No." Michael rejected her suggestion scornfully. "You can't stand outside calling, 'Here Nuisance, here Nuisance.' What do you think, Sean?"

"Well, now." Sean pursed his lips and tapped a finger to his chin. "We've got Boots and Bear and Brandy, right?" Michael nodded, taking his gaze from the cat and kittens to study his hero.

"How about Beau? Kind of fits with the others, don't you think?"

"Yeah." Michael nodded enthusiastically. Then, as though remembering, he turned a solemn gaze to his mother. "What do you think, Ma? Is Beau all right with you, too?"

"You mean like Bo Peep?" She couldn't resist teasing. "That's a sweet name."

"No! Not like Bo Peep." Her son's face reddened and he turned to Sean for support. "You didn't mean Bo Peep, did you Sean?"

"Let's see." Sean squatted down on his heels beside the box and gently extracted the striped kitten from the nest. He flipped it over, taking a quick look under its tail, and returned it to its mother. "Not Bo Peep," he pronounced. "He's definitely Beau, as in Beau Brummel. He'll make a fine dandy."

"You're sure?" Lottie pulled a long face. "I rather fancied Bo Peep."

"Aw, Ma!"

"Ignore her, Michael." Sean winked at Lottie, then turned a serious face to her son. "She's just wishing she had a little girl to play with." His glance collided with hers, sending shivers of awareness rocketing down her spine. If Patrick had come home, there would have been more children to fill this big house. Their feet would have worn paths through the garden. Their laughter would have filled the empty rooms upstairs. One of them might have been a little girl with shiny brown hair and soft eyes. Involuntarily she wrapped her arms about herself, hiding her empty womb.

She caught Sean watching her, saw the understanding in his gaze, and wondered how he could read her so easily. Even Patrick hadn't known what she was thinking before she told him.

"Girls. Ugh!" Michael scrambled up from kneeling beside the kittens. "Are we going to eat soon? I'm starving."

"You look it." Lottie's eyes rested lovingly on his sturdy form. "You can make toast while the eggs boil. Then you'll have to hurry or you'll be late for school."

"I've put extra feed for Cloud in your saddlebags," Sean said. "He'll need it with the cold and the heavy snow. Have you got matches and extra socks and mitts, just in case?"

"You're as bad as Ma." Michael grinned. "I ain't going to get lost or fall in a creek, or get stuck in a snowbank. I'm not a baby anymore."

"And no shortcuts." Sean shook a warning finger at him. "You don't know what's buried under the snow."

"Eat your breakfast now." Lottie placed bowls of steaming porridge on the table, a small glow of pleasure warming her heart. She worried about Michael every day he rode off to school. It eased her fear to know Sean was watching out for him as well.

"There you go, puss," Lottie crooned, rubbing a gentle finger under the cat's chin. The little cat surrounded by her frisking kittens had brightened the kitchen for nearly a week, bringing a welcome distraction to Lottie's days. She was as unsettled as the weather. One minute she was glad that Sean had made no further attempt to kiss her, the next she was dreaming of the taste of his mouth on hers. She picked up Brandy and nestled him under her chin.

She heard the door open. "Is that you, Michael?"

"Yes, Ma."

She set the kitten back in his box and stood up, breathing a little easier. Her son was safely home. Night fell so quickly and completely these days. It was dark by four in the afternoon.

"I'm hungry." Michael tramped into the kitchen, leaving puddles of melting snow on the clean floor. He rummaged in the cookie jar and drew out a handful of treats.

"Just one. Supper will be in half an hour."

He sighed mightily and replaced three of the cookies in the jar.

"What's new at school?"

"Nothing," he mumbled through a mouthful of oatmeal and raisins. "I'm going to find Sean." He slammed out of the house, leaving her to mop up the puddles.

"Take heed, Tiger"—she shook an admonishing finger at the cat contentedly nursing her babies— "they'll grow up into ungrateful brats."

She opened the oven door to check on the roast, tested the potatoes, and then drained and mashed them, setting them on the back of the stove to keep warm. From the pantry she brought out the apple pie she'd made earlier in the day and put it in the warming oven. She'd discovered Sean liked his pie slightly heated.

When Michael and Sean returned to the house she had the table set, her plain white dishes gleaming against a deep blue cloth she'd unearthed from the cedar chest. "Wash up," she called over her shoulder while she honed the carving knife. "Dinner's ready." She cut into the succulent roast and laid the slices onto a serving platter. Along with the meat and mashed potatoes she served bowls of carrots and turnips and a basket of fresh baked bread.

"Ma, are we going to the Christmas party?" Michael asked the minute she'd finished saying grace.

"Oh, Michael. Do we have to talk about that now?"

"We could talk about the Indian raids instead."

All her pleasure in the cozy scene around the kitchen table evaporated, replaced with a cold dread. "What raids?"

"Billy Jackson says his dad lost four head last night. Billy didn't hear anything, though. He says he wishes they'd yelled and hollered and wakened him up. He's real mad he missed all the excitement. Do you think they'll raid us?"

"Eat your turnips, Michael." Sean frowned at the boy, who instantly looked conscience-stricken.

"Sorry," he muttered, pushing mashed turnip about with his fork. "I forgot."

"Forgot what?" Lottie's glance flicked between Michael's red face and Sean's glowering one. "Would someone please explain to me what's going on?" Her question was greeted with only silence. "Michael?"

Her son shot a quick look toward Sean, received some invisible signal, and went back to studying his uneaten vegetables.

"Sean?"

"It's just a small thing, Lottie girl. Nothing to fret yourself over."

"And what is this 'small thing'?"

Sean sighed and set down his knife and fork. "Michael told me about the latest raid. I've decided to start doing night patrols, that's all." He asked Michael a question about his geography assignment. "Did Miss Douglas like your map of County Clare?"

But Lottie was not to be put off. "We'll bring the cattle into the closest corral tomorrow. It'll mean more work but we'll manage. If you want to take the night patrol tonight, I'll do it tomorrow."

"Don't be daft, girl. That's a man's work."

She couldn't believe her ears. "I've been 'the man' on this farm for ten years, Sean O'Connor. I'll protect my cattle without any say-so from you."

"You think I can't do it?" He fixed her with a challenging stare.

"That's not what I meant."

"Then you think I won't do it? That I'll sleep through the night and leave the cattle at risk?"

"No." How had she ended up on the defensive? She was in the right, and yet Sean had her twisting in her chair and imitating Michael as she shoved food around on her plate without eating it.

"That's settled then." Sean loaded his fork with roast beef. "Wonderful dinner, Lottie." He turned his attention to Michael. "What did Miss Douglas say?"

"She liked the leprechauns."

"You put leprechauns on a school assignment?" Lottie temporarily forgot her argument with Sean.

"Just for fun. I know they're not really there, but it made the map more interesting. Miss Douglas thought so too."

She raised her eyes to meet Sean's gaze. "Fairy dust," she said, and shook her head. She rose from her place and collected the empty bowls. She carried them to the sink, then took the pie out of the warming oven.

"Russets?" Sean's eyes gleamed with hope.

"Of course." She set the pie on the table and went to fetch a pie-lifter and fresh plates.

"Your ma makes the best pies I've ever tasted," Sean told Michael. "She says it's because of the apples but I think it's because of the cook." A little glow of womanly pride eased her irritation over the cattle.

"We sure get more pie since you came." Michael had recovered from his discomfiture. "We used to just get stewed apples."

Lottie stood with a knife poised over the pie and felt as though it had stabbed her heart. She'd hoped Michael hadn't missed what he'd never had.

"Well, pie's a lot of work." Sean's voice slid into the sudden silence. "I reckon your ma had her hands full with feeding cattle and horses. Besides, what's a little squirt like you need with pie?"

"I'm growing every day." Michael thrust out his childish chest and thumped it with his fists. "My new shirt's not too big anymore. If Ma keeps baking pies, I'll soon be as big as you."

"It's turnips, not pie, that'll make you grow." She sliced the knife through the piecrust. Despite her words, she made Michael's portion as generous as Sean's, then lifted a smaller piece for herself.

At midnight she lay in the darkness of her room, listening to Sean's firm steps on the stairs. For what was surely only a few minutes but seemed like hours she lay rigid and alert—ears straining, heart thumping—until she heard the click of the door that signaled his return. She sighed deeply and rolled over, asleep before he reached the top of the stairs.

The next night the pattern was repeated, and the night after. She tempered her resentment of his high-handed decision with gratitude for his support and baked more pies.

"Ma?" Michael was home early, and calling from the kitchen.

She brushed a floury hand across her forehead and stuck her head out of the pantry. "Michael? What are you doing home so early?"

"Miss Douglas gave us all a half-day holiday to collect decorations for the schoolhouse. She wants it to be all fancied up for the party." His face fell and he slumped into a chair by the table, his boots leaving puddles of melted snow on the floor. "It's not fair," he grumbled. "I have to do all this stuff to get ready and I won't get to go." He kicked the chair legs in a steady thud designed to irritate his mother.

"Stop it, Michael," she said almost automatically, her mind busy considering the possible decorations she could contribute to the party. She had grown up with lavish Christmas celebrations, complete with a huge tree in the front hall, garlanded with strings of popcorn and cranberries, each branch adorned with knots of lace or ribbon. She and her sisters had spent wonderful, exciting weeks making the decorations in anticipation of the day their father brought home the tree and the season officially began.

But when Michael was a baby she had been far too busy to make much of a fuss over Christmas and she had never got into the way of it again. The twenty-fifth of December passed much like any other day at Pine Creek Farm, except that she would give Michael new mitts or socks that she had knitted for him, and he would give her the card he had created for her under his teacher's watchful eye. She had never bothered with the fuss and extra work of decorations and a tree.

Seeing Michael's dejected figure slumped against the table her heart smote her. Sean was right. In her determination to keep her farm and to protect her son, she had robbed Michael of many of childhood's joys. At least this year, she decided, so long as Sean was here to see to the outside work of the farm, Michael would have a proper Christmas, with a tree and all the trimmings. As for the Christmas party at the schoolhouse, she'd think about it.

"There's a set of miniature ruby stemware in the big cabinet in the dining room," she said. "You can take that. If you turn the glasses upside down and tie them onto a long ribbon, they'll look very pretty hanging in a window or on the tree, wherever Miss Douglas wants them. After supper we'll go into the attic and see what else we can find."

If she had hoped to clear the scowl from her son's face, she was disappointed. "I'll go ask Sean." Michael gave the chair legs one last kick and marched out of the house.

"You're welcome," she called after him, but her sarcasm went unheard.

She sighed and picked up the fuzzy black kitten, holding him before her face. He gazed at her with innocent blue eyes and twitched curious white whiskers when she tickled him under the chin. "What do you think, Bear?" she asked. "Should Cinderella go to the ball?"

The kitten squirmed and clutched her finger with both front paws, then clamped his baby teeth onto her knuckle. "Ouch! You ungrateful little beast." She laughed, and put him back on the floor where he promptly attacked his mother's tail.

If only it were as simple as *Cinderella*. Her reluctance to attend a party in Prospect had nothing to do with needing a fine gown and a coach, and everything to do with fear. Sean wanted her to go, for Michael's sake, he said, and for her own as well, but she couldn't give up her old beliefs so readily. What if people laughed at her or shunned her?

"You're exaggerating," he'd said. "You can't judge the whole town by a couple of spiteful gossips. What about Jed Barclay? He's always glad to see you."

"Jed doesn't have a wife."

"Then he'll be glad to dance with you. Besides"— he'd looked sly—"I deserve to see you in a yellow silk gown."

"Well, you're not going to," she'd promised him, and shoved another stick of wood into the stove, putting an end to the discussion. Even if she agreed to attend the party, she didn't have time to make herself a new dress.

Still, on this dark December afternoon, she climbed the stairs to her bedroom and pulled the cedar trunk out from under the bed, opened the lid, and pondered its contents.

The package of yellow silk she lifted out and set aside before reaching for the cornflower-blue gown. She lifted it carefully from the trunk, shook out the tissue paper from between its folds and held it up to the window, examining broken threads and a torn flounce. It could be mended in time. She hung it on the back of the door and smoothed the creases from the skirt. It was a beautiful dress for dancing. She ran downstairs for her needle and thread. Cinderella would go to the ball and let the gossips be hanged.

"Sean says they used to collect pinecones for decorations when he and Pa were little," Michael informed her at dinner. He wore his sulky look and pushed carrots around on his plate without actually eating any.

"You could do that." She hadn't told them her decision yet, waiting for the right moment. "We could dip them in sugar frosting, too, to brighten them up, but I'm afraid you won't have time before tomorrow. I wish you'd told me sooner that Miss Douglas wanted everyone to contribute to the decorations. We hardly have enough time now to get ready for the party."

Michael's mouth dropped open, and he gave up

trying to hide his carrots under the edge of his plate. "You mean we're going?"

"If you and Sean think it's a good idea, I suppose we can." She tried to keep her face severe but couldn't resist sneaking a peek at Sean. The look of warm approval in his eyes brought a lift to her heart. She didn't like being at odds with him.

Her smile broadened to a chuckle when she glanced back to her astonished son. "Close your mouth, Michael," she said. "It's not polite to gape. And yes, we'll all go to the party, and we'll put up a Christmas tree in the front parlor, and you can hang frosted pinecones on it, and Duke can have an extra bone on Christmas Day."

"Yippee!" Michael raced around the table to give her an impulsive hug. "Can we have candy, too?"

"Candy and cake and oranges, if Jed Barclay has any, and we'll ask the widow Jones if she has any young birds for sale, and we'll have roast chicken for dinner. Satisfied?"

"Sounds like a fine Christmas to me." Sean leaned his elbows on the table, steepling his fingers and resting his chin on them.

"Well"—she wished Sean's smile didn't make her blush so easily—"I guess we should make an effort to celebrate Christ's birth."

The rest of the week flew by in a flurry of sewing and baking and laughter and stretched nerves. Although Lottie had made up her mind to go to the party, and put on a brave face, in her heart she still feared the inevitable whispers and haughty looks. When she put on her blue gown on the night of the party, she nearly lost her nerve.

In the mirror her reflection glowed like a jewel, surrounded by the twinkling flames from the candles on her dressing table. Her dress rustled with a soft, enticing whisper when she walked. She did look like Cinderella, but her bared arms and neck made her feel exposed and vulnerable. She couldn't face the people of Prospect dressed like this. She should have donned her gray skirt and modest blouse. In a panic she reached to undo the fastenings of her bodice but before she could change, Sean knocked on her door.

"Are you ready, Lottie? We mustn't keep the horses standing in the cold."

Too late. She would have to follow the path she had set for herself. She picked up the knitted shawl from where it lay on the bed, wrapped it snugly around her shoulders, blew out the lamp and opened the door.

Sean was waiting for her, dressed in his Sunday suit, his hair slicked down. He looked so handsome and so like Patrick he took her breath away. For one brief moment she felt as though she had stepped back to the time when she hadn't a care in the world and love sweetened every waking moment.

His eyes lit with appreciation and he bowed, extending his arm to her. "May I have the pleasure, my lady?"

Though her throat felt tight, she managed a small chuckle and placed her fingers lightly upon his arm. "Why thank you, kind sir," she said, hiding her nervousness behind a facade of teasing.

"Hurry up, Ma."

Michael shouting at her from downstairs shattered the illusion of fairyland but still she smiled. Despite the hardships of the last ten years she had a son and she wouldn't trade him for all the fairy castles in the world. The man at her side would drive Thelma Black mad with jealousy. She placed her fingers on his arm and allowed him to lead her along the hall.

"The front stairs, I believe," he said when she would have turned toward the narrow ones that led directly to the kitchen. They walked the full length of the house and, in regal style, descended the wide steps of the front stairs. At the bottom step, Sean bowed low and raised her hand to his lips. "Thank you, my lady."

"Oh, sir!" She flirted an imaginary fan before her face, doing her best to enter into the spirit of the evening.

"It'll be all right." Sean dropped his teasing manner and did his best to reassure her. "I'll be right beside you."

She nodded but she was already steeling herself not to mind if the evening turned into a disaster. They walked through to the kitchen in silence.

"No, Duke, you can't come." Michael, his face flushed with excitement, his hair combed in perfect imitation of Sean, argued with his dog, trying to persuade him inside. Duke stood stubbornly in the open doorway, tail wagging.

Her heart warmed at the sight of her strong, healthy son. By the time they reached Prospect, his rebellious forelock would be hanging over his brow and the clean white shirt would be creased and smudged, but just at this instant he filled her with pride.

"Duke, stay." Sean pointed to his mat beside the stove and, with one last, soulful look, the dog obeyed.

"Good boy," Michael said, patting him. "I'll bring you a treat," he promised and pulled on his mitts.

Lottie layered on a heavy coat over her finery, Sean retrieved the bricks warming in the oven and placed them on the floor of the sleigh, then they all piled into the cutter for the trip into town. The harnesses jingled, the snow creaked under the runners, and the steady tramp of the horses' hooves whisked them over the frozen landscape. For Lottie, the night had a fairy tale feeling, and she gave herself up to it. Perhaps Sean had been right. Perhaps her fears had been exaggerated.

Their first stop was the livery stable, where they left the horses in the ostler's care before walking the short distance to the schoolhouse. Along the way they met other people bound on the same errand. She watched as couples and families came together in happy groups, forming and reforming as they walked, but no one joined her party. No one called a merry greeting or held out a hand in friendship.

Lottie grew silent and tense. She felt Sean's arm holding hers stiffen, and he quickened their pace. By the time they arrived at the schoolhouse she was hot and breathless.

"I'll be waiting for you," he whispered as he left her at the door of the girls' cloakroom.

She nodded briefly and stepped into the feminine enclave to remove her outer garments and tidy her hair before entering the main room, just in time to hear Mary Jane Lewis exclaim, "Did you see her? Crazy Lottie's coming to the party!"

The little cloakroom was crowded, but miraculously the women managed to clear a space around Lottie, squeezing themselves into corners and staring openly as she came face to face with Mary Jane.

"Still talking when you should be silent?" She faced her former pupil. "No wonder you failed your provincial exams."

A small titter ran around the room. Mary Jane tossed her head and flounced away. Most of the other women melted away as well; the ones who were left shifting uncomfortably about, trying to pretend they'd not overheard.

Stone-faced, Lottie turned to the mirror, lifting and replacing the combs that held her hair, gathering her courage. Defiantly, she straightened her shawl about her arms, letting it drape to expose her neck and shoulders. Then, with her head high, her back straight, and her heart in her throat, she stepped out into the schoolroom.

The students' desks had all been pushed to one side of the room, and a double row of chairs placed down the other. In one corner stood a magnificent fir tree beribboned with tinsel and festooned with symbols of the season. Her ruby stemware held a place of honor high up in the top boughs, out of reach of little hands.

Michael had already disappeared into a crowd of boys but Sean stood waiting for her. "That's my girl," he whispered, coming to stand beside her. "Don't forget, we're in this together."

She flashed him a grateful smile and tried not to notice that the room had grown quiet and every eye was turned upon them. The taut silence seemed to stretch out forever. Her face grew hotter still while her fingers turned to ice. If her legs had obeyed her wishes she would have fled, but she seemed to have lost the ability to command her limbs. Rooted to the spot, she wished the floor would open beneath her feet and swallow her up, anything but this awful staring.

"Charlotte!" Sadie Gardener came bustling across the room, her arms outstretched. "Good heavens, dear, don't stand there like a stump. Come and join us."

Beside her, she heard Sean let out his pent-up

breath, and all three of them moved across the room, Sadie keeping up a steady stream of chatter as she took Lottie's hand and led her toward a cluster of people seated beside the Christmas tree.

The hum of conversation resumed, the band tuned up their instruments, and the party began in earnest. If the occasional hard stare was sent in her direction, Lottie appeared not to notice. Sean was quick to see that she had tea and sandwiches and lemonade and anything else that was in his power to give that would make this evening bearable.

His attendance was so assiduous that Sadie finally ordered him to go away. "You're standing over Charlotte like a dog guarding a bone," she complained. "Go mingle."

Reluctantly he moved a little distance away. When the dancing started, he took his turn on the floor with Miss Douglas and Sadie Gardener before claiming Lottie for the last dance.

When the music ended, the drummer sounded a great flourish, and a Santa Claus in a red suit and white beard bounded onto the makeshift stage to shouts of laughter from the adults, who recognized the portly figure of Jed Barclay, and squeals of delight from the children, who saw only a packsack filled with treats.

"Oh, no," Lottie whispered, still standing in the circle of Sean's arm. "I didn't bring anything to put in the sack for Michael."

"It's all taken care of," he whispered back.

When Santa dug into his sack and called Michael's name, the boy's face was transfixed with surprise. "Wow," he murmured as he joined his mother to show her the small wooden flute carved from a willow branch. "Look what Santa gave me."

Lottie smoothed his hair back from his forehead. "It's wonderful." She looked directly at Sean, not caring if she caused a fresh wave of gossip.

"I'm going to see what Billy got." Michael scooted across the dance floor to where a group of boys huddled in a corner.

"Thank you." She turned gratefully to the man beside her. "I didn't realize there would be a Santa."

"I guess Michael forgot to tell you."

"Seems to me he's forgotten to tell me a lot of things." She nodded toward the group of boys. "Do you know what's going on there?"

"Just boy stuff." He grinned and caught her arm. "Come on. Sadie wants to talk to you." He jerked his chin to the corner where her friend sat, waving an impatient hand in their direction.

"Charlotte, you must meet Miss Douglas," Sadie said the instant she got close. "Charlotte was the schoolteacher here years ago," she explained to the young woman sitting beside her.

"Hello, Miss Graham." The schoolmarm held out her hand and Lottie noticed she was much younger than she'd first imagined. "I've heard about—" The new schoolteacher broke off as a flush came over her face. "I mean, it's a pleasure to meet Michael's mother."

"How do you do, Miss Douglas? I hope Michael isn't a trouble to you." She shook the young woman's hand and wondered what had brought the sadness to Miss Douglas's eyes. For one so young, she seemed to bear a heavy load. "If you ever want to borrow some books from me, or come to the farm for a chat, you're welcome," she added impulsively.

"Thank you." Miss Douglas's smile was swift and genuine.

"I knew you'd have lots in common." Sadie nodded her head and beamed at the two women. "Come along, Mr. North." She linked arms with the nattily dressed gentleman who hovered close by. "You can help me fetch a plate of sweets and leave these two to get acquainted."

The party broke up soon afterward, but it was well past midnight by the time Sean tucked the buffalo robes around her in the cutter for the ride back to the farm. Michael, exhausted by excitement and the late hour, snuggled down beside her and was soon asleep.

Wedged tightly between her son and Sean, Lottie was too keyed up from the party and far too aware of the man beside her to feel the least bit drowsy. Wrapped together as they were beneath the buffalo robes, the heat from his body warmed her. His leg pressed tightly against her own; his arm brushed against her breast as he adjusted the reins. Despite her layers of petticoats and furs, she felt almost intimate with him.

Trying to calm herself and banish such thoughts from her mind, she tipped her head back and looked up at the heavens. The moon rode high and white in a velvet sky. Stars twinkled like myriad candles, so bright they seemed within reach of her hand. She caught her breath in awe.

"Beautiful, isn't it?" Sean murmured.

"Perfect," she whispered back, keeping her voice low lest she break the spell of the night. Sean seemed to sense her mood, for he said no more, but their eyes met with perfect understanding. Under the moonlit sky, in the vastness of the wilderness, she felt their two souls drawn together. No words were necessary.

They topped the rise that led down to the farm and the horses, sensing home, quickened their pace, kicking up clods of snow and setting the cutter swaying as they raced toward the warmth of the stable. "Easy now"—Sean tightened the reins—"your oats will wait."

Before driving on to the barn, he pulled the cutter to a halt close by the verandah steps, wrapped the reins about the brake handle, and leaped out of the sleigh. Then he turned to help Lottie, catching her about the waist and swinging her to the ground as easily as he might have picked up one of Tiger's kittens. Her hands rested on his shoulders and she tipped her head back to look into his face, her lips parted with laughter. For one long, tension-fraught moment she gazed into his eyes and knew he wanted to kiss her. Knew, too, that she would welcome that kiss on this most magical of nights.

"Are we home?" Michael asked sleepily, climbing out from under the coverings she had piled over him while he slept.

Sean dropped his hands and she jumped away with a guilty start. "Yes, Michael." Her voice sounded high and breathless. "Let's go inside and get you to bed before you fall asleep in the snow." She took her son's hand and hurried him up the steps and into the house. For once Michael was too sleepy to protest being treated like a baby.

Without waiting to remove her coat she lit a candle and went upstairs after Michael. He had already climbed into bed, leaving his clothes scattered in a trail that led from the door to the side of the bed. She picked up his shirt and pants, folding them neatly and laying them on a chair as she had so often in the past. She pulled the quilt up to his chin, tucking him in, then bent and dropped a kiss on his cheek. She had loved this nighttime ritual when he was a baby. But he was growing so quickly, and there were no more babies to fill her arms. She banished the rebellious yearnings and brushed a lock of hair back from his face. "Good night, my son. Sleep well."

Gliding soundlessly back down the stairs to the kitchen, she lit a lamp and placed it in the window to guide Sean back to the house, then removed her coat and boots. Taking the poker, she stirred up the fire in the stove, making the kitchen warm and welcoming.

Restless, she paced about the room, her ears tuned for the sound of Sean's feet on the step. She went from the window to the door, looking out toward the barn. Was it only her imagination or was Sean taking an extraordinarily long time to bed down the horses? She didn't need to wait up for him, of course, yet she hesitated. After all they had shared this evening, she was reluctant for it to end without a proper good-night. At the very least she should thank him for taking a gift for Michael.

Duke whined at the door and she opened it for him. "Go find him, boy," she murmured as the dog set out at a trot toward the barn. She closed the door and stood listening to the tick of the grandfather clock in the otherwise silent house. There was nothing to keep her from her bed.

"Bah!" she exclaimed aloud, irritated with herself for mooning about like a lovesick schoolgirl. Leaving the lamp burning in the window, she picked up the candle and trod up the stairs to her room. She dropped her shawl on the bed and went to stand in front of the mirror, astonished by the image that looked back at her. Could this dewy-eyed woman really be "Crazy Lottie"?

She raised her arms to pull the combs from her hair, and watched as it fell in waves, thick and shiny, to just below her ears. Her long, heavy braid was gone but she liked the soft curls that replaced it. She sat down and reached for her hairbrush, drawing out the magic of the night as long as she could. In the morning she would be herself again.

Sean stayed in the stable as long as he reasonably could. The horses were fed, brushed, and bedded in fresh straw, their mangers full of hay. He had walked all around the barn, checked every door, gone outside and walked the corral fences. The cattle were all accounted for and content. Duke joined him as he made his way toward the henhouse on another pointless errand meant only to delay his return to the house . . . and Lottie.

It would be so easy to believe all this was his. The farm, the dog, the boy, the woman. He could give up his dream of riches in the gold fields, stay here with Lottie, grow old with her, have children with her. It wouldn't be hard to win her heart. Despite their differences, they were friends already, sharing in the work of the farm, and he had seen the glow of something more in her eyes tonight.

From the first instant of their meeting he had admired her fine eyes and slender figure. After the fire, when he had changed the bandages on her hands and breathed in the sweet perfume of her skin, he had known desire. In the weeks since, he had enjoyed her wit and tenacity and even her bad temper.

But tonight, he thought with gut wrenching urgency, tonight he had seen her dressed in a fine gown: the soft, white skin of her breasts rounding above the bodice; the slender column of her throat exposed in heartbreaking vulnerability. He had wanted to fling her shawl about her shoulders, sweep her up into his arms and carry her out of the schoolhouse, away from the lascivious stares of the rude miners. He had wanted to whisk her back to Pine Creek Farm and lay claim to her as his own.

He hadn't, of course—that would have been a fool's mission. Instead, he had followed meekly in her wake, brought her tea and sandwiches, and, for one heart-stopping waltz, held her in his arms.

Duke shoved his head into Sean's hand, begging for a pat or a kind word. He ruffled the dog's ears and patted his shoulder. He was cold and there was nothing to keep him prowling about outside in the dark of night.

"Time to go in, hey Duke?" he said and at last wended his way along the snowy track from the barn to the welcoming warmth of the house. The lamp in the window threw a path of gold across the snow to guide his steps.

Gold. Riches, power, ease. Gold was his dream, not a woman and a boy and a farm. His desire for Lottie was merely the natural reaction of a lonely man in the middle of the wilderness, thrust into close proximity with an attractive woman. He must not let a passing fancy dissuade him from his true mission.

Entering the kitchen, he doused his own lantern and picked up the lamp that Lottie had left for him. Quietly, he climbed the stairs toward his solitary bed.

Lottie, with her hair unbound, stood waiting in the open door of her room. He stumbled and nearly dropped the lamp. "What are you doing still up?" His voice held a raspy edge and he couldn't take his eyes off the deep cleft between her breasts, which disappeared into the tight bodice of her dress.

A blush warmed her skin, adding to her allure and his own mounting desire. "I just wanted to say good night and thank you," she murmured, dropping her eyes and raising her hands to cover her nakedness. The gesture only served to emphasize the seductive nature of her garments.

"You're welcome," he said gruffly, his eyes still fixed on her enticing curves.

"Well, then," she stammered, reaching behind her for the door handle, "I'll . . . uh . . . good night."

But neither of them moved, held fast by an irresistible and inevitable force. It was more than a man could stand.

"Ah, Lottie," he groaned, reaching out to haul her into his arms.

With one quick movement he lifted her feet off the floor, whirled her into her bedroom and pushed the door closed behind them. Only then did he allow her to stand on her own feet, but still he held her with one arm tight about her. With his free hand he stroked her cheek, allowing his fingers to play along the smooth line of her jaw, trailing down her neck, skimming lightly along the neckline of her low-cut bodice.

Desire tightened his gut, sending his breath into his throat in raw gasps. He tipped her chin up, looking into her eyes, seeking and finding an answering hunger.

"Darlin' girl," he murmured against her lips while his fingers worked to loosen the fastenings of her gown. All evening he'd been mesmerized by the soft swell of her bosom, tantalized by the shadow of her cleavage.

For three months he had lived in the same house with her, worked side by side with her, shared her burdens, cared for her and her child. He had admired her courage, marveled at her strength and appreciated her knowledge. But tonight he saw her only as a warm, desirable woman. A woman whose lithe figure filled him with yearning. A woman with soft curves and feminine mystery who reminded him remorselessly that he was a man. A man who needed a woman.

"We mustn't," she protested weakly even as she softened in his embrace. It felt so good to be held again, to be admired and adored. She had been alone too long, spending her youth in grieving. Now, as a woman, with a woman's mind and a woman's body, she welcomed Sean O'Connor as a lover.

Her hooks and buttons dealt with, Sean loosened the laces of her corset, freeing her breasts from their constraints. They spilled out, lush and full and throbbing with heat, the nipples hard and erect. He gathered their fullness in his hands, lifting them, testing them, kneading them to even greater yearning. He cupped them high, burying his face between their roundness. His thumbs brushed lightly over the nipples, drawing a gasp of surrender from her.

"Sean!" she cried, grasping his shoulders and digging in her fingers.

"Let me love you, darlin' girl," he murmured, the Irish lilt in his voice warm and enticing, drawing her under his spell, robbing her of her will to resist.

Her heart beating high, her cheeks hot with confusion, she attempted to cover herself, tried to beat back the throbbing yearning of her body, sought to bring Patrick's face between herself and Sean, but her efforts were in vain. The shadowy memory of her lost lover could not compete with the virile presence of his cousin.

Over the weeks of his enforced presence in her home she had come to rely on his physical strength as he handled with ease the chores that had strained her muscles to their limit. She had come to treasure his company in the long, dark evenings, listening as he told tales of a land she would never see. She had already shared much of herself with him, reading to him from her favorite poets, confiding in him her hopes for Michael. She had even learned to trust his judgment, discussing the business of Pine Creek Farm and recognizing the wisdom of his advice. Despite their few, forbidden kisses, he had never tried to push her beyond the line she drew between them and she had appreciated and respected him for his restraint.

But tonight he had stepped over the invisible barrier that separated them and she was powerless to push him away. In a blinding flash of honesty she admitted that she had no wish to resist the forces that drew them together.

As though sensing her capitulation, Sean swept her up and carried her swiftly to the bed, laying her down into its welcoming depths. Quickly, he shed his shirt and followed her down, lying close beside her, their bodies touching from hip to shoulder. His eyes never left hers as his hands continued to play havoc with her clothes and her senses.

"You're so beautiful," he murmured, running his fingers through her tumbled hair, nuzzling his face against her neck, driving her wild with desire. "When I make my strike," he whispered, raising himself on his elbow to look down into her face, "I'll buy emeralds to dangle from your ears, ropes of gold to twine in your hair and diamonds to shine around your neck."

The words acted on her like a deluge of icy rain. In an instant she changed from compliant, eager lover to rigid, relentless foe. With all her strength she pushed him away from her, taking him unawares and heaving him onto the floor in a welter of confusion.

"Lottie, what the—" he shouted, scrambling to his feet, but she was ahead of him, pushing him over again before he had regained his balance. Angry tears streamed down her cheeks and she raised her fists to strike him.

"Stop that." He grasped her wrists and held her fast. "What's the matter with you, woman?" His voice was harsh, his grip on her arms unbreakable. Still she fought him.

"Let me go!" she cried, panting and sobbing and gasping for breath.

"Not until you tell me what's wrong."

"Gold!" She spat the word at him. "You're just like Patrick, blinded by that golden whore. I loved him, body and soul, and he left me to chase a dream across the wilderness, a glittering, heartless sprite who promised him riches if only he would follow her over one more mountain, through one more valley, up one more nameless creek. He left me and his unborn son and this good land, and for what? For an illusion! I'll not be left again, Sean O'Connor. If you want me, you turn your back on the gold rush."

"Lottie"—he held out his hand pleadingly—"you can't mean that. I've dreamed of the gold creeks for years. That dream has sustained me. I've risked everything I have for my chance to strike it rich. Now I've found you, it's more important than ever. I want to give you things, jewels and furs and a fine house and servants so you never have to bruise your hands with hard work again. You could live like a lady."

"Stop it." She covered her face with her hands, sobs shaking her, tears streaming from between her fingers. She had lost . . . again. "Patrick said the same things." She laughed bitterly and held out her work-hardened hands for him to see. "I'm content with my farmer's hands and I'll not play second fiddle to the gold fever again."

"Lottie." Sean's face was ashen in the candlelight as he pleaded with her. "Lottie, trust me, love. I'll not hurt you."

"You must choose," she said, hardening her heart, looking away from the pain she saw in his eyes. "You can stay with me and Michael, make Pine Creek Farm your home, and be my lover, or you can follow the golden trail to hell. You can't have both."

He tried one more time, his voice soft and tender. "How can I live in the same house with you and not touch you?"

"Then you had better go," she said, each word dropping like a stone into the pit that suddenly yawned between them.

As she watched, disbelief, anguish, and finally a hard resolution played across his face. His shoulders had sagged when she issued her ultimatum. Now he straightened, standing tall and true before her, the lines in his face etched deep, the laughter gone from his eyes. He would not ask her again.

"I'll pack my things and be gone in the morning." He strode from the room, closing the door with quiet finality behind him.

Chapter 9

She crumpled into a heap on the floor, her legs no longer strong enough to hold her upright. Alone and heartbroken, she huddled on the hard boards, unmoving, trying to think, trying to plan for the morrow, but her brain refused to function, unable to get past Sean's final words. He'd be gone in the morning.

After a long time she grew cold and began to shiver, the demands of her body pushing past the misery of her heart. Calling on the strength that had seen her through every crisis of the past ten years, she dragged herself to the bed, pulling off what remained of her clothing and dropping it in a tumbled mass beside the bed before climbing under the quilt. She could not sleep, but lay shivering and aching with unfulfilled longing, miserable and lonely, as the moon outside her window crossed from the zenith of the heavens to ride the western horizon.

In the darkest hour before the dawn she heard

the sound of horses galloping past and the blood-curdling cries of Indian raiders. Cattle bellowed and bawled, and downstairs Duke set up a din to wake the dead. Her worst fears were realized.

At least the need for action released her from the icy grip of despair. In an instant she was out of bed, and scrambling into her shirt and trousers. She stuffed her feet into her boots and raced down the back stairs, seizing her rifle from the wall rack. "Stay here!" she yelled to Michael who was sleepily clumping along behind her, and yanked open the kitchen door.

Before she had gone two steps, Sean was beside her. "Get behind me, girl. They'll have rifles."

"They're long gone," she yelled back, "and those are *my* cattle."

Sean made a noise between a growl and a roar but raised no more objections as she fought her way beside him through the deep snow to the barn. The corral gate hung open, jammed into a snowdrift. Some cattle still milled about inside; others had bolted for the open when the rustlers had ridden among them.

"Wait here," Sean said tersely, leaving her to close the gate herself. "I'll check there's no one hiding in the barn."

Although her spirit rose in protest, this time she obeyed. She didn't believe any of the Indians would have remained behind, yet she quailed from facing the darkness inside the barn. She struggled to close the gate in the deep snow, then walked among the cattle still remaining in their pen, ensuring there were no broken legs or bleeding flanks, her nerves stretched to the limit as she waited for Sean to return.

Finally, when she thought she could stand the waiting no longer, she saw him coming toward her, riding his horse and leading hers, already saddled.

"The barn's safe." He held out her reins but made no effort to help her into the saddle. "We'd best round up the strays while we can."

Wordlessly she accepted his decision, throwing herself onto Titian's back and setting her feet in the stirrups. With only the light of a lantern and the setting moon for guidance, they followed the tracks through the snow until they had gathered up all the scattered herd, driving them into a second corral.

"That's it then," Sean said when they had finished. "You'd best go inside and get warm. I'll tend to the horses." He took the reins from her hand. "I'll spend the rest of the night in the barn."

She nodded, trying to ignore the curt tone of his voice. "You'll be in for breakfast?" she asked at last, afraid that when it was fully light he would ride away without a backward glance or even a nod of farewell.

For what seemed like an eternity, silence stretched between them. She waited, her nerves taut. So much depended on his answer. Finally, he muttered a brief "Yes," then turned on his heel and left her.

She returned to the house, keeping Duke beside her, needing the comfort of the dog's company and his unquestioning loyalty.

"Ma?" Michael, his arms full of firewood, greeted her the minute she stepped inside. "Ma, what happened? Where's Sean?" He dropped his burden into the woodbox.

"Oh, Michael." She sighed in relief. "You've built up the fire. Thank you." She hurried forward, holding her frozen hands out to the welcome heat.

"Was it Indians, Ma? Did Sean kill them?" She recoiled from the bloodthirsty gleam in her son's eyes.

"It was Indians." She opened the oven door and pulled a chair close. Would she ever be warm again? It wasn't only the cold of a winter night that chilled her bones. An icy hand of fear clutched her heart as surely as the frost nipped at her fingers and ears. "And no, Sean did not kill anyone."

"Where is he, then?" She heard a small echo of her own fear in her son's voice and hastily explained Sean's decision to stay in the barn.

"The sun will be up soon," she assured him, pulling herself together. "You can set the table while I make breakfast. I'm sure Sean will be hungry."

She forced herself to leave her chair and get on with the work at hand, setting the kettle to boil, measuring oatmeal into a big pot for porridge, putting bacon in the frypan and breaking eggs into a bowl, as though she could somehow fortify her home from danger by spreading a feast of plenty on her table.

When Sean came in, he reported that they had lost a half-dozen cattle. "Maybe I should ride around the district and talk to the other farmers, make up a posse, and go after those thieving blackguards." He paced about the kitchen, slamming a closed fist into his open palm.

"No!" Lottie whirled about, feeling the blood drain from her face. "No posses. It'll only stir up more trouble. We'll just have to accept the loss as the price of farming in the Kootenays."

"And what of the next time?" He smacked his hand against the back of a chair. "Dammit, Lottie, we've a right to protect ourselves and our property. Do you intend to huddle under your bed while they make off with all our stock?"

"That's not fair," she flashed with some of her old spirit. "I'll protect my herd but I'll not be party to starting an Indian war." She dished up steaming bowls of porridge, slopping it over the edge of the bowls with an unsteady hand. "Come and eat," she said, not looking at him. "We'll think better with something in our stomachs."

Sean looked unconvinced, but finally took his place across the table from her. "If you let them get away with it this time, they'll get bolder, taking more and more until it's not safe for anyone."

"It's not up to us to take the law into our own hands." She poured cream over her cereal, spilling that too. "We've a constable in Prospect. We'll report the theft and let him deal with the Indians. That's his job."

"One constable against the whole Kootenay tribe? What do you think he can do?"

"I don't know. Talk to Chief Isadore. Send out a call for reinforcements. I don't know, but I'm not fighting the whole Kootenay nation either. Whites are highly outnumbered here, Sean. We have to let the chief deal with his own people."

Sean didn't reply and they finished their breakfast in heavy silence. Even Michael was quelled by the palpable tension that throbbed between her and Sean. Finally, pushing away his empty plate and draining the last of his coffee, Sean rose to his feet and said, "I'll saddle up and go now."

Lottie stood too, her hands gripping the back of her chair until her knuckles whitened. He really was going. Somehow she had hoped . . . She should have known better. Too much had passed between them to think they could ever go back.

"I'll write Jed Barclay a letter," she said through

stiff lips, "authorizing him to charge your supplies to my account."

"There's no need." His eyes met hers for a fleeting second of understanding before he turned his back. "I'll be back before noon."

She let out her breath in a long hiss before collapsing onto her chair. For once her pride could not cover her true feelings.

"Can I go with you?" Michael begged, clearly eager to discuss Indians and posses and daring midnight raids without his mother's eye upon him.

"Sure and you can," Sean said, his taut face relaxing into the wry grin she had come to love so well. "If your mother can spare you."

"Go." Lottie waved her hand, unequal to the argument.

When Sean and Michael had gone, she gathered up the dirty dishes, washed and dried them, fed Tiger the milky remains of the porridge bowls, swept the floor and blacked the stove, comforting herself with all the small rituals of home. When it was time to feed the chickens and collect the eggs, she slung her rifle over her arm, whistled for Duke and trudged doggedly out to the chicken coop.

The rooster strutted about, watching her with bright, beady eyes. The biddies clucked sleepily as she lifted them and rummaged about their nests for eggs, but no fearsome animals attacked her; no hidden enemy leaped from the shadows.

She made her way back inside. She could spend the rest of the morning baking for the Christmas she'd promised Michael. At noon, Sean would be in for his dinner. She'd make the biscuits he favored.

For the rest of the week she and Sean and Michael

kept busy preparing for the Christmas Day they had promised themselves. If Michael noticed that the adults avoided each other, he said nothing. When Sean brought in a fragrant fir tree and set it up in the hall, Lottie watched from the kitchen. When Michael, let loose in the attic, unearthed a trunk full of trinkets abandoned by the farm's previous owner, it was Sean alone who climbed the narrow stairs to help him carry down their trove. They ate their meals together, but it was Michael who kept the table lively with chatter.

Lottie baked pies and cakes, washed the fine china also left behind by the young English lord, and tried not to notice that the sparkle had gone out of her days. When she knew he couldn't see, she watched out the window, seeking a glimpse of Sean working in the yard, taking comfort from his strength and hoarding the days against the loneliness that was sure to come.

"Merry Christmas! Merry Christmas!" Sean woke them all early Christmas morning, walking through the house and ringing a cowbell. He must have been up most of the night. Since the raid, he'd taken to checking on the herd twice a night. Lottie had learned to sleep through his frequent journeys past her bedroom door.

"Wake up, sleepy head." She heard him open the door to Michael's room. "You want to miss the whole day?"

"Oh no," Michael's groggy voice answered. "I'm sorry, Sean. Can we still do it?"

"All done, young 'un. Now get yourself downstairs."

She heard Michael's footsteps pound down the steps. He didn't pause to wish her a merry Christmas.

There was a tap at the door. "I've brought you hot water," Sean called from the hall. "I'll leave it here."

She rolled out of bed then, and scuttled across the room in her nightgown. She opened the door to find a pail of steaming hot water but Sean had disappeared. "Thank you," she called out, "and merry Christmas." She enjoyed the unusual luxury of warm water for her morning ablutions, then hastened into her skirt and blouse. She could smell bacon frying and dreaded the havoc that Michael could wreak in the kitchen.

"Merry Christmas, Ma!" Michael stood by the stove stirring the porridge with a wooden spoon while Sean broke eggs into a fry pan and flipped the bacon sizzling in another.

"What's all this?" Her gaze took in the table already set, the coffeepot burbling on the back of the stove, and Michael's shining face.

"It was Sean's idea. Are you pleased?"

Her gaze flew to Sean. He had his back to her, yet something in his stillness told her he was waiting for her reply as eagerly as Michael.

"It's perfect," she said, "and a wonderful Christmas present. Thank you, both." The rigid set to Sean's shoulders relaxed.

"Come and sit down." Michael darted away from the stove to hold her chair. "Sean taught me how to do that, too," he confided as Lottie took her seat.

"You're turning into a real gentleman."

"Let's eat!" Michael dished up hearty bowls of porridge and set them about the table. "I want to get to the presents."

"What about your chores? Cloud needs his feed of oats even on Christmas morning."

"Sean already did it. I slept in," Michael confessed sheepishly. "Everything's done."

"Everything?" She raised questioning eyes to Sean as he finally took his place at the table.

"Merry Christmas," he said with a slight nod. "Thought you might like a morning off." He gave his attention to the porridge.

"It was very thoughtful of you," she said to the top of his head, "but I don't expect you to do my chores."

"Still don't know how to accept a present?" He looked up then, his eyes boring into hers, reminding her of what had happened the last time he'd brought her a gift.

She dropped her spoon and picked up her nearly empty porridge bowl, bending down to hide her face under the table. "Here, Tiger," she said. "Come, puss." She made a great business out of petting the cat and talking to the kittens. When she sat up straight again, Sean had left the table to fetch the coffeepot. She sighed with relief.

"Coward," he whispered in her ear as he leaned over her shoulder to pour steaming black coffee into her cup.

"Thank you," she replied, too loudly, and tried to pretend they were speaking of the coffee.

"Can we go in to the tree now?" Michael bolted a mouthful of bacon and eggs and pushed his plate away.

"Not yet, boyo." Sean grinned at the lad's impatience and buttered a slice of toast with slow deliberation. "You want to take this gift-opening business slow and easy. Savor the anticipation. Make the moment last." His words were for Michael, but his gaze rested on Lottie's face.

He would make love the same way, she thought, *unhurried, taking time over each exquisite step, letting the anticipation build.* She blew a strand of hair out of her eyes, wishing the kitchen wasn't quite so warm.

"Something bothering you, Lottie?" He cradled a cup of coffee between his hands.

"No." She fanned her face with the back of her hand. "You've got the stove fired up pretty hot, don't you think."

"Seems just about right to me." He raised the cup to his lips, watching her over its rim.

"I think Michael's right." She got up and began clearing the dishes from the table. "It's time to get to the tree."

This time Sean made no objection. "I'll do the dishes, Ma," Michael volunteered after a speaking glance from Sean, "but can I do them after we open the presents?"

Lottie agreed and Sean chuckled. "Come on, boyo; let's go see what Santa brought." He dropped an arm about Michael's shoulder and the three of them went into the gaily decorated parlor.

"I don't really believe in Santa Claus," Michael said, but his eyes brimmed with excitement as he studied the gifts waiting under the boughs of the Christmas tree. "Who goes first?"

"Why don't you get out one present for each of us," Lottie said, "then you can open all of yours."

He dove gleefully into the mysterious parcels, distributing all of them, then settling down on the floor to open each of his own. He said a dutiful "thank you" for the scarf and mittens she had knitted for him and ate a couple of candies from the sack of candy, nuts, and oranges from Santa Claus. Then he turned his attention to the package from Sean, ripping it open in his excitement.

"Wow, Ma, look!" he exclaimed. "It's a compass." He snapped the case open and stared in delight at the wobbling needle. "I'll never get lost now." He scrambled to his feet to race about the whole house, checking every corner against true north.

Without Michael to bridge the space between them, she and Sean sat silently beside the tree. Sean cleared his throat and held up the heavy woolen socks she had knit. "Thank you, Lottie, they'll keep me warm."

"You're welcome." She touched the embroidered needle case in her lap. "This is lovely. Thank you."

"Glad you like it." Another long silence ensued.

"Well, maybe I'll just go do those dishes." She headed for the kitchen, feeling as though she were escaping from the principal's office.

"That's Michael's job. You're supposed to get a day off."

"I don't mind. He's having such a good time. Besides"—she paused in the doorway to look back at him—"I can't afford to go soft."

His jaw tightened but he made no further comment.

When Sadie Gardener, driving her own one-horse sleigh, came calling in the afternoon, Lottie welcomed her even more warmly than usual.

"Oh my, Charlotte!" her friend exclaimed as Lottie ushered her into the front parlor.

"Sit here, by the fire"—Lottie pulled up the softest chair in the room—"while I get you a cup of tea." She hurried off to the kitchen and returned with a pair of china teacups on a silver tray.

"I've never known you so grand before."

"Well"—Lottie shrugged, pulling a wry face—"it is Christmas, and with Sean's help this year, I've had more time for niceties."

"And about time, too." Sadie accepted a dainty shortbread cookie from the proffered tray. "I'm delighted you're enjoying the fine things in this house. It must feel like the old days in Toronto for you."

"Not quite." Lottie laughed ruefully. "The parsonage was handsome and well-appointed, but a preacher's salary never stretched to Spode china and Waterford crystal."

"I suppose not," Sadie conceded, munching thoughtfully on the shortbread. "Do you ever miss it, Lottie?"

Lottie considered for a moment but answered truthfully that her heart was now in the Kootenays. "I confess to wishing I had more access to books, and just lately I've missed my sister, Louisa, but I came west for the adventure and the freedom. I don't regret my choice. Why do you ask? Are you feeling nostalgic?"

"Not in the least." Sadie set her teacup into its saucer. "But one does tend to reminisce on Christmas Day. When I was a girl . . ." She was off on a ramble down memory lane that soon had Lottie laughing over the exploits of the young Sadie and brought Sean in to see what all the fun was about.

"Play us a tune, Charlotte," Sadie said. "What's Christmas without music, after all."

Willingly Lottie went to the organ and began to play, humming the familiar carols as her fingers touched the keys. She waited for Sean to join her, but when she turned her head she found he'd already left.

"Thank you, my dear. That was lovely." Sadie applauded. "Now, I must be off home. Abner will be getting anxious for his dinner."

Standing on the verandah in the pale winter sunshine, the two women hugged each other and said good-bye. "Merry Christmas, Charlotte," Sadie said. "I hope the new year brings you happiness." She turned her head to look directly at Sean. "Much happiness."

"And to you," Lottie replied, her heart full of gratitude for this stalwart friend. "Come and visit me again. I'll bring out the fine china anytime you call."

"I'll hold you to that." Sadie climbed into her sleigh, picked up the reins and set off at a spanking pace toward her own home.

Sean and Lottie stood side by side watching her out of sight. "It's been quite a day," Sean said as they went inside, Lottie hugging herself against the cold. She noticed that he did not offer her the warmth of his arm but stood well back, allowing her to precede him.

The incident, although small in itself, held a portent for the future. As winter wore on and the snow grew deeper, Sean worked through the short daylight hours, tending the cattle, feeding the horses, chopping firewood and keeping a vigilant watch for more raids against their stock. Lottie kept the kitchen warm and the table set with tasty meals. She washed his clothes and darned his socks, but the light seemed to have gone out of her days as surely as the sun had faded from the winter sky.

There was no more reading together or story-telling about the kitchen table. No more impromptu music-making around the pump organ in the parlor, and no more intimate moments when their glances met and held and when understanding and attraction flowed between them. If not for Michael, Lottie thought, there would be not a word exchanged in the house.

The only excitement came in March, and she would rather have lived out her life in dreary boredom than hear the news Sean brought with him from Prospect. An Indian, suspected of murdering two white miners three years ago, had been arrested and jailed but before he could be brought to trial, Chief Isadore had led a raid on the jail and freed the offender. The provincial constable had ridden to Vancouver in quest of assistance, leaving Prospect without any representative of the law.

"There's talk of forming a vigilante group."

"Surely not." Lottie's stomach tied itself in knots. "A raid on Isadore's territory could provoke more lawlessness. The settlers would be overrun."

"That's what Jed says. I don't believe there will be any attacks on Isadore's tribe but people are mighty scared. You can feel the fear. It's running like a river through town."

"And what of the farms? We're even more vulnerable." She cast her eyes toward her rifle.

Sean's glance followed hers and his mouth tightened. "Keep your gun loaded and close by your side," he said. "Carry it with you even if only to gather eggs. I bought more ammunition." He dropped a large box of cartridges on the table and began filling the chamber of his own rifle. "Perhaps it would be just as well if Michael stayed out of school for a time."

"Yes," she whispered and felt the authority at Pine Creek Farm shift toward Sean.

They passed the rest of the winter in uneasy peace. Sean stepped up his nighttime patrols of the barn and corrals. Lottie's face grew haggard from sleep-lessness, and Michael grew taller and more inde-pendent, looking to Sean for guidance and fretting at his mother's strictures.

Finally it was spring. Icicles dripped from the eaves of the house, sap flowed in the trees and the ice cracked and broke apart in the creeks. Still there was no constable in Prospect and Sean made no move to depart for the gold fields. Lottie said nothing, afraid to disturb the fragile truce that lay between them, but in her heart she was glad, grate-ful for Sean's presence, whatever his reasons.

For ten years she had managed by herself. She was a good shot and had no quarrel with the sur-rounding Indian tribe. She had even bartered with them, exchanging fruits and vegetables from her garden for the medicines and ointments of their healers. But this year everything had changed. This year they had raided Pine Creek Farm and openly defied the law as appointed by Her Majesty's Government. An Indian war could break out at any moment.

"It's Judge Parker's fault," Sean fumed after a trip into Prospect. "If he had let things alone, let the Indians continue to graze their cattle on Norton's Flats, none of this would have happened. He's just a little popinjay playing the great man. Thinks be-cause he bought himself a commission in the army he's entitled to more privileges than other men. It's time fools like him learned that this is a new country where a man must earn his way, not ride on the backs of others."

"You talk more like a farmer than a prospector." She couldn't resist challenging him.

"How so?" He paused in his work of unloading the sleigh and turned to face her.

"All that 'sweat of your brow' philosophy," she explained, enjoying the way his eyes glinted bright blue in the spring sunshine. "A prospector wants to strike it rich and then live like Judge Parker, enjoying the privileges of wealth and moving into society and politics with all their proscriptions and rules about etiquette and behavior. If you truly want to be a free man, Sean O'Connor, you'll stay here, on the frontier."

"Here, Lottie?" he asked with no trace of laughter in his voice. "On Pine Creek Farm?"

She felt her stomach drop. She had been speaking in the abstract, not the particular, and yet . . . "You could," she said slowly, not looking at him but fixing her gaze on some spot on the horizon just past his shoulder, "trade your labor for a share of the property."

"Do you mean that, Lottie?" She heard a tenderness in his voice that had been missing since the disastrous night of the school Christmas party. "You would consider parting with a share of your precious farm?"

For a long moment she considered the question, her eyes roving over the meadows just emerging from the winter snows, before coming back to rest a moment on his face. "If the terms were right," she said, finally.

To give up even a tiny part of Pine Creek Farm would be like giving up a piece of her soul. She would be admitting, finally, that Patrick would never come home to claim his family. She would be surrendering a sliver of the precious freedom and independence she held so dear. But her sacrifice would be rewarded. The farm would have a man's strength, Michael would have a man's guidance, and she would have Sean by her side. Perhaps, one day, she might have his love.

"But there would be no prospecting." She raised her chin, flinty resolve in her voice.

"You'd ask me to give up my dream for yours?"

All her defiance and determination dropped away like a kite that has lost the wind. Her hope spiraled downward and crashed in a crumpled tangle at the feet of the goddess of gold. "No," she said tonelessly, turning her back. "Follow your own dreams, Sean." She walked away, moving like an old woman, seeking the protection of her house.

Sean watched her go and felt like a scoundrel. She had offered him what she held most precious in life and he had refused her. He struggled with the desire to race after her, catch her in his arms, kiss away her sadness, and promise to live with her on these acres for the rest of his life. He longed for Lottie, longed for the love they could know together. What more could he ask, than the woman of his heart, a good farm, food on the table and fodder in the granary? He looked toward the barnyard and saw cattle and horses and chickens— enough to supply the necessities of life with plenty to spare.

He could have it all if he accepted Lottie's terms. His choice should be so simple. He loved her. He would marry her and settle down on Pine Creek Farm. They would have children and grow old and comfortable together.

But therein lay the problem that plagued his heart. Apart from the gold fever that burned in his veins, he did not want to tie himself with the steely, gossamer ties of home and family. He had abandoned his native land to seek fortune and adventure. Why should he squander his chances by stepping back into the same old trap? He kicked angrily at a clump of snow stuck to the runners. Besides, what did he want with a wife who was wedded to a ghost? Gold. That's where his future lay. He would not give up his dream, not even for Lottie's sake.

As soon as the Indian trouble was settled, as soon as it was safe to leave her, he would collect his supplies and head for the Big Bend. Perhaps, when he had filled his saddlebags with gold, perhaps then he could come back to Lottie, a rich man who could offer her anything money could buy. Perhaps then he could make her forget Patrick.

He let his gaze rove over the sloping fields, still buried under mounds of snow, but underneath he could feel the water beginning to run, knew the ground was softening, preparing for new grass. In a few weeks the land would come alive. He wished spring would come to Lottie Graham as well.

Chapter 10

As the weather warmed and the days grew longer, Michael returned to school. The fears of the winter receded along with the snowdrifts. A faint hint of new green covered the mountainsides while snowdrops and shy violets showed their faces in the garden. Lottie decided to make a trip into Prospect. Soon it would be time for seeding and her plough needed repairs.

Sean offered to come with her, and even though she didn't really need his help, she was glad of his company. It was the first trip she had made since the Christmas party. Perhaps Prospect had changed its attitude toward her, but she had too long an experience of wagging tongues not to dread encountering the gossips again. At least with Sean beside her, no one would dare to be openly rude.

"Got your rifle?" he asked as she climbed up into the seat beside him.

"Right here." She laid the weapon across her lap. "Do you really think we'll need it in broad daylight?"

"Probably not, but there's still no lawman in Prospect and emotions are running high."

"Do you think I was wrong to send Michael back to school?"

"Probably not," he said again. "The days are longer now so the lad travels in good light."

They didn't speak again until they stopped at the blacksmith's shop on the edge of town. "Did you hear the news?" The smith's broad face was flushed and beaming.

Sean handed the reins to Lottie and jumped to the ground. "What news is that?" he asked as he went around to the back of the wagon to lift out the heavy plough.

"There's a detachment of Northwest Mounted Police on its way to Prospect. They'll soon deal with them Indians. Yes, sir"—he rubbed his hands together in emphatic satisfaction—"and high time too. The whole town's been scared to death all winter. My missus won't even walk to Barclay's Mercantile by herself. Scared some redskin's going to jump out of the bushes and make off with her." He chuckled. "I told her if he did I felt sorry for the Indian, but she said it was no laughing matter and fed me cold beans for supper." He laughed at his own joke. "I heard you lost some cattle, Lottie. How many?"

"Six. More if you count the calves those cows were carrying."

"It's a shame"—the smithy shook his head—"a bloody shame. Still, once the Mounted Police are here, your worries will be over. You going prospecting soon?" He squinted at Sean. "You don't go soon you'll miss the season again. You hear about the big strike up the Wild Horse?"

"I thought that creek was all played out," Sean

said shortly. "Jed Barclay told me last fall there wasn't any use even looking there."

"Sure enough," the smithy agreed. "It was an old claim, sold to some feller from down in Oregon. Bill Creedle thought he'd done pretty well for himself, persuading a greenhorn to pay him a good price for a worthless piece of creekbed. Well"—he laughed heartily, wheezing a little in his glee—"Bill Creedle's madder 'n hell now. The greenhorn found a nugget worth twice what he paid for the claim, and he says he's getting good pay in his pan besides."

While the blacksmith talked, Lottie watched Sean, saw the way his eyes changed, losing their dull, brooding look. Saw their blue depths turn to sparkling azure, as eager as the wavelets that hurried along the surface of the Kootenay River. Her heart clenched as she remembered those same eyes as dark as a thundercloud when he gazed out at the fields of her beloved Pine Creek Farm. As she listened to the smith's excited talk, a leaden weight of foreboding settled in her chest.

Their business with the blacksmith concluded, Sean leaped up into the driver's seat and set the horses trotting down Prospect's main street. Silent and troubled, Lottie sat beside him, wishing with all her heart that she had not chosen this day to visit Prospect.

There was no escaping the gold fever that filled the town. A paper boy ran down the street shouting the headline and waving a newspaper. As they drove past the assay office, she saw the government agent placing a notice in the window. Even the clutch of loafers normally clustered about Jed Barclay's stove were gone, some buying supplies, others hurrying to reregister their claims.

"Afternoon, Lottie." Jed weighed out flour and sugar for her. "Big doings today."

"So I hear."

"Need anything else? I got some new hats in." His eyes flicked to the battered headgear she'd worn for the past three years.

"Not today." She fidgeted, anxious to get away. "Thanks."

"Guess you'll be going any day now." Jed directed this remark at Sean. "Weather's lookin' good."

"Good for seeding," Lottie said shortly.

She completed her business as quickly as possible, but the damage had been done. Beside her in the wagon, heading back to the farm, Sean said not a word but the stern, set look on his face told its own story. She had known this day would come, dreaded it, prayed that some miracle might occur to turn Sean from his chosen course. She should have known better.

The only reason he wasn't already on the gold fields was because of his sense of responsibility to her and Michael. It was in her power to hold him here, forever a hostage to her need, or to set him free. It was an agonizing choice but by the time they topped the rise and looked down on Pine Creek Farm spread out before them in all its verdant glory, she had made up her mind.

"Stop the horses," she said gruffly.

Casting her a puzzled glance, Sean obediently pulled in the reins. For a long time the two of them sat silently gazing out at the meadows and the mountains. The farm was so beautiful, so lush, so generous and eternal. Why couldn't he be content here? She hardened her heart against the love that longed for expression. Once the gold fever took hold of a man it never let him go.

At last she spoke on a long, shuddering breath. "Go. Follow your golden harpy. She is your dream. This"—she spread her hands to indicate the land— "this is mine. I can't relinquish my dreams. I won't deny you yours."

"I can't leave you, Lottie." His voice was harsh, his jaw set in a hard line, his eyes fixed straight ahead. "It's not right. You and Michael here alone."

The words were right, and she had no doubt Sean would do his duty as he saw it, but she had seen the telltale flicker of hope in his eyes. She wouldn't hold him to his own mistaken notion of chivalry. Because she loved him, she had to let him go.

"Go." She twisted sideways on the wagon seat and gently touched her finger to his lips. "I cannot compete with gold fever. If you remain with me, all your life you will harbor regret. Your regret will grow to resentment and anger. You'll end by hating me. I couldn't bear that." Her voice quavered briefly but she quickly regained her control. "Go. Follow in Patrick's footsteps. It is your destiny. As it is mine to remain behind."

Once again she saw the quick flash of excitement in his eyes, the undeniable eagerness to be gone. He caught her hand and pressed it to his cheek. "The Mounted Police are coming." His voice filled with excitement. He released her hand and set the horses trotting toward the stable. "They'll put an end to the Indian trouble. And I'll hire a man to come and help you get the new seeding in. And I'll be back, Lottie, you'll see." His words tumbled over each other in his eagerness to persuade her, and perhaps himself, that his defection was excusable. "I'll be back with bags of gold. I'll shower you with riches, girl, anything you want."

"What I want you cannot buy." She turned her face away.

It took only a couple of days for Sean to pack up his belongings, saddle his mare and ride into Prospect for the last time. Lottie made sure that his pack was filled with food from her larder and his old blankets were exchanged for the warm, thick ones from the bed he had slept in all winter. What she would not do was wish him good-bye and good luck. Nor would she listen to his promises to return.

"Don't look so sad, girl," he begged her on his last morning. "Let me see you smiling. Let me carry that image in my heart until I return."

But she would not yield. "Once you go," she told him, firm in her resolution but with an aching heart, "you are gone forever. I'll not welcome a prospector here again." She turned her back and walked into the house, trying to shut her ears to the sound of his horse's hooves as he rode away.

That evening a sturdy young man named Tom arrived at her door. "Sean O'Connor sent me," he explained. "I'm to help you with the seeding and look after the horses and the herd, at least until the Mounted Police arrive."

She would have sent him away—she had managed alone before, she could do so again—but this night she felt too defeated to summon the energy. "Come in," she said and led him up the stairs to the room that had been Sean's.

Even though spring had come to the Kootenay Valley, the days lay dull and heavy on Lottie's heart. Buds in the apple trees burst into fragrant pink and white bloom. Fresh green grass colored the pastures. New calves appeared on wobbly legs, leaning into their mothers' flanks. The days grew warmer, the earth smelled damp and fecund, but the Sweetheart Tree stayed barren.

Going through the round of her days, she planted her garden, rode herd on her cattle, and gave up her Sunday skirts. Michael talked incessantly of Sean but she wanted only to forget him and their brief time of happiness. Young Tom appeared at her table for meals; otherwise he kept himself to himself, and she was glad.

As the evenings lengthened and the days warmed she returned to her old routine, sitting on the bench beneath the gnarled old apple tree, watching the horizon, waiting and wishing. But what she wished for she no longer knew. It was merely the comfort of familiarity that drew her day after day to the old Sweetheart Tree.

One evening in June, when the chores were done and Michael had gone to bed, she sat at her desk and took up her pen. After that one cruel letter from her father, she'd heard not another word from her family, nor had she sent a letter of her own. But Louisa's picture on her dresser greeted her each morning, and the loneliness in her heart needed some release. *No doubt you will be surprised to hear from me,* she wrote to her sister.

It has been so long since we saw each other. I've missed you, but I knew Father would never forgive me. For years I've hoped that Patrick would somehow, miraculously, come back. I longed to send news that my faith in him had been rewarded. It pains me to admit my pride has been as unyielding as Father's.

You wouldn't recognize me now, Louisa. I'm an inde-

pendent woman. I wear men's pants, and I work in the fields and the stable. I doubt any of the genteel ladies we used to know would invite me into the front parlor. Remember those awful calls we used to make on the church ladies? Father would drone on and on while our hostess poured tea from her best service. You and I would sit primly on a hard sofa, hands neatly folded in our laps, feet flat on the floor, backs straight. And then when we got home to our bedroom, you would imitate everybody, and we'd laugh until our sides hurt. I've missed your laughter, dear sister.

Do you think you might come and visit me for a while? Michael is almost grown up. I'd like him to meet his Auntie Louisa. There's a train now. You could reach the railhead in three days. If you come before freeze-up, you can take a paddle wheeler down the river to Prospect and be here in a matter of days. Imagine! It took me weeks to reach the town when I came west.

I'm sending this letter to the church rather than the manse. I pray someone there will know your whereabouts and pass it on to you. Do come, Louisa. Your loving sister, Lottie.

She folded the letter, placed it in an envelope and wrote the address. Tomorrow she'd ride into Prospect and post it. It would be wonderful to see Louisa again, and strange. Would they still laugh together or had the years stolen that from her as well?

Abruptly she rose from her chair and went downstairs and out through the kitchen door into the warm night. Tonight she didn't go to the Sweetheart Tree, but sat on the verandah steps instead. "Hello, Duke." The dog nudged his nose under her hand. "Did I wake you up?" She dropped an arm about his neck and hugged him close to her body, rubbing her cheek against the smooth fur on the top of his head. She gazed skyward and mocked herself for spending a moonlit night with only a dog for company.

Soon it was high summer with dust hanging in the air and bees buzzing incessantly about the clover tops. Lottie doggedly drove her team round and round the hay field, gathering in the winter's feed. Tom energetically pitched hay onto the wagon but Michael had disappeared. Probably taken his dog and gone fishing, she thought, vexed with his sulks and his shirking. She wished Sean O'Connor had never set sail for Canada, never set foot in Prospect, and never set her frozen heart to feeling again.

She took a deep breath, filling her nostrils with the sweet smell of fresh hay, seeking to lift her spirits. She had always rejoiced in the bounty of her farm, tallying up her crops the way a miser counted his money. But this year, even the sight of filled hay mows and grazing cattle was unable to lighten her heavy heart. The farm, her pride and her protection, had become one more burden on her overladen shoulders.

The wagon was full and she set the horses toward the barn, setting her face to the work at hand, trying to shake off her apathy. "You unload," she said to Tom as they drove onto the barn floor. "I'll tend the horses."

"I can do that," Tom protested. "Mr. O'Connor said I was to—"

"I don't give a fig for what Mr. O'Connor said," she snapped and wrapped the reins about the brake with a vicious twist. "If you want to keep your place here, you'll take your orders from me and no arguing."

"Yes ma'am." Tom shrugged, shook his head, and climbed onto the wagon to begin the task of unloading the hay. She unclipped the traces and led the horses away to their stalls.

Tom was strong and a good worker, but she wished he had more spunk. Sean wouldn't have let her get away with such a display of bad temper. Angrily she stalked into the horse stalls.

"There you go, my beauties," she crooned, lifting the heavy collars from the Clydes. She felt the heat rising from their backs, smelled the strong odor of horseflesh. All the minutiae of life on a farm that should have calmed her and restored her spirit. Yet today, even the soothing, rhythmic task of brushing the sweat from the horses' coats seemed only pointless drudgery.

Day followed day in the same wearying round of toil with never the yeast of laughter or song to leaven it. Soon it was September and she was in the grain field with Tom, preparing for the threshers. She tried not to remember her last harvest, when Sean had come riding into her life like a knight errant, and swept her up in the whirlwind of his vitality.

Instead she focused on her irritation with Michael, who was missing again. All summer long, the boy had managed to disappear whenever there was work to do, returning in the evening with a creel full of trout and a look of bland innocence on his face when she took him to task for shirking. She was at her wit's end with him. She could only hope that when school started next week, his teacher could break through his tough shell of indifference.

She heard a shout and looked over her shoulder to see her wayward son running across the stubble toward her, waving his hand. "Hey, Ma!" he shouted, "Ma, look! We got a letter. I bet it's from Sean."

"Where have you been?" She straightened her back, brushing the hair out of her eyes and pushing it under her hat. "You were supposed to be helping Tom."

"Aw, Ma." Her son ignored her scolding, and thrust a thick vellum envelope into her hand. "Is it from Sean?"

She looked at the letter, turning the envelope over to look at the fine curling letters that spelled out her name and the name of Pine Creek Farm and Prospect, British Columbia. She frowned. "Where did you get this?" she demanded, still angry with him for playing hooky from his chores.

"At the post office, of course."

"You went into Prospect alone, without telling me?" She forgot about the letter as she realized the full extent of Michael's truancy. "You know that's forbidden. What if you'd been lost or attacked by Indians or fallen off your horse? I wouldn't have known where to look for you."

"Aw, Ma." Michael thrust his hands into his pockets and kicked up a dust cloud in the dirt at their feet. "I won't get lost. I've got my compass. Besides, the Mounted Police are here now so the Indians aren't going to attack anybody. They're building a fort in Prospect and I went and talked to the sergeant and he showed me around. They've got a hospital and jail cells and a blacksmith shop and everything."

How had it happened that her son could be gone for hours without her knowing? It seemed only yesterday that she had carried him on her back while she worked, always ready to tend to his needs, never letting him out of her sight. She felt a stab of apprehension. Who knew what tales he had heard in town, tales of adventure and gold strikes?

"You had no business going into Prospect without permission when there were oats to be stooked," she scolded. "Now go and help Tom. It's the least you can do."

His face reddened but he held his ground. "What about the letter?" he asked. "Aren't you even going to open it? It could be from Sean."

"It's not from Sean." She had recognized Louisa's handwriting even after all this time. "You can read it after supper, when you've finished your chores. Now go and help Tom."

Michael spun around on his heel and stomped off toward the other end of the grain field. "I hate you!" he shouted back over his shoulder. "Crazy Lottie!"

Cut to the quick, she sank to her knees beside a sheaf of oats and watched her son's fleeing figure. *It's not my fault!* she wanted to cry after him. *It's not my fault that first Patrick and then Sean abandoned you. It was the gold fever that took them.*

But it was her fault. She had allowed Sean to stay, and had indulged Michael's hero worship, condoned his affection for Patrick's cousin, trusting that Sean would teach him to be a man. She had been wrong. For a second time she'd been beguiled by a pair of Irish eyes. Through ten long years of hardship and loneliness, she had learned nothing. And now Michael was paying the price.

Tiger came and wrapped herself about Lottie's ankles, purring and butting her knees, begging a scratch behind the ears. Now that her kittens were grown, the cat had returned to her old haunts, giving up the soft comforts of her box behind the stove in favor of the freedom to roam and the excitement of the hunt.

Lottie gave the tabby an absentminded pat and wished her life could be so simple, but try as she might, she could not return to her old ways and her old peace of mind. Since Sean had gone she had been restless and discontent, rebelling against the endless toil and soul-deep loneliness that was her lot. With a heavy heart she tucked the letter into her pocket and made her way to the house. There, safely hidden in her own bedroom, she at last broke the seal.

My dearest sister, she read. *You cannot know of the shock and joy your letter brought me. I had thought you were dead.* She read on, learning that Louisa still lived with her father. Their other sisters had married and had babies and often came to visit, but Louisa had remained a spinster, keeping house for their father since their mother had died only two years after Lottie had left them all to travel west. As Lottie had suspected, her father had refused to hear her name spoken once he had learned of her disgrace and had informed his family that she was lost to them forever.

I know it was a cruel and heartless thing to do, Louisa wrote, *but he is old now, Lottie, and crippled with arthritis. I have told him I am writing to you, and he has not forbidden me. I wish I could come to Prospect, as you suggest, but Father is ill. That is why it has taken so long for me to reply to your letter. We moved out of the parsonage three years ago because Father could no longer serve as a minister. He was so poorly earlier this summer that, for*

*several weeks, I didn't even attend church. He's a little
better now, but I could not leave him to undertake a journey to British Columbia.*

*But I've another idea. I know he will not ask you him-
self, but for his sake and mine, Lottie, dearest, please
come home. I cannot bear the thought of you alone in the
wilderness. I want to meet Michael and I think Father
should know his grandson. He's different now, dear. Age
and illness have softened his heart. He will not turn you
away.*

Thoughtfully, she read the letter through twice,
then folded it and placed it under her pillow. She
went to the window and gazed out, although there
was no need. She knew every inch of Pine Creek
Farm. She didn't need her eyes to see the pastures
sloping down to the valley floor, didn't need her
ears to hear the burble of the creek wending its
way across her acres, didn't need her tongue to
taste the sweetness of the air.

Come home. But home was here in this fertile valley, in this bountiful wilderness. And yet . . . She
turned away from the window, crossing the room
to pick up the picture of herself and Louisa that
now stood on her dresser. Wasn't home with family? Shouldn't Michael meet his grandfather and
his cousins?

It was the boy's need for family that had led him
to put Sean on a pedestal, after all. Perhaps she
owed her son a family, more than she owed him a
farm, and the city offered good schools, even a
university. Michael could be a doctor or a lawyer or
a preacher like his grandfather. Good, safe, *respectable* professions. If they stayed in Prospect he
could be lured away from the farm anyway, going
prospecting or joining the Mounted Police.

She returned to the window and saw him racing across the freshly cut fields, Duke at his heels. His arms outstretched, his head leaning forward. As she watched, he tripped and tumbled to the ground, rolling onto his back. Duke leaped on his chest and the two of them wrestled playfully in the stubble. She sighed and turned her back, going slowly down the stairs to the kitchen.

After supper, while Michael grudgingly helped her do dishes, she told him about Louisa's letter. "You have a grandfather in Toronto, and your Aunt Louisa wants us to go there and stay with them."

"We can't do that." Michael was aghast at the idea. "We have to be here for when Sean comes back. And besides, who would feed the horses and look after the cows and gather the eggs and . . ." He ran out of words, overwhelmed by the enormity of abandoning the farm.

"We'd have to sell up," Lottie said, for the first time putting into words the horrible idea that had nagged at her ever since she had read Louisa's letter. *Sell up.* How could she even consider it? Pine Creek Farm was her life. Yet to keep Michael safe, she would sacrifice even that.

"No." Patrick's blue eyes, dark and stormy, glowered at her from Michael's face. "Pa might come home—and Sean. We have to be here."

"Michael, listen to me." She took her hands from the dishpan and wiped them dry on a towel. She looked full at her son. "Your father will not be coming home. It was foolish of me to believe in him for so long."

"No." The boy's chin quivered as he fought back babyish tears. "No!" he shouted, stamping his foot and hurling the dish towel onto the floor. "I won't listen to you. He will come home, and Sean too. You'll see. In the fall, before the snow comes. Sean promised me." He turned and ran from the house, slamming the door so hard the windows rattled.

If he had hoped to dissuade her, Michael had chosen the wrong method. More than anything, his outburst convinced her that she must move away from Prospect. She would not have the boy spend his life in limbo, always waiting, always dreaming of "someday," never content. Whatever her mistakes, Michael deserved better.

Sadly, she returned to her tasks, automatically tidying her kitchen, sweeping a broom across the floor, setting the table for the morrow's breakfast.

Tomorrow she would go to see Sadie Gardener. Her heart quailed at the thought of telling her friend her decision, but Sadie was the only one she could trust. She would ask Sadie and Abner to see to the sale of her cattle in the fall. Tom could stay on until then. She would put his wages in Abner's hands, to be paid out when the disposal of her livestock was complete. She had enough in the bank to buy tickets for herself and Michael on the new Canadian Pacific Railway.

She heard the front door slam and the sound of Michael's footsteps crossing the hall and going up the front stairs, avoiding her. She made a move to go to him, to talk with him, try to explain the hard realities of life here on the farm and the possibilities that awaited him in the city, but she hadn't the heart.

Instead she turned and went outside, seeking the solace of the bench beneath the Sweetheart Tree. This evening she did not look to the horizon but let her gaze move in loving detail over every inch of her land, memorizing the color of the grass along the creek bank, impressing the lines of the fences on her mind, engraving on her heart the gentle slope of the pastures.

The next morning Michael didn't appear for breakfast, but Tom informed her he had seen the lad very early in the morning talking to Tiger in the barn.

"Well," she sighed, setting a full bowl of porridge before Tom, "he'll be in when he gets hungry."

By lunchtime Michael had still not appeared but his fishing pole and his dog were missing as well. He would be home for supper, Lottie assured herself, bringing his catch with him and bragging about the "big one" he would get tomorrow. A day on his own would do him no harm.

But when suppertime came and still he hadn't returned, she began to worry. "Did you see where Michael went fishing?" she asked Tom as the evening hours dragged by.

"Didn't see him put a line in the water," Tom replied. "He was riding along the creek, though, and I watched him until he went into the bush. I guess there's better pools there than out in the open."

"I don't care how good the fishing is." She whipped up her anger as a terrible dread formed into a hard knot in the pit of her stomach. "He shouldn't have stayed away so long."

"I could go and look for him," Tom offered.

"Just a minute, before you go," she replied and went with dragging footsteps toward the back stairs. "I'll check his room, just in case." There was no chance that Michael could have come home and fallen asleep in his own bed without her knowing, but she clung to even that flimsy straw rather than face the real reason that drew her steps onward.

In her mind she relived every word she and Michael had spoken over the summer, every harsh comment, every angry scowl. Since the day Sean had ridden out of their lives, Michael had changed, his sunny disposition disappearing behind a cloud of resentment and morose silence. She had believed—hoped—that it was only a phase in his inevitable growing up and had tried to ignore his black moods. Besides, she too had been troubled. She'd faced too many changes too quickly.

Sean had come bursting into her life, unfreezing her heart and making her vulnerable. The Indian raids had shaken her belief in the safety of her farm, and then Michael had turned into a sullen stranger. She hadn't had time to make peace with this new life. She'd lacked the patience to deal with Michael's moods.

With a trembling hand and quaking heart she pushed open the door to his bedroom and went inside. One swift glance confirmed her dread. The bed was too neat. The door of his wardrobe stood open and some of his clothes were missing. On the washstand, a folded note leaned against the ewer.

She snatched up the paper and scanned the brief message.

"Oh, no," she whispered aloud, sinking onto the bed, the letter gripped in her hand. Fed up with the cheerlessness of their days and adamant that he would not go to Toronto, Michael had gone in search of his father and Sean. *You'll see*, he'd written. *I'll find Pa and then we'll all be happy again.*

"No, no," she moaned, rocking herself on his bed,

touching her hand to the pillow where he had laid his head. "Not you too, Michael. Not you, too."

She lay down on the bed, hugging his pillow to her, cradling it as she had cradled Michael as a baby, while the blackest grief of her life shook her heart, overwhelming her very soul, blocking out the last spark of her will.

When young Tom came knocking at the door asking if he should set out to look for the boy, she turned such a ravaged face toward him she saw him flinch. *Crazy Lottie.* No doubt the whispers would fly that she had finally lost her mind. Yet, strangely, the idea gave her strength, gave her courage, reminded her that she was a survivor.

She got up from the bed and stood tall, fixing her young helper with a resolute eye. "No, Tom," she said. "Michael has run away. I will find him."

She walked down the stairs and out to the stables, her mind racing ahead. She would need supplies. Michael would be hungry and maybe cold. She collected the saddlebags and brought them back to the house to fill. Michael had a twelve-hour start, but if she set out now and traveled all night, she could narrow the gap, perhaps even catch up to him. Michael was still only a boy. He would sleep long past sunup.

"Ma'am, you should wait until morning," Tom tried to remonstrate with her. "It's just asking for trouble to set out at dark. Besides, after a night out the youngster will probably change his mind and come home on his own."

"I wish I could believe you," she said as hope flared and died in an instant, "but this isn't a childish prank. Michael is on a mission. I must go. There's a full moon tonight and I know the path along the creek. Now, if you want to help, go and saddle my horse."

As she went upstairs to fetch blankets and extra socks, she heard him leave the house muttering under his breath, the word *crazy* clearly audible as he passed beneath her window.

Chapter 11

When he left Pine Creek Farm, Sean rode directly to the government office in Prospect and registered Patrick's old claim at the Big Bend in his own name. There might be nothing left on it, but it gave him a place to start and would save him the necessity of journeying out to register a new stake.

He collected the rest of his supplies from Jed Barclay's Mercantile, located and hired young Tom to help Lottie during the summer, and set his face to the west, determined to make his dream of riches a reality. As he rode out of Prospect he kept his eyes fixed straight ahead. No looking back in regret. He must focus on the adventure that lay ahead and try to forget the despair he'd glimpsed in Lottie's eyes before she'd turned her back on him.

It grieved him to cause her more pain, but he had to follow his own destiny or live forever with bitterness and what-might-have-been. Even Lottie had known he could not call himself a man if he turned back from his chosen course.

When he came back, he vowed, then they could speak of love. He would meet her as an equal with wealth of his own. He would have earned her trust. He didn't believe her assertion that she wouldn't wait. Where would she go? Her land held her in thrall as surely as the Emerald Isle held its leprechauns. Come freeze up, he would return to Pine Creek Farm and Lottie.

He lifted his eyes to scan the mountains and the mighty forests. Excitement stirred in his veins. His years of waiting were over. He let out a loud whoop and listened to his voice echoing between the hills and down the valley until it was lost in the vastness of the land. His horse tossed her head, jangling the bit. He laughed aloud and patted her neck. "That's right, old girl. Nothing will stop us now."

Following the Dewdney Trail as it wound westward, he kept his ears open for any mention of Patrick among the many prospectors he encountered but learned nothing. He chided himself for being as foolish as Lottie. Patrick was the past. The future lay before him.

The wilderness had changed since the first prospectors had raced across it to find the mother lode. Roads and trains and steamships eased the journey from Prospect to Big Bend. Where Patrick would have trekked the whole way on foot or on horseback, Sean spent only a few days on horseback before boarding a paddlewheeler to travel up the Kootenay Lakes.

Once on board he left his mare in a stall belowdecks and joined the crowd of men lounging against the rail or packed tightly onto the benches on deck. Excitement prickled his scalp and ran like the tingle of lightning down his spine as he watched the paddlewheel, each turn taking him closer to the

Big Bend. After so many years of waiting and so much sacrifice, at last he was on the gold trail, his dream within his grasp.

Leaning against the rail, he listened to miners' tales, soaking up the lore of the gold fields, filling his mind with bits of old-timer wisdom and his imagination with visions of wealth.

"There's still gold for the panner," a young man argued, not wanting to listen to the grizzled veteran who warned that only big companies could afford to work the deep diggings.

"There's no gold left in the shallow gravels," the old-timer contended, only to be shouted down by other, ever hopeful prospectors.

He heard stories of fabulous riches and raucous yarns of the high living a successful miner could enjoy when he hit the big cities. The saga of Billy Barker was repeated over and over, sometimes as a warning to the foolish, other times as a fable to encourage the fainthearted.

"He didn't get rich in the California rush," Sean heard, "but that didn't stop him, no sirree. Billy Barker knew there was gold for the taking. You just have to find it."

"I heard he went down fifty-two feet before he made his strike."

"That's right. Lots of men gave up but Billy, there, he had a dream about the number fifty-two, and he kept going."

"Is it true he took out over a thousand dollars in just two days?"

"Yep, and that was just the beginning. Billy made a fortune in that strike. He's been living like a king ever since."

"I heard he's going broke."

"Don't matter. He can always go back and work

his claim again. There's lots more gold in these here mountains."

Sean listened to it all, feeling the fever in his veins. *Thousands of dollars,* he thought, *in just a few weeks.* He'd be rich before the snow flew. Then he'd head back and court Lottie as she deserved. No more the poor relation begging work for the price of his keep. He'd buy her jewels and dresses and all the cattle and horses she could want. They would travel, first class. Visit New York and Vancouver and San Francisco.

His grand imaginings stumbled a little as he thought of persuading Lottie to leave Pine Creek Farm but his optimism soon overrode that small worry. Once he showed her how easy life could be, she'd be eager to leave the hard work behind. He repeated this assurance over and over to himself as the realization grew that his dream for the future now included Lottie and Michael. He still wanted the gold, but he wanted it for Lottie.

At the head of the lakes he disembarked and the trek grew more difficult. A trail of sorts had been hewn out of the wilderness by the thousands of miners who had traveled that way before him, but those same miners had left behind piles of tailings and rotting flumes and gouged-out creek beds that forced those following to cut new routes deep into the forest. Often he had to dismount and lead his horse along treacherous, narrow paths, skirting the edges of canyons, only inches from a plunge into the depths and certain death. His fear of heights dogged his footsteps, often making him hesitate, setting his heart to pounding in his chest, earning him the curses of the men following behind.

He pressed on, learning to keep his face turned toward the mountainside, never allowing himself to peer into the chasms that yawned just inches from his feet. When he couldn't force his legs to move, he let his surefooted mare lead the way, while he clung to a rope tied to her saddle. He shut his ears to the sound of stones and pebbles rattling down a cliff, closed his mind to all but the call of gold.

The flimsy, makeshift bridges thrown in haste across creeks too deep to ford were the worst of his nightmares. Every step along these swaying death traps brought a cold sweat to his brow and nausea to his throat. But he gritted his teeth and persisted.

Day after day, he plodded on. The trail grew crowded with miners, some going in with hope, others coming out. Then, finally, beyond the Dalles des Morts, he reined in at the top of a rise and looked down on the Big Bend of the Columbia River.

At home, in Ireland, he'd imagined himself a lone prospector in the midst of a pristine wilderness. Instead he gazed upon a tent city thronged with hundreds of miners. The forest close by the river had been plundered to build rude cabins and rockers and flumes. It was doubtful there was a stick of firewood within easy reach of the stream. Piles of tailings choked the riverbanks, while dozens of men knelt in the water, plying their gold pans.

Tired and dirty, he surveyed the scene. He'd made it. After all this time, gold was within his grasp. "Hallelujah," he whispered softly, then nudged his heels against his horse and rode down the slope toward the camp. The smell of crowded, unwashed humanity assailed his nostrils. In the heat of the day, flies by the thousands plagued both men and horses. A drunken brawl broke out in the doorway of one of the tiny saloons that dotted the shanty town and spilled into the muddy street. No one paid any attention.

Watched by suspicious eyes, he made his way along the riverbank, past claim posts and workings and the belligerent men who guarded them. Where French Creek joined the river, he came upon a rude log building, a little larger than the miners' shacks, that sported a sign reading GENERAL STORE. He dismounted and dropped the reins of his tired horse over the hitching rail and stepped into the dim interior.

After the brightness of the outdoors, it took a moment before his eyes adjusted to the dark room but eventually he made out sacks of flour and sugar and beans behind the rough counter. A sign over a back door indicated feed and grain for sale. A slim, dark man with a French-Canadian accent was waiting on another customer when Sean entered, so he had plenty of time to assess the meager supply of goods and the exorbitant prices attached to them. Tobacco was fifteen dollars a pound, and he wouldn't be surprised if it had been soaked in the river overnight to make it heavier. He fingered the roll of bills in his pocket. He'd need to find gold just to pay his expenses.

The previous customer went out grumbling and weighing his poke, now considerably lighter, in his hand.

"I'll be needing—" Sean said, stepping forward, but before he could ask for the few items he needed to replace, the shopkeeper came around the counter, his face creased in a huge smile, his arms outstretched in welcome. *"Bon, bon!"* he shouted joyfully. "Beeg Ireesh. You come back."

Sean's hand was grasped and pumped in an extravagance of bonhomie while the little Frenchman rattled on in a mixture of French-Canadian patois and rough English, all the while smiling and thumping Sean on the shoulder with delight. "How you come back here? Where your woman?" The man peered around Sean's shoulder. "You hiding the pretty Lottie, eh?" he asked, grinning and winking and squinting at the door, as though expecting to see a lady come tripping over its threshold.

Sean freed himself from the storekeeper's exuberant grasp and stared at him in astonishment. The man must be mad. But his new friend continued to beam at him from intelligent black eyes. Slowly, understanding dawned. "Would you be talking about one Patrick Malone?" he asked, guessing that his uncanny likeness to his missing cousin had confused the storekeeper as much as it had startled Lottie when she first set eyes on him.

"*Oui, oui,*" the man babbled volubly. "Beeg Pat, that you."

"No, it's not," Sean replied firmly. "Your 'Big Pat' was my cousin. My name's Sean O'Connor."

"*Non!*" The little man fell back in amazement. "*C'est impossible.*" He struck his hand to his forehead in disbelief and walked around Sean, eyeing him from all directions as though convinced he were the victim of a practical joke.

"When was the last time you saw my cousin?"

"Oh, long time." The Frenchman shook his head and pursed his lips. "Five, ten years, maybe. He came say good-bye. He say, 'Henri, I go now. I go home to Lottie.' "

Sean felt the air rush out of his lungs. If he had needed any convincing that Henri had known Patrick Malone, the repeated reference to Lottie dispelled any lingering doubts.

"Did he say anything else? What route he planned to take? If he had partners or traveled alone?"

"*Non*, he go alone," Henri declared. "Beeg Pat, 'e never 'ave a partner. 'E say, go down the lakes, then maybe try the Moyie, but already 'is poke full of gold, and 'is saddlebags, too. You want Beeg Pat, you go find Lottie in Prospect."

"No." Sean shook his head sadly. "Whatever happened to my cousin, he never made it back to Lottie. She's been waiting for him for ten years."

"Ah, *c'est triste.*" Henri wrung his hands in sympathy. "*La pauvre* Lottie."

"You never heard of him again? No rumors he'd been seen somewhere else or"—he hesitated to put his worst fear into words—"or that he was dead?"

"*Peut-être.*" Henri shrugged expressively, spreading his hands in a typical Gallic gesture. "Always there are accidents, robberies, shootings. Who knows?"

Who knew, indeed, but the conviction was growing in Sean's mind that Patrick Malone had met with some mischance along the way. Would it break Lottie's heart to learn the truth? Or would it set her free to love again?

He shook his head, clearing his mind. That was a question for the future. Today he needed fresh supplies. When he'd filled his pockets with gold, then he would set about wooing and winning the woman who haunted his dreams.

"Well, Henri," he got down to business, "I need oats for my horse, and beans and bacon for myself."

"*Oui*, you come right place." Henri bustled about weighing and measuring, handing Sean the miner's

rations in exchange for the lion's share of his remaining cash.

On a sudden inspiration he asked Henri if he
knew the location of Big Pat's claim.

"Everybody know," Henri replied. "Your cousin,
he always talk and laugh. He one 'appy feller, your
Pat. His claim out on Charlotte Creek; 'e name it
for 'is lady, *n'est-ce pas?* You go up river about two
mile, then go west on the creek about 'alf mile.
You find his claim post still there.

"Thanks, Henri." Sean picked up his provisions,
loaded them onto his horse and set off upriver. It was
slow going on foot, but his little mare was weighed
down with supplies and couldn't carry him as well.
By evening he had located Charlotte Creek. Turning
up the waterway, he followed an old path until he
came upon a dilapidated log cabin and a weathered claim stake with the inscription, *P. Malone,* still
faintly discernible, carved into its length.

He had finally reached the end of his rainbow.
He stood in the tall grass and looked about him,
savoring each second of the time. He reached into
the saddlebag and drew out the deed to the claim.
Two hundred and fifty feet along the creek was
his. Excitement drove out his fatigue.

He tied his horse to a scrubby bush and stepped
up to the cabin, pushing on the rough plank door.
It sagged on its hinges and he put his shoulder to
it to force it open. Inside, the cabin was dark and
filled with cobwebs and the droppings of animals
who had made their nests in the hut over the
years, but there was a stove and a table and even
the remains of a bunk bed.

He held his nose and walked inside, pulling a
ragged curtain off what had been a back window.
There was no glass, but at the moment he would

rather have fresh air. He'd have a campfire and sleep outside tonight, he decided, but in the morning he would set about making the cabin habitable. He'd be glad of a roof over his head and a hot stove to sit beside when the weather turned bad.

He left the cabin and walked down to the creek. No doubt other prospectors had worked the claim since Patrick's disappearance, but that didn't stop him from dipping his gold pan into the water and bringing up a load of gravel. Squatting on his haunches, he swirled the black sand in the stream, letting the water carry away the lighter rock and gravel, leaving a residue of fine pebbles and sand. He tilted the pan more steeply, submerging it in the water and swirling it around, watching as more pebbles floated free. Finally, when only fine particles remained, he took a pair of tweezers from his pocket and picked through the leavings, squinting his eyes against the setting sun.

There! The glint of gold caught his eye. Excitement gripped his throat as he used the tweezers to lift the yellow grit from the debris of worthless sand. *Gold!* He held it up to the light, turning it this way and that with the tweezers, watching in delight as the sun caught it, throwing glittering splinters of light from its yellow surface.

He sat back on his heels, holding the gold aloft with the tweezers, staring at it, mesmerized. After all the years of waiting and planning and hoping and fighting, after all that, he had finally struck gold. Only a pittance, he admitted honestly, but it was an omen. He was meant to be here. He had been right to come. He wished he could have come with Lottie's blessing.

He dropped the speck of gold into the poke he now wore about his neck. The first deposit on his fortune. He strode up to the old claim post and carved his own name under Patrick's. He could build a rocker and sift through the old tailings, pick up the pay that had been missed the first time. Unlike his cousin, he was a patient man and thorough. He might even sink a shaft, he thought, remembering the tales of Billy Barker.

Glancing once more at the sun, already sinking behind the peaks of the Monashee range, he left the creek's edge and made his way back to the cabin. In the lee of the hut, he built himself a fire and heated beans and bacon in a frypan, set a coffeepot over the flames and settled down, his back resting against his saddle, his horse contentedly munching on the long grass that grew against the cabin walls.

The evening drew in, cool enough to drive the flies away. Stars flickered overhead. An owl hooted in the forest. He ate his dinner, then lay looking up at the sky, wondering if Lottie gazed from her window at those same stars and thought of him.

It was his last night of ease. From then on he worked feverishly, making the cabin habitable and building a rocker. During the days he shoveled gravel, bailed water, and sorted the coarser gravel caught in the riffles of the sluice. In the evenings he panned the fine sand that had been washed out of the apron in the first sorting. It was laborious, back-breaking toil, but the reward was a steadily growing hoard of fine particles of gold.

He met other prospectors on the creek, some of them like himself, working alone on a small claim, others having thrown in their lot with the big out-fits like Consolation. Whenever he met an old-timer, he asked about Patrick.

Little by little, he gleaned a history of his cousin's life on the creek. Apparently Patrick had been lucky in his claim, striking pay in the first pan. It wasn't long before he was known as a rich man. But Patrick had loved to spend his money as well, frequenting the rude saloons that sprang up overnight in a mining camp, and becoming a favorite among the hurdy-gurdy girls.

Anyone who remembered Pat Malone spoke of laughter and singing, and always at the end of an evening, with a tear in the eye, made a maudlin toast to Lottie. When Patrick had struck out for home, everyone knew he carried a rich payload in his saddlebags and love in his heart for the "girl he'd left behind." No one had heard of him since.

But he hadn't time for brooding over Patrick. As the weeks wore on, bone-chilling fatigue eroded his initial fascination for the golden dust. Sorting through the washings of the rocker apron, dipping his pan into the water, levering out a dishful of black sand, swishing it round and round, and picking through the rubble that remained in the bottom filled him with weariness. Flies, cold, heat and poor food took their toll on his body, but worse was the emptiness that ate at his heart. Even a golden glitter in the bottom of his pan ceased to fascinate him.

He missed Lottie. Missed the timbre of her voice as she read aloud from her favorite poets. Missed the understanding that flowed between them when they chuckled together over one of Michael's escapades. Missed the sight of her welcoming him home. The gleam of sunshine on Lottie's hair had replaced the gleam of gold in his dreams.

One morning, too tired to pick up his shovel, he stood in the door of Patrick's old cabin, staring out at the ugly tailings and scarred landscape of the creek, but in his mind's eye he saw the fertile soil of Pine Creek Farm and fat cattle grazing in its lush meadows. In memory he strode down the path from the house into a barn filled with sweet-smelling hay. The grain would be ripening soon, ready for cutting and stooking.

He hoped Lottie would leave the work to Tom but knew in his heart she'd be working alongside the hired hand, matching her strength to his, challenging him to keep pace with her. He scowled and picked up his shovel, heading down to his workings at the creek.

Days passed and the gold dust in his poke grew heavier and the emptiness in his heart grew greater. Listening to the whiskey jacks calling for their mates, his loneliness increased. At night, when he gazed at the stars, instead of seeing the glint of gold and the lights of New York City reflected in their sparkle, he saw the tears glinting in Lottie's eyes when he bade her good-bye. The gurgle of the creek outside the cabin, which used to murmur *riches, . . . riches, . . . riches . . .* now seemed to whisper *dross . . . dross . . . dross . . .* He felt as though his soul had passed through the refiner's fire, purifying him of old, worn-out beliefs, leaving only the tempered steel of truth.

He'd reached the end of his rainbow, only to discover the pot of gold was empty. He'd left his true treasure at Pine Creek Farm. He dreamed now of a lamp in the window and bread baking in the oven, Michael chattering at his side, and Lottie. Lottie welcoming him in from the dark and the cold, Lottie working beside him, sharing her dreams. Those were the visions that filled his heart as he looked into the sand in the bottom of his pan.

Yet, he would not crawl back to her like a whipped

puppy, a disillusioned dreamer, to hang on her skirts. The image of Patrick's father—drunk, maudlin, full of apologies until the next time—filled him with disgust. He would never be just another drunken Irishman, dependent on his wife for the price of a whiskey. He had promised Lottie riches, and Sean O'Connor was not one to break his promises.

He attacked his claim with renewed vigor, working from sunup to sundown, sinking a shaft into the soft bank of the creek, digging deeper, working with a frenzied determination that yielded up the wealth others had left behind. His were hard diggings but the reward was great. By summer's end he felt he had earned the right to go home.

He had gold in his pockets to shower her with jewels and fine gowns, or more acres and more cattle, if she chose. He could meet her as an equal, a man who could provide for her, cherish her and make up to her for all the hardship she had known.

With a cheerful heart he bought a mule to carry out his gear, and packed his saddlebags. The evening before he headed out he made one last trip into Henri's little store.

Just as in Jed Barclay's more expansive Mercantile, a group of miners sat about the potbellied stove, soaking up the heat and swapping tall tales. In good spirits, he decided to join them.

"Did you hear about Old Man Rawlins?" asked one.

"What about him?"

"Heard he got himself a bath and a shave, put on his Sunday suit, and went a-calling on the Widow Jenkins."

The series of raucous guffaws that greeted this piece of news left Sean bewildered and confused.

"Heard she run him off with a shotgun," continued the narrator of the tale, much to the amusement of his cronies.

"Is the Widow Jenkins so formidable, then?" Sean asked.

"That's the word for it," came the reply, "but she ain't a widow."

"Then why—"

"It's like this," explained his raconteur. "Bill Jenkins came out here at the start of the rush, in sixty-five. Brought his young bride with him. They staked a claim and worked it for maybe ten years, give or take, had a couple of young 'uns. Life was good. Then, the easy pay ran out, so Jenkins, he decides to try further north. He leaves his missus to hold their claim here and off he goes. Last anyone heard of him for five years. Everyone but his wife figured he was dead, but then, one day, home he comes, spent the winter here, then in the spring, he's off again.

"But this time he's been gone so long, new fellers think his missus is a widow but she won't have it. Swears her man is coming home, same as last time."

"Crazy woman," another man grunted. "I tried to buy that stake from her. Would have paid her enough so she could've moved back to her own people in San Francisco. She wouldn't budge. Said she wasn't going anywhere without her husband."

"If she wants a husband, there's plenty on offer." The first man took up the tale again. "She could do real well for herself too. Plenty of fellers here with rich diggings looking for a wife."

"*Mais non.*" Henri broke into the conversation. "Mrs. Jenkins, she is in love." He struck a dramatic pose with his hand on his heart. "Me, I understand. Once I had love. My Isabella, she had the beautiful face, the gentle heart. I love her with my life. But 'er papa"—the little French Canadian shrugged expressively—" 'er papa, 'e an important man in Montreal. 'E say, Isabella marry a rich man, not poor Henri. She cry, she say she love me, but . . ." He spread his hands in a helpless gesture. "She marry Papa's rich friend and I come west."

"You're not poor now, Henri," chided one of the miners, scowling at the pouch of tobacco he'd just paid for. "You could have a wife."

Non, non—the little man sighed—"never do I love again. Always I see my Isabella's face. Maybe, when I am old and she is old, and 'er papa and 'er rich 'usband are gone, maybe then we will meet again. Until then . . ." He shrugged his shoulders with Gallic resignation and fell silent.

Suddenly the room lost its warmth and its camaraderie for Sean. He shivered, as though a ghost had trod on his grave. Abruptly he left the cheerful group by the potbellied stove and strode out into the frosty night. With long, angry steps he retraced the path to his cabin, cursing Patrick all the way. At last he understood and the knowledge was bitter. He'd been so smug, so caught up in his own conceit, he'd believed all he had to do was show up with gold in his pocket and Lottie would fall into his arms. He hadn't understood the depths of her passion. The miners at Big Bend laughed at Mrs. Jenkins for her loyalty and the women in Prospect scorned Lottie for hers. None of them were capable of understanding a love so intense it could survive even in the face of apparent desertion.

Even loving Lottie as he did, he had failed to recognize the sincerity and steadfastness of her nature. Even if she succumbed to the loneliness of her life and allowed him to love her, so long as his cousin haunted her heart, Lottie could never be truly his.

Filled with frustration and longing, he picked up the whiskey bottle he kept and took a long swallow. The fiery liquid burned all the way down. He took another swig, seeking the oblivion of a drunken stupor. But the bottle was only half full, and even after he had emptied it, he was wide awake and hurting.

In the morning he went back to working his claim, undecided whether to stay or strike out. But strike out for where? There was no place he wanted to be except with Lottie. His notion of rich living in the city now seemed more absurd than the leprechaun's magic. Next week, he thought, swinging his pick against a large boulder, next week he'd decide on winter lodgings.

A week passed. Each day, he delayed, unwilling to take a step that would remove him once and for all from Prospect and Lottie Graham. But the days were running out. If he stayed much longer on Charlotte Creek he would be trapped for the winter, paying out a big portion of his earnings to little Henri for flour and sugar and ammunition.

On a cold, rainy morning he walked down to the creek, picked up a flat stone and sent it skipping across the surface of the water, remembering the first day he'd met Lottie. Wild and windblown she'd been, yet with a dauntless quality about her, fighting the storm with only a child for help. A reluctant chuckle rose in his throat as he remembered how she had threatened to shoot him.

He picked up another stone and sent it skimming after the first, remembering too the heartbreak in her eyes when she had realized he was not Patrick Malone come home at last. And then he knew, the knowledge coming upon him as blindingly bright as the sun breaking through the clouds.

If Lottie were ever to be free, he had to discover Patrick's fate. She had spurned his promise of gold and jewels but he could bring her a better gift. He would give her freedom and a whole heart.

And what if Patrick was still alive? He quailed at the thought but determined, if by some miracle his wayward cousin was still in the land of the living, he would drag him back to Pine Creek Farm, by force if necessary, and compel him to do right by Lottie. If, as was more likely, Patrick had perished, he would discover the story by whatever means it took and bring that knowledge to Lottie. Once she knew the truth and was free of Patrick's ghost, he would beg her to marry him. Then he would throw his heart and soul into making her happy.

His decision made, he lost no time in repacking his gear and heading out. Over and over, as he worked his way down the river and detoured along the little creeks, he asked the questions. "How long have you been on the gold fields? Did you ever meet a man called Patrick Malone? About ten years ago. He looked a lot like me." Day after day he received the same puzzled stare, careless shrug, and sometimes a muttered curse or a fearful glower as a superstitious miner turned his back.

As he trekked down the Columbia, away from the gold fields, he was joined by other miners, some cursing their bad luck, others with furtive, secretive eyes scanning each man's saddlebags, assessing the possibility of striking gold in a different way. A few were openly boastful, bragging of the richness of their claim, vowing to return the following spring. It was one of these men, a longtime prospector, who finally answered Sean's question with a glimmer of new information.

"I remember a man," he said. "Black Irish, we used to call him. You have the look of him, all right, except he was always laughing. Never met a man that beat him for finding the joke in everything. I mind one time we had a storm, put the river into flood, washed the bank right out from under his tent.

"There he was looking at his blankets floating in mud, his kettle and frypan missing, himself drenched to the skin and filthy. Well, blamed if he didn't just pick himself up and jump in the river. We all thought he was trying to kill himself but then he gets out, laughing his head off, and says he figures the Lord was telling him it was time for a bath." The old prospector shook his head, incredulous still. "Never met a man could laugh like that, before or since."

"Ever hear what happened to him?" Sean's idle tone belied the urgency of his question.

"Expect he's sitting on his own front porch with his sweetheart, Lolly, Laura, something like that. He used to talk about her no end. Soon as he struck it rich he would be off home to . . . Lottie! That was her name."

"Well, he never made it," Sean said. "You remember him saying anything about the route he'd take?"

"Dunno exactly." His informant scratched his head and thought a while. "I mind he was talking of going to Kootenay Landing. Figured he'd buy some finery for his lady there. Never heard no more after that. Pity if he didn't get back to his Lottie. He'd done all right on his claim but it was all for her. She was a lady, he said, and now he could treat her like she deserved."

Armed with this new knowledge Sean pressed on, convinced he was following the right path. Patrick had traveled the Kootenay Lakes route rather than the Arrow Lakes or the Columbia River itself. He would look for more news at Kootenay Landing. There must be someone, a shopkeeper or saloon owner, who would remember a man with his looks and a hearty laugh.

A few days later, footsore and weary, he finally reached Kootenay Landing. His sturdy mule, stubborn and ugly but surefooted on the treacherous passes and tough enough to withstand the hardships of a rough trail and poor forage, had withstood the journey without mishap, but his little mare needed a rest and a feed of oats. When he reached the livery stable he led his hardworking beasts inside and purchased fresh hay and clean stalls for them. Then he took himself to the hotel, ordered a room and a bath, and lay down on a soft bed to rest. Later he'd go down to the bar for a drink and a hot meal and pursue his quest for recollections of Patrick.

Chapter 12

While Sean was heading south to the Kootenay Lakes and filled with renewed hope, Lottie was traveling northwest and filled with dread. She'd been on the trail for four days. She was weary and saddle-sore and wracked with worry and guilt. If only she hadn't quarreled with Michael. If only she hadn't allowed her own unhappiness to blind her to her son's distress. "Dear God!" she cried aloud as she sat by her small campfire and gazed at the stars overhead. "Where is my son? Please don't take my son, too."

The stars continued to twinkle high above and a night creature rustled in the underbrush, but no voice answered her prayers. She pulled her blanket about her and wondered if Michael was warm enough. Was he alone and frightened in the vastness of the wilderness? Or worse, had he met with evil men?

She had stuck to the Dewdney trail but had wasted many hours going partway along some of

the creeks and secondary tracks that crossed it. She believed Michael would travel the main trail but he could easily have wandered onto another path and gotten lost. Panic rose in her throat as she considered the impossibility of finding one boy in this immense landscape. But she fought it back, convinced in her heart that Michael had followed Sean and Sean had taken the quickest route to the Kootenay Lakes and the Big Bend.

She shivered as a nighthawk swooped low over her head. An evil omen? Already she had met miners coming out of the gold fields, heading for winter lodgings in town, and none of them had seen a boy with a dog. She got up from the fire and collected more wood to feed its flame, using the physical action to calm her mental strain. It was a useless exercise. Until she had Michael safe in her arms, nothing would lessen the awful terror that flooded every cell of her being.

To fight her fear she turned to rage. Rage against the man who had brought this latest calamity upon her. If Sean O'Connor hadn't come conniving and worming his way into her home, Michael would be safe in his own bed. It was Sean who had filled the boy's head with tales of gold, Sean who had stolen her trust and then betrayed her.

In an agony of suspense she rose, saddled her horse, and doused the smoldering fire. She could not wait until light. Every hour she delayed took Michael farther from her. Knowing her haste was foolish, yet unable to wait for the dawn, she mounted her horse and set off, trusting in a fitful moon to light the trail.

Sensing her anxiety, Titian shied at every shadow, dancing sideways at every stir in the undergrowth.

She fought to control him, but when a hare leaped across the path, she was lost. Titian reared, tossing her to the ground, and fled into the night.

"Whoa!" she screamed, recovering her wind and making a futile lunge for the reins. It was too late. Her horse was gone. She could hear him crashing through the underbrush and flung herself into the bushes in one last effort to catch him but she only frightened him more. The sound of his hooves thundering down the trail grew fainter and she was alone. She sank onto the ground, huddling her knees to her chin, and wished she could die.

But when morning came, she called on the last of her spirit and got up. So long as she had breath in her body, she would search for Michael. On foot, bruised and with blood oozing from a cut on her cheek, she pressed forward, stopping only to drink from the creeks she crossed. Her canteen, food and rifle had all disappeared with her horse. She had only the money she wore in a money belt about her waist.

For two more days she walked, ignoring the pain in her blistered feet, ignoring the hunger that gnawed at her stomach, pushing herself beyond exhaustion until at last she boarded the paddlewheeler for Kootenay Landing. Not caring that she looked like a madwoman, she approached the captain, demanding to know if a boy and a dog had boarded his vessel lately.

"No ma'am." The captain shook his head. About to turn away, he seemed to change his mind and turned back to her. "Are you ill, ma'am?"

"No." She gripped the rail of the boat, faint with hunger and weary to the bone. "I'm a little hungry, and I've lost my son."

"Come in here." The captain took her arm and led her into the pilothouse. "You can sit there"—he pointed to a small bench beside a stove—"and get warm." He dug into a duffel bag under the bench and withdrew a sandwich wrapped in paper. "Have a bite of this. My missus makes the best bread and cheese on the lakes."

"I can pay," she whispered and fumbled with the money belt.

"Don't be ridiculous." The captain thrust the sandwich into her hand, then turned his back. He pulled a cord, sounding the ship's whistle, and began maneuvering them away from the shore.

Too tired to argue and grateful for the man's kindness, Lottie bit into the sandwich. Once they were out in the middle of the lake, the captain glanced at her again. "Now, what's all this about losing your son?"

Overwhelmed by the man's gruff kindness, she poured out her story, not sparing herself in the telling. "I should have kept a closer watch on him," she finished on a whisper. "It's all my fault."

"I doubt that." The captain spoke into one of the tubes close by the wheel, ordering more speed from the engine room. "Never met a boy yet that didn't kick at the traces when he started getting older. What's his name?"

"Michael Graham."

"Well, Mrs. Graham, I'm sorry I can't tell you I saw him, but there's more than one ship on these lakes. Could be you'll hear more news of him at Kootenay Landing."

She clutched at the straw of hope he'd thrown her. When the paddlewheeler docked, she thanked the captain for his kindness and stumbled down the gangway with the rest of the passengers. She searched up and down the dock, asking everyone she met if they'd seen a boy. Her questions were met with shakes of the head and sometimes a rude demand to go away.

Exhausted and near hysteria, she made her way down the rutted main street before staggering into the only hotel in town. Someone here must have seen him, a young boy, alone. Surely someone would have news of her son.

Curious eyes turned to stare as she stood weaving in the doorway, a figure of ridicule, but even in despair she knew how to face down the curious and the hostile. Summoning all her hauteur, she stared straight ahead and announced in clear, carrying tones, "I'm looking for a boy with a dog."

Lottie! Sean wheeled, dropping his whiskey onto the bar. Lottie, covered in dirt, her hair a wild tangle, hollow-cheeked, her eyes sunken in her face. The woman of his dreams now stood before him in the flesh.

"Lottie!" He leaped to catch her as she seemed about to faint. "Lottie, darlin'." He wrapped his arms about her, unmindful of her dirt. "It's all right, girl, I'm here now."

His illusions of love and gratitude quickly shattered as she pushed hard against his chest, sending him staggering backward.

"You!" she shrieked, nearly demented with rage. "You!" In her anguish she leaped at him, pounding him with her fists, clawing at his arms, screaming her agony. "Where is my son! What have you done with Michael?"

He caught her hands as they flailed uselessly against his superior strength. "Lottie, stop it." He held her arms at her side, forcing her to stand still and listen. "Hush now." He gently pulled her outside, away from the gleeful eyes of the saloon's patrons.

"Where is he?" she whimpered, the fight gone out of her. She slid weakly out of his arms, collapsing onto the boardwalk, her face buried against her knees.

"Hush, love, hush." He knelt beside her, holding her trembling body against his own. Beneath her heavy shirt he could feel the sharpness of her bones. Her cheeks were hollow and her long, graceful neck seemed too thin to support the weight of her head. *Dear God, what has happened to her?* Fear touched his heart as he imagined an Indian raid. Was that why she was wandering the countryside in such a state, searching for Michael?

"Tell me," he urged, his voice a hoarse whisper while his imagination conjured up a host of unspeakable terrors: Pine Creek Farm in flames, Michael kidnapped, Tom killed, Lottie—

His gut contracted with horror. He had been so sure she was safe, with young Tom to guard the farm and the police to guard the town. He would never have left her alone if he'd thought there was still danger. "Ah, Lottie," he groaned, a wave of guilt breaking over him as he held her closer, trying now, when it was too late, to protect her. "Tell me, darlin'."

"Michael is gone!" She raised desperate, hate-filled eyes to his. "He went after you! If Michael is dead, Sean O'Connor, you'll have killed him." Her voice broke on the words, and she covered her face with her hands, rocking herself back and forth in her agony.

Transfixed by the magnitude of her pain and the horror of having played a part, however unwittingly, in her trouble, he could do nothing but hold her close while anguish shuddered through her body.

"Thought you might be wanting this." The bartender appeared beside him, holding out his untouched whiskey. "My missus says to bring the lady around to the kitchen if you want a woman's help."

Grateful, Sean took the proffered drink and pressed it to Lottie's lips. "Here you are, my girl. Drink a little of this. It'll steady you."

Lottie shook her head and tried to push his hand away, but he gently insisted, tipping the strong spirit into her mouth while he continued to soothe her with soft words. "We'll find him, darlin'," he promised, holding his own fear in check. "We'll find him. We're in this together now."

At last her sobs grew quieter and he was able to persuade her to accept the landlady's help. He took her around to the kitchen door of the hotel, shielding her from the stares of rude men in the tavern, then left her to that kind lady's ministrations while he went to make his own arrangements. Lottie needed rest and good food and clean clothes. She would also need a horse.

When he returned Lottie was drinking a restorative cup of tea with the landlady. Her face was washed and she was in control of herself once more, but the deep, haunted look in her eyes remained unchanged. It nearly broke his heart.

She followed him without argument when he escorted her to his room, hers now, but the light had gone from her. He almost wished she would scream and rave at him. This quiet, obedient automaton frightened him even more than the hysterical dervish who had flung herself at him and tried to claw his eyes out.

Once in the privacy of his room, he showed her the fresh clothes he had bought for her and the bath he had ordered. "You'll feel better," he said, emptying pails of hot water into the tin tub, "once you've bathed and eaten. Then we'll talk and make our plans."

Lottie only turned dull, lifeless eyes upon him. "It's too late," she whispered. "My son is dead."

"No!" He caught her hands, rubbing them in his own, trying to restore warmth and blood to her frozen soul through his own physical heat. "No, Lottie. You must not think that. Come now, have your bath while I go and order a meal. Later you can tell me everything." He held out a new cotton nightgown to her. "Put your old clothes outside the door when you've finished and I'll get rid of them. You can wear this tonight and I've brought you new clothes for the morning." She didn't answer, only stared listlessly at the floor.

"Lottie"—he gave her arm a small shake— "promise me."

She nodded halfheartedly without looking at him but he took it as a sign of acquiescence and withdrew. He stood in the hallway, his ear pressed against the door until he heard the small splash of water. Satisfied that she had obeyed his instructions, he went down to the kitchen and persuaded the landlady to set a tray with thick slices of bread and a bowl of soup from the pot that simmered on her big black stove. When it was ready, he carried it upstairs himself.

He knocked briefly on the door, then opened it and went in. Lottie stood in the middle of the room, her hair hanging in a wet tangle down her back. She wore the nightgown he had left for her and he saw her disreputable old clothes in a heap beside the door. The first chance he got he'd burn them.

Placing the tray on the washstand, he took her hand and led her over to the high feather bed. "Climb in," he said, pulling back the covers and waiting until she had complied.

Once she was tucked in with the pillows stacked behind her and the blankets about her waist, he placed the tray across her lap and stood over her until she picked up the spoon and began to eat. Then he dragged up a chair to sit beside her. "Now, tell me everything, from the beginning."

He listened without comment as she related the events that had preceded Michael's disappearance, including her decision to leave Pine Creek Farm and Prospect forever. "I thought he'd gone fishing to get over his temper." Her eyes beseeched him to understand how she had come to wait almost a whole day before setting out in pursuit. "He'd done it before."

"Ah, Lottie, love, don't blame yourself. Finish your soup." He nodded to the half-eaten meal, then fell silent, pondering what she had told him. "Think now," he said at last. "Did Michael ever say he was coming after me? Or was it Patrick he wanted to find?"

"It's the same thing, isn't it?" she flung at him, the spoon stopped halfway to her mouth.

"Only in your fevered imagination. Michael never confused me with his father." He sucked in his breath, reminding himself of all she'd been through. "You remember the map, Lottie?" He spoke more gently. "The map on the back of Patrick's letter to me? Michael may have copied it. If he set out to look for his father, you've been following the wrong trail."

"But that's not possible." She dropped her spoon with a clatter onto the tray and pushed it away. She threw the blankets off her lap and struggled out of the soft confines of the feather mattress, gaining her feet on the side of the bed away from him. She glared at him across its protective width. "I know he was following you." Her old spirit flared in defiance and accusation.

"How do you know? Did he tell you? Think carefully, my girl. What did his note say, exactly?"

He watched, without leaving his chair, as she drew a deep, shuddering breath and moved away. Lottie paced to the tiny window on the other side of the room and stared out, but he knew she was not seeing the short, muddy street that ran behind the hotel. She closed her eyes and pinched the bridge of her nose. She seemed to be dredging up a long buried secret.

"He said he wanted his father," she intoned in a harsh, dry whisper. "He said I didn't understand, but you did."

He felt her heart break with every word she repeated.

"He said he was going to find Patrick."

Finally she turned from the window and faced him again, her eyes dull and flat as though it hurt her to see his face. Inwardly he winced at the stark despair in her gaze, the bleak hopelessness of her voice. Lottie had already borne more than enough pain for one lifetime. He feared for her if she lost Michael too.

"To find Patrick," he repeated, crossing the room to stand beside her. "Don't you see, Lottie? You equated Patrick with me, but Michael had seen the map. Patrick wrote in words that he was heading for the Big Bend, but he also drew a map of a second site, south of Prospect. Michael has gone downriver, not up."

Ashen-faced, Lottie stared at him. He could see her inner struggle as she thought back over the exact words of Michael's farewell letter. His heart ached as he watched dismay, disbelief and despair chase each other across her face. Instead of helping her, she looked as though he had taken away her last reason for living.

"Lottie, darlin', don't look so bleak. Michael's a smart lad, more mature than most boys his age. He's used to the land. He knows how to hunt and fish and track game. He has a good horse, you told me so yourself. He has Duke with him. A week or two on the trail isn't going to kill him. We'll find him, you'll see."

He wrapped his arms around her, pressing her face into his shoulder, rocking her in his arms. This time she did not pull away.

If it weren't for Michael's danger, he thought, holding himself in check even as he breathed in the warm, feminine scent of her skin and savored the soft swell of her breasts beneath the modest nightgown. If it weren't for Michael's danger, he would ask nothing more than to hold Lottie, to feel her body surrender to his.

He'd learned in those days on Charlotte Creek that the cold glitter of a gold nugget in the stream was no match for the warm flicker of firelight in the hearth, or the golden lights that shone in his true love's eyes when she was happy. And she would be happy again. He'd make damn sure of that. Once they found Michael and returned safely home, he would devote the rest of his life to making Lottie Graham happy. Except he planned to make her Lottie O'Connor at the first possible moment.

It was growing late; the square of light from the window faded to gloaming. She needed her rest. Reluctantly he dropped his arms from about her and led her back to the bed, urging her into its soft embrace. "Rest now, darlin'," he said, and pulled the covers up to her chin before bending down to brush a fleeting kiss across her brow. "Good night." He turned and crossed to the door.

Watching him, Lottie felt a deep yearning of loneliness that had nothing to do with Patrick or Michael and everything to do with Sean O'Connor. She had fought her love for this man, tried to deny it, but her heart refused to listen. Lonely and frightened as she was, she needed him, needed to love and be loved in return.

"Sean," she whispered, her voice a mere thread in the darkness.

"Yes?"

A wave of hot embarrassment washed up from her toes to the top of her head. She should have held her tongue. She bit her lip, her fingers curled over the blankets, holding them close under her chin. She stared into the fading light, unable to speak. Foolishly she wished she could pull the covers over her head and become invisible.

"Lottie?" Sean took a half step toward her. "Do you need something?"

Unable to speak, she merely nodded, while inwardly she cried aloud for her need. She needed Sean. She needed him with a deep hunger that could only be satisfied by complete intimacy.

"What is it?" He was beside her now. She could see the worry on his face as he bent over her.

"I . . ." She licked her dry lips.

"Tell me, Lottie," he murmured, his hand cupping her cheek, his weight sagging the bed as he sat beside her. Even in the gathering darkness, she could see the flame leaping in his eyes and knew he already understood and shared her need.

"Tell me what you need, Lottie." His lips were only inches from hers.

"I need you," she confessed, and then caught her breath as his mouth touched hers with aching tenderness.

"Ah, my darlin' girl." He pushed away from her while his fingers tangled with the fastenings of her nightdress, catching the ribbon at her neck, holding it taut for a moment, then tugging gently until it yielded, loosening the knot, letting the ruffle fall open. She bit her lip in a soundless gasp. A second ribbon, much lower, held the cotton closed across her body. Again he caught the slip of satin and gently pulled it free, letting the fabric fall open, exposing her breasts. For a long moment he merely gazed at the gentle swell of her bosom, not touching her, not speaking, but she saw his face soften.

She felt as though she couldn't move, couldn't breathe. Of their own accord her nipples hardened, thrusting themselves upright, begging for the touch of his hand, pleading for the warm release of his mouth. Still he did not move. Her embarrassment grew.

"Are you sure, Lottie darlin'?" he muttered, his voice a hoarse growl, deep in his throat. "I would not hurt you for the world, girl, but there will be no turning back if I stay with you now."

"I'm sure," she said, her voice low but steady. "Love me, Sean. Make me forget."

He came to her then, in a storm of lovemaking that had her gasping and wanting more. He skimmed his hands over her body, sending shivers racing up and down her spine. He touched his lips and his tongue to her swollen nipples and she arched her back in a fever of desire. He rained kisses on her face and down her throat. His hands caught her hair and spread it on the pillow behind her. She lifted her arms to him and he slipped the nightgown from her body.

The moonlight crept in the window and gleamed upon her naked flesh, making her feel like a pagan goddess. "Come to me!" she cried, reaching for him when he continued to delight and torment her with whispering caresses that tantalized but no longer satisfied. She arched and twisted, catching him by the shoulders, pulling him down to her. Eagerly she tore at the buttons on his clothes, urging him to join her in a wild dance to Eros.

When she felt driven to frenzy with desire, he caught her in love's deepest embrace, joining their two bodies as one, carrying them both upward in a spiraling, soaring flight toward the stars, holding her to him as she slipped over the edge of gravity and plunged with reckless abandon into the abyss of pleasure.

Clinging to him, her arms and legs wrapped tightly about his body, she reveled in the joy of her power, for, even as all control slipped from her grasp, she'd felt him shudder and collapse upon her, his weight driving her into the mattress, the convulsive shudders that rippled through his body an echo of the storm that raged deep within her being.

At last she lay still beneath him, holding him to her when he would have moved away. She wanted to stay in his arms. For a brief time he had made her forget, forget her fear for Michael, forget the years of waiting for Patrick. Now she remembered. But even in her remembering she clung to him, a shield against her pain.

* * *

When she woke at dawn Sean was already gone. She lay for a moment, replete and languid. Despite her desperate worry over Michael, she felt oddly content. Knowing that Sean was beside her in the search for her son eased her mind and sharpened her intelligence. There would be no more rushing blindly into the night.

She tossed back the covers and slid out of bed, then wrapped a sheet about herself while she located the clothes Sean had brought her yesterday. Once she was dressed in clean shirt and trousers, her face washed and her tangled hair pulled into a neat braid, she went downstairs in search of breakfast and Sean.

There were few others astir at this early hour, but she followed the smell of fresh coffee to the hotel's public room and sat down at one of five small tables. Sean wasn't there but she didn't worry. He would come back. A girl came quickly from the kitchen to serve her, except she wasn't a girl. A fiery, red-haired woman whose sapphire eyes raked Lottie's face with undisguised scorn stood beside the table.

"You the woman who rode in here all covered in dirt yesterday? Told the landlady you was Lottie Graham?"

"Yes." She was startled by the hostility in the woman's voice but assumed it was because she'd made extra work. "I'm sorry to have caused you trouble."

"Trouble, is it?" The waitress sneered. "I'll show you trouble." She planted her hands on her hips and leaned forward, thrusting her face so close Lottie could smell the stale stench of her breath. "So you're Patrick's fine lady," she jeered, making no attempt to take the breakfast order.

Lottie flinched, the suddenness of the attack sliding beneath her defenses. "What do you know of Patrick?" she asked, her voice a cracked whisper.

"A sight more than you, I'll be bound," the red-head answered.

"I don't believe you."

"Hah!" The woman tossed her head, throwing back her thick mane of hair. "I know he came through here in the spring of seventy-six, all handsome and laughing and full of hope."

"You saw him then?" Lottie's heart began to hammer. "You spoke to him?"

"Oh, aye. I spoke to him all right. He fair knocked me for a loop with his silver tongue and his brawny shoulders. But he'd none of me. True to his Lottie he was, his fine lady." The woman nearly spat the word.

"Did you ever see him again? Did you ever know what happened to him?"

"Of course I did. I was here, wasn't I, still eating my heart out for your big Irishman when he came through a year later. As handsome as ever and rich to boot."

"Did you say a whole year had passed?" Lottie whispered, passing her tongue over her lips. "He didn't come out until the spring of seventy-seven?"

"That's what I said, didn't I? He only meant to spend the summer at Big Bend, but the takings were good and he stayed too late, got wintered in."

"But he was alive in seventy-seven?" Lottie persisted, too focused on getting information about Patrick to notice the other woman's rudeness.

"Why should I tell you?"

"Please," Lottie begged, abject in her need to hear of Patrick. "Please tell me all you know."

"You mean you never saw him after that?" The

redhead laughed, a harsh, bitter cackle. "Well, I'm glad." The woman's mouth turned down in scorn. She thrust her face forward, forcing Lottie to draw back. "You may have had Patrick's loyalty and his love, but at least you didn't get his gold."

"Did you?" Lottie was on her feet, her hand locked hard about her rival's arm. Her years of toil made her strength more than a match for the insolent harlot. "Did you follow my Patrick? Did you creep up on him in the night and rob him?"

"I never stole anything from Patrick Malone. He's the thief." She tried to shake her arm free.

"That's a lie. Patrick never stole from you." Lottie's grip on the woman tightened until her nails dug into the flesh.

"Let go!" Her rival screeched and swung her free hand to land a blow on Lottie's shoulder.

"What do you mean, Patrick was a thief?" Lottie persisted, not slackening her hold on the woman's arm by so much as an ounce.

"He stole my heart, didn't he? And gave me nothing in return. Stole yours too, I'd say."

"What's all this then?"

Lottie had been so intent on her dispute with the unknown woman, she hadn't noticed Sean's return. Now he stood beside her, his face dark with concern.

"Sean"—she turned pleading eyes to his—"make her tell me. She saw Patrick. She saw him after he'd left Big Bend."

"Is that true?" Sean fixed a stern glare on Lottie's tormenter. "What's your name, girl?"

"Patrick!" There was no mistaking the shock on the girl's face. "Patrick, don't you remember? It's me, Nan."

"Well, Nan," Sean said, easing out a chair from the table and pushing it under Nan's knees. "In the first place, I'm not Patrick—I'm his cousin, Sean—and in the second place, I want you to tell me anything you know of him."

"Never." Nan reared back in the chair, Lottie having finally released her arm, and stared at Sean with all the intensity of an assayer studying a nugget. "Get away with you, Patrick." She slapped at his knee. "What kind of a trick are you playing now?"

"It's no trick," Sean said while Lottie stood helplessly by, frozen by her need to know what Nan could tell her. "Now, tell me, when did you last see my cousin, Patrick Malone?"

"No." There was no mistaking the sullen determination in the woman's pouting face.

"You must, Nan. Patrick has a son. He has disappeared; he's looking for his father. You must tell us, Nan. Everything you know."

"Well." The woman's face softened only slightly. "How old's his boy?"

"Ten. He'll be eleven in a few more weeks."

Lottie saw Nan sag in her chair as she worked out the date of Michael's conception.

Sean pulled up another chair and sat down, facing the redhead, his urgency compelling her to tell what she knew. "For Patrick's sake, Nan."

"Well, it's like I told her." She darted a venomous glance at Lottie. "It was after he'd spent a summer and a winter and a summer at the Big Bend. He'd struck it rich. His pockets were full of gold dust. He didn't need to go anywhere, least of all to some dirt farm." Her voice grew shrill as she recalled her grievances. "But he wouldn't listen to me. Oh no. It was Lottie this and Lottie that and help me buy a gown for Lottie, Nan." She raised her hands, her fingers curled into claws.

"Was he heading home for Prospect, then?" Sean interposed himself between the two women.

"Sort of. He was going down the Moyie first, and then, he said, he was going home for good. Home to Lottie, he said. But I see"—she cast one more scornful glance at Lottie before jumping to her feet and flouncing out of the room—"his precious Lottie couldn't wait for him."

In the stunned silence Nan left behind, Lottie faced Sean in an agony of remorse and self-recrimination. What had she done? Even in her panic for Michael, how could she have forgotten Patrick? Patrick who, for her sake, had turned away from Nan's eager charms.

"Darlin'?" Sean stretched out his hand to her but she backed away, her hands behind her back, her eyes wide.

"Don't," she croaked harshly. "Don't touch me."

"Lottie, love . . ." Sean's voice beseeched her; his eyes, full of the most intimate knowledge, bored into hers.

"No," she said, the magnitude of her betrayal overwhelming her. "Don't you see?"

"You'll have to tell me, Lottie girl. All I see is the woman I want to make my wife."

"No, no. You mustn't speak so!" she cried, her heart torn with love, both for Patrick and for Sean. But Patrick had first claim. "Patrick . . ."

"And are we back to that, then?" Sean dropped heavily into the chair Nan had vacated. "Why can't you let him go, girl? We could have a good life together, you and I. We could be happy, and Michael too."

"We must go," she said, refusing to look into his face. "We must find Michael and then search for news of Patrick. I must know the truth, Sean."

"And until then?" he asked, his face falling into the hard, hopeless lines she had known when first they met.

"Until then there can be nothing between you and me." She turned away from the pain she saw in his eyes. How could she ever have thought he had Patrick's eyes? True, they were the same shade of blue but it was Sean's own soul that looked out at her, not Patrick's, and that soul was seared with suffering. She couldn't bear knowing that she was the cause. "We must go," she said, keeping her back to him.

"The horses are already saddled and waiting." She heard the cold, flat voice of a stranger.

Chapter 13

After a silent breakfast served by the sullen Nan, they set out, riding fresh horses, Sean's mule loaded down with supplies. On the trip down the lower Kootenay Lake by paddlewheeler, Lottie watched Sean's tense face with an ache in her heart. She longed to comfort him, to reach out her hand and smooth away the tense lines about his mouth. But she could not. The vows she had spoken to Patrick were inviolable. She had been wrong to turn to Sean. Resolutely she turned her back, glad when he left her to tend to the horses.

By midday they had disembarked and begun the trek overland to the Moyie, asking everyone they encountered on the trail if they had seen a boy with a dog in the last several days. Mostly they were met with a regretful shrug and a shake of the head, but finally one man, a greenhorn limping along in ill-fitting boots, recalled seeing just such a one about a day or so back.

"He said he was looking for his pa," the tenderfoot said.

"Michael!" Lottie exclaimed, some of the weight lifting from her heart. "It must have been Michael. Was he all right?" Hope buoyed her spirits, making her forget the ache of her body after so many hours in the saddle and the ache that struck her heart every time she looked at Sean's drawn face.

"Seemed a mite young to be out here alone," came the reply, "and maybe a bit scared, but he flat out refused when I asked if he wanted to travel with me. Said I was going in the wrong direction."

Sean thanked the man for his help and they set off again. After the agony of the past several days, Lottie's heart lifted with hope. Michael was all right and he was only a day ahead of them on the trail. Whatever had befallen Patrick, at least Michael could be restored to her. "Hurry," she said to Sean, forgetting, in her eagerness, that she had no right to ask for his aid.

"The sun's too low," he said, shaking his head, "and the trail is unmarked. Even with Patrick's map we might miss a turning. Better to make camp now and start early in the morning."

But his caution was not proof against her greater eagerness to be gone and she finally gained his reluctant agreement. "But only while the sun is fully visible," he said, casting a worried eye toward the sky. "We stop the minute it begins to sink."

When she would have argued further, he stopped her with a reminder that she had already lost one horse to impatience and he had no intention of losing another. "You can't find Michael if you fall into a creek and drown."

She could not refute his decision but neither could she accept it easily. She set her mouth in a tight line and urged her horse forward. In a taut silence, they followed the Moyie upstream, Sean studying the landmarks and comparing them to Patrick's map, Lottie searching the ground for footprints, especially dog tracks.

When they came to an enormous boulder guarding the mouth of a smaller creek, Sean pulled up. "That's it." He pulled the much creased map from his pocket. "Right here." He pointed to a faded *X* on Patrick's map and the words *big rock* with an arrow indicating a small stream. About two miles on he had drawn a gold pan and a pickax.

"We're almost there!" Lottie cried. "We'll find him by nightfall."

Sean merely grunted, unwilling to bolster what could turn out to be false hope.

On foot, leading the horses, studying the ground for tracks, they moved upstream. Amazingly, Sean found he was not even tempted to pan the black sands swirled into bars in the middle of the stream or trapped in crevices along its edge. The fever for gold had left him, replaced by the hunger for love.

Raised as he was, firmly rooted in the Catholic faith, he could understand Lottie's conviction that she was honor-bound to Patrick, but understanding did nothing to ease his anger and frustration. To have traveled all this way and finally found the woman who made his life complete and then to lose her to a ghost was more than a man should have to bear.

"Time to make camp," he announced as the sun touched the highest peak of the mountains.

"But we're so close. There's at least an hour of daylight left."

His heart ached for her but he stood firm. "It's folly to go on in poor light on an unmarked trail. I won't risk it, Lottie."

He dismounted and unhooked the canteen from

his saddle. "I'll start a fire." He held out the empty flask, refusing to meet her eyes. "You can fetch some water from the creek."

Lottie slid to the ground and took the canteen from his hand, then tramped down to the stream without a word. Sean sighed and set about collecting wood and chips for the fire. Crickets chirped in the tall grass; a thrush's fluting call wafted through the evergreens; peaceful sounds of evening that failed to soothe his spirit. He felt more akin to the furtive rustling of a small animal in the underbrush or the mournful wolf cry coming from upstream. He scowled and kicked hard at the ground, making a circle for the fire. He'd been right to make camp, despite Lottie's silently accusing eyes.

"Sean!" He heard her screaming and turned to see her running, slipping, and scrambling up the slippery bank of the creek. "Sean, come quick."

But he was already racing toward her, rifle in hand, set to fend off a bear or cougar attack. He caught her as she stumbled into his arms. "What's wrong?"

"Sh." She held her finger to her lips, then caught his hand and dragged him to the edge of the creek. Her canteen lay abandoned on the bank. "Listen," she whispered, her eyes and ears strained as she faced upstream.

The wolf howled again and she gasped. "Did you hear?"

"It's a wolf." He was puzzled by her excitement. "It won't bother us, Lottie. Not with a fire."

"It's not a wolf." Her eyes glistened as they listened to the howling. "It's a dog. It's Duke. I'm positive that is Michael's dog. Listen!"

The cry came again, carried faintly on the night breeze.

"I suppose it could be a dog"—Sean cocked his head, listening carefully—"but even if it is, you can't know it's Duke." He didn't tell her that if it was Duke howling, it was a bad omen. A dog with a master would not be baying at the sky, calling to his wild brethren. A dog with a master would be resting beside a campfire, head on his paws, eyes watching the boy he had followed his whole life.

"It is. I know it." She would have dashed head-long into the forest that lined the high bank of the creek had he not caught her arm.

"Let me go." She tried to shake herself free of his restraining hand. "I must go."

Acknowledging the futility of further argument, he agreed. In silence, ears straining, they made their way upstream, without the horses. The ground grew rougher, rising sharply, forcing them away from the water's edge onto a rocky cliff. Several times Lottie tripped over hidden tree roots and fell to her knees, scraping her hands, but when he would have helped her she shook him off.

Setting his mouth in a grim line, he followed as she rushed ahead of him.

"There!" she exclaimed as they reached a high, flat promontory. "Look!" She pointed a shaking finger across the deep gorge of the creek far below.

Duke, nose pointed skyward, sat at the very edge of the cliff on the other side of the stream, howling disconsolately. Lottie whistled, and he broke into a frenzy of barking, jumping in the air, crawling on his belly toward the precipice, backing and circling. Of Michael there was no sign.

"Michael!" she cried into the emptiness, and he could hear her euphoria dying away. She'd finally understood the grim significance of the scene.

"Michael!" she shrieked. The mountains echoed her cry, as wild and primeval as the creatures that haunted the forest.

A fallen tree stretching across the chasm hinted at what had happened. Michael's horse was tethered on the same side as Lottie and Sean, the dog stood on the other, and far below, on a tiny spit of sand, lay a huddled shape, the size of a ten-year-old boy.

Sean's eyes scanned the cliff edge, looking for a route down the steep rock face but found nothing. It wouldn't have done him any good if he had; the stream was swift and deep on this side of the chasm. He'd have to try to reach the boy from the other side.

"Michael," Lottie whimpered. She stood on the edge of the cliff, her arms wrapped around herself, her body shivering under the strain of her overwrought nerves.

He grasped her by the shoulders, forcing her to look at him, pulling her away from the cliff. "Go back and get the horses," he commanded, trying to reach through her panic. "Do you hear me, Lottie! We need the horses and supplies if we're to help him."

"I can't leave him here alone," she whispered, staring at Sean with blank eyes.

"He won't be alone, I'll get to him."

"But how?" she asked, her voice trailing off as she gazed at the fallen log. "Oh, no." She finally looked fully into his face. "Sean, you can't."

"I'll have to," he replied, his jaw set. "Now go, girl, there's less than an hour of light left." He could see the rebellion in her eyes, knew she wanted to defy him, but she had too much respect for the wilderness to argue further.

"You're right," she whispered. "Be careful." She wheeled and headed back the way they had come.

He watched her disappear into the trees and wished he could have gone with her, looked for an easier crossing, but there was no time. If he was to cross the gorge he had to do it now, while there was still light. He took the rope from the saddle on Michael's horse, looped it over his shoulder and strode toward the downed tree. His fear of heights must not stop him, he told himself. He'd crossed the narrow, swaying bridges that took him to the Big Bend. He could manage a fat, steady log.

He tried to ignore the voice in his head that reminded him the bridges were at least three times as wide as this fallen log and were made of flat planks, not rounded, slippery, roughened tree bark.

Go on, he told himself when his legs began to shake. Other men could scale mountains and climb the rigging of a ship. He could cross a twenty-foot span.

His heart pounding, he inched his way carefully out onto the narrow bridge, high above the rocky creek bed. His legs, shaking with terror, wouldn't support his weight, so he dropped onto his stomach and wrapped both arms and legs about the fallen tree. Sweat poured off his face, running into his eyes and making them burn. His hands were so slippery he could barely grasp the rough bark of the log. But he would not go back. He would not abandon Michael and he would not fail Lottie.

In the twilight the stream below gleamed like silver. He could hear the rushing of the water, knew it ran swift and cold, bristling with rocks, set to pound a man to death if he was foolish enough to fall in.

He turned his face into his shoulder to clear the sweat from his eyes. He couldn't lift a hand from the log even for a moment.

Don't look down. The words resounded in his head. Gritting his teeth, he fixed his eyes on the far bank. *It's only twenty feet away. Anyone with an ounce of manhood in him can manage twenty feet.*

His mouth filled with fear. His heart beat as though to burst through his chest. The sound of his blood pounding in his ears obliterated the rushing of the stream. He couldn't do it. He had no head for heights, never had, never would. He inched backward but the thought of facing Lottie with his weakness and his failure stopped him. His love must be stronger than his fear.

Holy Mary, Mother of God, pray for us now . . . He recited the words, long since unsaid, but burned so deeply into his heart and soul that they came to mind without conscious thought. Over and over he recited the prayer in his mind, using it to block out all other thought, to block out the terrifying sensation of hanging in space, the certain knowledge that death lurked only inches away.

One slip, one false move, and he would plunge onto the rocks. He, who could not climb a ladder in a haymow, was now suspended on a fallen log above a fifty-foot chasm. His teeth were clenched so hard his jaw hurt, but he was barely aware of the ache. *Pray for me . . . Pray for me.* Inch by torturous inch he pressed forward. Hands, arms, legs, feet— every fiber of his being straining against the log, every ounce of his willpower straining against his fear.

He slid one hand forward, grasped a shred of rotten bark, and nearly fell when it came away in his fist. He froze. Icy fingers of fear clutched his spine, spreading out along his nerve endings, paralyzing him. The terror was so great that for a fleeting instant he contemplated letting go. Surely the plunge toward death would be preferable to the horror of clinging here, suspended high above the earth.

Lottie. I can't desert her now. She has borne too much, lost too much. I must not fail her.

Biting down so hard he felt he might crack his teeth, he reached forward again, tearing away the soft bark until he came to solid wood. The bridge would hold. He took a deep breath and crept forward. If his heart burst within him, at least he would have died with courage. *Ten feet more. Reach, push, rest. Pray for me. Nine feet.* The dog was so excited, his frenzied jumping and scratching at the log caused it to quiver. Again Sean halted, his dread overpowering his will. He tried to speak to calm the dog, but though his throat worked and his mouth opened, no sound came forth.

Duke barked again and even ventured a few steps onto the log bridge. "No!" His voice was a mere thread of sound, but the dog heard and obeyed, backing off the log. "Lie down."

Duke whined and wagged his tail, his nose straining forward, sensing a man he knew and trusted.

"Lie down," he said again, more firmly this time, and the dog reluctantly lowered his belly onto the ground, his nose resting on his paws, pressed tight to the fallen log.

Eight feet more. With just a few more shrugs forward he'd be able to grasp the dog's head with his hands. *Pull the knees forward, stretch the arm out, push, pray. One more foot.* He was almost there. His hand reached forward again, encountering Duke's coat, soft and warm and living beneath his fingers. He'd made it.

"Good dog." He rested a moment with his hands on the dog's head, gathering courage. With one last supreme effort he lunged forward, felt solid ground beneath his hands and feet, and collapsed in the dirt.

Exhausted more by terror than exertion, he lay on the ground breathing in great gulps of air, digging his fingers into the thin soil, feeling the sudden cold of the night air against his sweat-soaked clothes. Duke circled around him, uttering short, sharp yips of excitement, his tongue lolling out to sweep over Sean's face in a slobbering, grateful welcome.

"All right, then." He wiped his face on his sleeve and pushed himself onto his knees. He wrapped his arms about the dog, grateful for his sturdy warmth, and waited for the strength to return to his limbs. "Come on, mutt," he said at last, releasing the dog and getting to his feet. He had managed to cross to Michael's side of the chasm, but he still had to find a way down to the boy.

"Where's Michael?" he said to the dog and followed as Duke whined and ran down a faint trail at the top of the cliff. In the shadowy half-light he trusted the dog's instincts more than his own. Duke led him straight to the cliff edge and a sight that froze his blood.

A chunk of bank had recently given way, leaving a raw scar in the earth. A gold pan lay near the crumbled edge. He dropped to his stomach and wriggled forward until he could see over the rim of the cliff. Michael, small and still, lay directly below him.

Edging back from the precipice, he felt his way

cautiously along the cliff face, searching for anything that would allow him to get to the boy. With the dog padding beside him, he stumbled onto a stunted tree, its roots sunk into a stony crevice. It wasn't much but it was a chance. Swiftly he slipped the lariat off his shoulder, secured one end of it around the shrub, tested it for strength, then tied the other end to himself. "Stay here," he murmured to the dog, patting his head for reassurance. At least there would be a witness to his death if the tree didn't hold. He tried not to think of the drop into space that lay just a few feet in front of him. If he could cross the log, a simple descent at the end of a rope should be easy.

Lowering himself over the edge, he braced his feet against the stone wall, played out the rope through his hands and slid downward into darkness. Step by cautious step he slithered down the embankment until all the rope was played out but still his feet had not reached the bottom. It was completely dark now, the moon not yet risen.

Suspended in the air, he had no way of knowing how close he was to the ground or even if he hung over the sandbar or the craggy rocks, but there was no turning back. He could not climb back up the rope and leave Michael behind. He couldn't even use his trembling fingers to untie the knot, so he reached for the knife on his belt and cut himself loose, falling through the darkness into he knew not what.

His feet crunched into coarse gravel, the weight of his body forcing them deep into the soft sand, and he fell forward onto his hands and knees. He had hit the sandbar.

Still on his knees, his eyes straining to see, he

scrambled forward until he reached Michael. In an agony of suspense he touched the boy's neck, drawing a deep breath of relief when he found a pulse. Michael was hurt—probably with a broken leg by the look of him—and he was unconscious, but he was alive. Sean's heart was torn with pity as he imagined the pain and hunger and cold the boy had endured alone.

He peered about him, seeking some sort of shelter, and discovered that the spit of sand was part of a small beach extending into a shallow cave at the base of the cliff. Thanking God for His mercy, he scooped the boy up into his arms and carried him into the small shelter, out of the cold breeze that drifted along the creek bed. It was a start but he needed a fire.

He was searching for wood along the side of the creek when a beam of light from the top of the cliff stopped him. Looking up, he saw Lottie, with Duke at her side, waving her lantern back and forth, searching the depths of the canyon. Her feet were dangerously close to the crumbling lip. "Stay back!" he shouted. "Lottie, get back!"

She didn't move, but the lantern swung toward him, catching him in its feeble ray. "Is it Michael?" The suffering in her voice would stir compassion in the devil; for the man who loved her, it smote him to the heart.

"It's Michael, and he's alive, but he's cold and hurt," he called back, wishing he could protect her from more pain but knowing he could not. She had to know the truth and she had to be strong. "Did you bring the horses and supplies?"

"Yes."

"Then get the bedroll from the mule and my

saddlebags, there's matches and some food in them. Throw them down to me."

"I'm coming down." A small avalanche of gravel cascaded along the precipice as she stepped to the edge.

"No!" he yelled, his heart leaping into his throat. "Lottie, you can't help Michael if you're hurt yourself. Be sensible, girl." He hated to be so harsh with her when all he wanted to do was hold her and shield her and keep her safe, but she had to understand the danger. "Lie down on your stomach," he called to her, "and drop the supplies over the edge. They'll land right here beside us. When it's daylight, we'll find a way to get him back up. Please, Lottie," he insisted as she remained poised on the edge of the bank, "for Michael's sake, do as I say."

"But he's my son!" *Rachel crying for her children.*

The rising moon cast its feeble light from the sky, illuminating the pale oval of her face, betraying her anguish. It nearly broke his heart. He knew he seemed ruthless and cruel but if he relented and allowed her the luxury of coming to Michael's side, they all might perish. He hadn't beaten back his own terrors and crossed the chasm on a fallen log, or said his prayers and dropped into the darkness from the end of a rope to lose it all now.

"You must be strong!" he shouted back to her. "Michael needs you to nurse him, to love him, and to make him well again, but you can't do that if you fall down here yourself. Now do as I tell you."

For a long moment she didn't move, and he was afraid she would defy him. Her face showed all the grief of the world. His heart was wrung with pity. But at last she disappeared from the cliff's edge.

and a moment later a bedroll and his saddlebags landed at his feet.

"Do you have wood and kindling?" Her disembodied voice came from above him.

"There's a small cave here," he shouted back. "There's some driftwood inside and I've collected enough chips to start a fire. I'll keep him warm through the night. Come daylight, we'll find a way out of here."

"Then, I'll see you in the morning." Her reply was fainter than before. She must have moved back into the trees, seeking shelter for herself and the horses.

It didn't take him long to pile a few sticks of dry wood into a pyramid and set them ablaze near the mouth of the little cave. He spread out one blanket on the ground where the sand was soft and dry, then lifted the still unconscious boy into his arms and laid him on the blanket. The movement must have caused him pain, for Michael moaned and his eyes flickered open.

"It's all right, son," Sean murmured. "I've got you now. You'll be all right."

"Duke," Michael croaked.

"Your dog's fine." Sean lowered him onto the makeshift bed and piled another blanket on top. "He's waiting at the top of the cliff, along with your mother." He smiled a little, proud of the lad for worrying about his dog first. Michael was made of good stuff; he would grow into a fine man.

"So stupid," Michael whispered, gritting his teeth against the pain. "I was following the map and stepped too close to the edge."

"Rest now." Sean raised the boy's shoulders and gave him a cup of water. "We'll talk tomorrow."

Throughout the rest of the night, while Michael drifted in and out of troubled dreams, Sean kept him warm, soothed him when he cried out, kept the fire stoked and held vigil until the dawn. At first light he left the sleeping child and set out to explore.

Above the sandbar the cliff rose sheer and straight; the rope he had descended the night before dangled some fifteen feet above his head. Even if Michael weren't injured they would have a hard time climbing out of the canyon. As it was, such a route would be impossible. Across the stream a matching rock face offered the same bleak aspect. They would have to make their way downstream until they found a lower bank.

Stepping back into the shallow cave he stopped short, his eye caught by a gruesome sight. Away at the back of the cave was a cluster of whitened bones. They had been invisible in the dark but the sun's early rays sliced a band of light into the recesses of the cave, bathing them in ghastly brilliance. With his heart beating hard he slipped past the still sleeping Michael, whispered a quick prayer, and bent to examine the remains. They were human. A hole in the back of the head and a bullet lying inside the skull told the death story. But what stole his breath and dropped him to his knees was the gleam of gold that circled the neck. Reaching out a shaking hand he unclasped the gold chain and drew a locket into his hand. Turning it over he read the initials *CHG* on the back. *Charlotte Henrietta Graham.*

Kneeling in the sand, Sean was shaken by a storm of emotions. In his hand he held the answer to Patrick Malone's disappearance. To his surprise, his first emotion was pure grief. In coming at last upon proof that Patrick was dead, he forgot his anger and resentment toward his cousin and mourned only for the lighthearted pal of his youth.

"Sean?" Michael had awakened.

"Yes." He hurried back to the boy, thrusting the locket into his pocket. Before he could mourn the dead, he must help the living. He had to get Michael home and he had to tell Lottie the truth.

He knelt beside the boy, blocking out the sight of his father's bones. Already, as the sun climbed higher in the sky, the streak of light that had penetrated the far reaches of the cave was receding. In a few more minutes, Patrick's bones would lie in darkness once again.

"Did we find the gold? Is this the spot Pa marked on his map?"

"Gold?" A sense of melancholy softened his voice. "Yes, son, in a way, we found gold." A golden locket, a golden memory, a golden truth, and a golden love at the end of a long vigil.

"Michael!"

Sean jumped to his feet at the sound of Lottie's voice and the excited barking of a dog. He narrowed his eyes against the brilliant sunlight to see her standing in the cave entrance. Her hair streamed down her back in unkempt tangles, her eyes were black holes in a white face, mud spattered her heavy trousers, and she was wet to the knees.

"Michael!" she cried again, her voice breaking into a harsh sob as she lunged forward, falling to the ground beside her son. Tears streamed down her cheeks as she caught her child in her arms and held him close. "Michael," she sobbed over and over, while Duke squirmed about the boy in an ecstasy of joy.

Wordlessly Sean waited and watched, helpless to

ease her grief. Only Michael, alive and straining to free himself from her embrace, could do that. "Aw, Ma, I'm too big for hugs."

A harsh laugh mingled with Lottie's sobs, but she didn't take her hands from Michael's neck nor raise her cheek from his. "You're never too old for hugs from your mother."

Her words brought a lump to his throat. His Lottie was a survivor, but if Michael ever did anything again to cause her grief, he'd be in for a stern lesson from Sean O'Connor.

When Lottie's sobs grew quieter, he took her hands, drawing her to her feet and folding her into the warmth of his own embrace. "It's over now, darlin'," he murmured, holding her trembling body against the strength of his own. "We can all go home." She made no reply but at least she didn't push him away. "I'll try to find some straight sticks to make a splint for his leg."

"I've brought supplies." She pushed herself out of his grasp. "There's an ax and food. I'll start breakfast while you make the splint."

"You carried all that with you?"

"No." For the first time in two days he saw a faint glimmer of her old spirit shine through her eyes. "I left the horses up there"—she pointed to the top of the cliff—"and just took the mule and Duke. I knew there was no crossing downstream so we went up. About a mile and a half farther on the embankment flattens out. I got down to the streambed there and worked my way back."

"In the dark?"

"I trusted the mule. They're too stubborn to get killed." She flashed a weak smile. "Most of the time there was a narrow shoreline. When that disappeared, we went into the stream. We'll have to go out the same way." She looked at Michael's useless leg. "It'll be tough, but it's the only way."

While Lottie fried beans and bacon over the campfire, Sean constructed a rough litter and attached it to the mule's packsaddle. He would carry the other end of it himself. Hope buoyed his spirit. If he could cross the log, he could easily carry to safety the lad who was almost his son. Once they were back on the main trail they would look for a farmhouse and borrow a wagon to complete the journey to Pine Creek Farm. Amazingly, for all the trials they had been through, they were little more than two day's journey from home.

Before setting off, however, there was one more task he had to perform. Leaving Michael to rest in the sunshine outside, Sean drew Lottie into the dim coolness of the cave one last time.

"Lottie, love." He searched for the right words, praying he would be able to bring her release and not more pain. She had already withstood so much. Could she bear one last revelation? "Lottie, darlin' girl." He took her hand in his. "I've something to show you." Slowly, his eyes never leaving her face, he drew the locket from his pocket, cradled it gently in his palm and held it out to her. "The initials are yours," he said quietly, waiting while she absorbed the significance of his discovery.

He could see her fingers shaking as she reached out and touched the circlet of gold, tentatively, like a kitten exploring the world outside its basket. "Mine?" She raised pitiful eyes to his. "Patrick?" Her voice broke. "Where is he?"

Feeling like a murderer, Sean pulled her into his arms, stroking his hand over her tangled hair, cradling her head against his shoulder, seeking to take her hurt upon himself. She remained tense and rigid in his embrace, refusing to soften to him, holding herself as though in readiness for some terrible blow to fall on her unprotected head.

"He's here, Lottie," he said. "I found a skeleton at the back of the cave. There's a bullet hole in the skull and your locket was fastened around the neck. You were right, Lottie. Patrick was coming home—to you."

She leaned away from him, her hands coming up to cover her mouth. "Shot?" Her eyes filled with horror. "Oh, my poor Patrick."

"He wouldn't have known." Sean hoped he spoke the truth. "Don't torment yourself with that."

"Why?" she whispered. "Why would anyone harm Patrick?"

"A thief, I'd say. From what I've heard from the old-timers on the trail, Patrick was a great one for talking. He told everyone from Big Bend to Kootenay Landing that he'd struck it rich."

"But how did he get here?"

"I expect when he was shot, he went over the embankment here. High waters in the spring would have carried his body back into the cave. The thief wouldn't have worried about searching for him. He had Patrick's horse and the gold that was surely packed into his saddlebags."

"My poor Patrick," she whispered over and over again. "My poor Patrick."

"Don't grieve, girl," Sean begged. "Remember him as he lived, big and laughing and vigorous. All those people along the trail who remembered him, they all said he loved to laugh and he talked always of his Lottie. Remember that Patrick loved you and was coming home to you."

"Nine years." She sagged against him as though

all the strength had drained from her body. "For nine years he lay here, only two days' journey away, and I didn't know."

"It wouldn't have mattered," he assured her. "You couldn't have done anything for Patrick had you known. But you bore his son and raised him and taught him to love his father. It's a fine thing you've done, Lottie. Fine and brave and noble. My cousin chose well when he left his heart with you."

"Michael." She raised her eyes. "Does he know?"

"Not yet. I wanted to tell you first."

"He must be told."

"Yes," he agreed, "and he should hear it from you."

"What will I say?" she asked piteously. "After all this time of waiting and hoping, how can I tell him it was all in vain?"

"Tell him the truth. Tell him that he set out to find his father, and in an odd way, he did. Because of his courage and determination, the mystery of Patrick's disappearance has been solved. Tell him his father would be proud of him."

"Yes," she whispered. He could see her struggling against her emotion. "Yes, that is what I'll tell him."

They walked outside into the sunshine where Michael waited on the makeshift litter. Duke sat beside him, his nose pressed against the boy's chest. Beside him, he felt Lottie shudder. "We came so close to losing him, and now I must tell him his father is dead."

"It'll be all right." He paused and caught her hand, squeezing it briefly between his own. "He's a survivor. Like his mother."

Later, as Lottie and Michael sat together talking, weeping and touching the locket as though through it they could touch Patrick himself, Sean went alone into the cave. He dug a grave and buried Patrick's remains and etched a cross on the rock with his miner's pick. Beneath it he inscribed the name of Patrick Malone and the dates 1852–1877.

Stepping back outside into the sunshine, he found Lottie and Michael waiting for him, trusting in him, depending upon him. Patrick's family. His family, more precious than all the gold in all the rivers of British Columbia.

"Let's go home," he said.

Chapter 14

On a rare warm day in October, Lottie sat on her own verandah and pondered the changes the past year had wrought. It had been almost twelve months to the day since Sean had ridden into her life on the winds of a hailstorm. She felt as though she had been in the midst of a storm ever since.

As fiercely as the hail battered down the grass in the fields, Sean had battered down her defenses, forcing her beyond the narrow, unhappy walls she had built around her life, blowing like a tempest through the icy shell she had erected around her heart. He had brought her into light and love once more.

It had hurt at first. She had grown comfortable in her isolation, invulnerable in her seclusion. She had resisted him, clinging to her old ways, cleaving to her rigid loyalty to Patrick, believing there was room in her heart for only one love.

She'd been wrong.

It had been two weeks now since they'd discovered Patrick's remains, and she'd learned that loving Sean in no way diminished her affection for her first love. But now she remembered Patrick with gentle melancholy, welcoming the tender memories that brought pleasure without pain. Even her tears for a life cut short were like a soft rain upon a parched earth. The acrid sting of bitterness no longer burned her eyes.

Her hands dropped into her lap, idle despite the apples that lay waiting to be peeled. Her gaze roamed over the fields until she caught sight of Sean riding along the far pasture, and her heart lifted with gladness. After so many years of watching in vain, she could never take his presence for granted. And therein lay the one taste of vinegar in her cup of contentment.

All the shadows of the past were gone. Patrick was decently laid to rest; Michael had been seen by Prospect's new doctor and pronounced healthy. His leg would heal and he had suffered no lasting effects from his fall. The harvest was complete, the threshing crew come and gone. With Tom to help, Sean had insisted there was no longer any need for Lottie to labor in the fields or the barn, and she had acquiesced, happy to spend her time caring for her garden and cooking for her menfolk. Life at Pine Creek Farm had settled into a placid rhythm.

And yet all was not well. After that one passionate declaration of love in Kootenay Landing, Sean had never again spoken to her of the future. Her heart was his for the asking, but he hadn't asked. Had he decided, after all, that he didn't want her? Life was good but it couldn't go on this way indefinitely. Sean had too much ambition and pride to remain indefinitely as her hired hand. And she had too much love and passion bursting for expression to be content with a platonic friendship.

She watched him riding among the cattle, admiring the easy way he sat his horse, letting her eyes linger on the breadth of his shoulders and the length of his legs. Memories of their night in Kootenay Landing brought a hot flush to her skin.

Restless, she got up, leaving the apples unpeeled. She went into the house, quickly climbing the stairs to her room. There she changed from the skirt that was now her habitual dress into her shirt and trousers.

"Michael," she called, coming downstairs and going into the sitting room where the boy lay on a sofa. "Michael, I'm going to ride out for a while."

"You going to meet Sean?"

"Yes. I'll be back in time to make supper. Do you want another book before I go out?"

"I'm tired of books," Michael groused, "and I'm tired of lying on this sofa."

"Just be glad you've a sofa to lie on," she retorted, then softened her rebuke by going to the barn and corralling one of Tiger's new kittens and bringing it back to the house to amuse Michael while she was out.

With some trepidation she saddled her horse, mounted and set out over the sloping fields, across the creek and on to the edge of the forest until she found Sean.

He raised his hand in greeting as she drew rein beside him. "Hello, my girl. What brings you out here?"

"You," she said breathlessly before she could change her mind.

"Something wrong? Is it Michael?" His voice sharpened with concern.

"No, no. I just wanted to talk to you."

"And what was so urgent it couldn't wait until

evening?" His eyes quizzed her, bringing the heat to her cheeks.

Her horse sidled restlessly, tossing his head, pulling on the reins, impatient to gallop over the meadows on such a fine day.

"Can we walk a little?" she asked. Now that she was here, she didn't know how to begin.

"If you like." Sean dismounted easily and reached out a hand to help her down.

"That's not necessary," she snapped, nerves making her edgy. She slid to the ground unaided.

"Now what's put a burr under your saddle?" Sean teased, but his eyes were wary.

"Nothing," she said shortly and then more quietly, "everything."

He took the reins from her hand to lead both their horses. "Care to tell me about it?"

For a little while they walked in silence, Lottie studying the ground, noting where night frosts had whitened the grasses, listening to the clink of the horses' bridles, feeling tongue-tied and shy and cross. "It's about Christmas," she said finally.

"Christmas!" There was no mistaking the surprise in Sean's voice, and she felt a little better, more in control.

"Yes." She plunged on without giving herself time to get cold feet. "I need to know if you'll be here for Christmas. If I'm to get a present for you I'll need time to prepare, and then of course there's Valentine's and Saint Patrick's Day and then Easter and . . ." Her words ran out along with her courage and she fell silent, her feet dragging to a halt.

Sean stopped too and dropped the reins to take both her hands in his. "Lottie girl," he said softly, "are you by any chance asking me my intentions?"

"The horses," she protested feebly.

"Never mind the horses," he replied. "Now, my love, I asked you a question." He placed two fingers under her chin and lifted her face so that he held her gaze.

His face was somber and unsmiling, and his eyes were the deep blue of an autumn sky, but she could see a fire burning there, a light that matched the fire that burned in her heart. His mouth was only inches from hers. If she stretched onto her tiptoes she could kiss him. Or he could bend his head and meet her halfway.

"Lottie?"

"Yes," she whispered, placing her hands on his chest and rising on her toes, "I'm asking your intentions."

"And what would you like me to say?" He bent his head until there was only the breadth of a blade of grass between them.

"I would wish to hear that they were honorable," she said, and felt herself crushed in an embrace that threatened to crack her ribs. His mouth took hers in a fierce, hungry kiss.

"Darlin' girl," he muttered when at last, he released her. "Are you sure? I thought you might be grieving still."

"Is that why you've been silent?" she asked, glad to have an explanation for his reticence. "I thought perhaps you'd had second thoughts."

"Me!" He dropped his arms from around her in astonishment. "Never, my love." He took her hands again and held them against his chest. "But I wanted you to be sure. When you come to me, Lottie, it's Sean O'Connor you'll be loving, not the image of Patrick Malone."

"Ah, love." Her voice broke with tenderness as she

understood the doubt that lay behind his words. "I've done with grieving and I well know the difference between you and your cousin." She reached up to touch her fingers to his cheek. "Shall I tell you now, that even before Michael ran away, it was your face that haunted my dreams, not Patrick's?"

She tapped her fingers against his lips, half scolding, half tender. "My heart has been yours long since, Sean O'Connor. How else could I have joined with you in love that night in Kootenay Landing? It was loyalty to Patrick and fealty to my vows that held me from you, never a lack of love."

"In that case." He dropped to one knee and took her hand. His eyes sparkled with laughter and tenderness. "I ask you, Charlotte Henrietta Graham, will you be my wife?"

"Don't be on your knees to me," she protested, then dropped down into the long grass beside him and threw her arms about his neck, sending them both toppling to the ground.

Laughing, they rolled together through the long, dried grasses until they came to rest with Lottie on her back and Sean leaning above her, holding her prisoner. "Say yes," he demanded.

"Yes."

"Say you love me."

"I love you, Sean O'Connor." She reached up to pull him down to her and showed him without words that there were no more doubts.

But when she would have carried their lovemaking to its natural conclusion, Sean drew away. "Not until you are my wife," he said, putting a stop to their kisses. "This time, Lottie, you are going to be properly and respectably married, in a church with Sadie Gardener to stand up with you and friends to witness."

"Oh Sean, no," she protested as he hauled her to her feet and brushed the dust from her clothes and the grasses and seeds from her hair. "We are the only ones who matter."

"I insist." He dropped a quick kiss on her hair, then plopped her hat back on her head. "We're going to live here, love, take our place in the community. Prospect won't be a gold rush town forever. There's a railroad coming and more people. There's no end to the possibilities for a strong man and a smart woman." He grinned at her, his smile as carefree as a boy's.

"I'll use my takings from the gold fields to expand the herd, buy more land. We'll be among Prospect's leading citizens, girl, and we'll start as we intend to go on. Besides"—he leaned down to kiss her under her ear—"you wouldn't deny me the sight of you in a yellow silk gown, now would you?"

The picture he painted tempted her, but old habits die hard. "What if they laugh at me?" she fretted. "Or refuse to come at all? I couldn't bear to bring disgrace upon you."

"They'll come," he said with breezy assurance. "How soon can you have your dress ready?"

Lottie sat beside Sean in the very back pew of Prospect's Presbyterian church and pinched herself. This was her wedding day. She looked down at the yellow silk that covered her lap and pinched herself again. There was no Roman Catholic church in Prospect but Sean had said he didn't care. So long as they were properly married, he was content.

She looked over the congregation. The church

was full. There must be as many as fifty people present. How had she let Sean talk her into a public wedding on a Sunday morning? They could have taken their vows before one of the traveling judges who came to Prospect periodically, or, if he was determined to have a religious service, they could have asked the minister to marry them privately in the manse. But Sean had been adamant. Lottie was to take her proper place in the community. Their wedding was just the beginning.

The minister pronounced the final *Amen*, turned a beaming face to the congregation, and announced, "Ladies and gentlemen, that concludes our service for this morning. I will be greeting you at the door in just a few moments, but I am pleased to announce that those of you who wish to remain behind are invited to witness the marriage of Miss Charlotte Henrietta Graham and Mr. Sean Liam O'Connor."

A rustle of surprise went around the church. A few people stood up, but they had to edge their way to the end of the pews past the knees of all those who had decided to remain. In no time at all the minister was back; and Lottie, feeling like a golden princess in her yellow silk dress, stood beside Sean at the front of the church. Sadie Gardener stood to her left, and Abner was at Sean's right.

"Join hands and repeat after me."

She linked her hand with Sean's, the outward symbol of the linking of their hearts, and spoke aloud in the presence of God and witnesses the vows that would bind her to him for the rest of their lives. She heard Sean promise to love and cherish her "till death do us part" and felt her heart fill with peace.

"I now pronounce you man and wife."

Safe in the shelter of Sean's love, her shoulder

touching his, she turned to face the congregation.
She let her eyes drift over the assembly. Some were
merely curious, and some whispered behind their
hands, but Jed Barclay was there and she couldn't
mistake the sincerity of his congratulations as he
bounded up the aisle to shake Sean's hand. Miss
Douglas from the schoolhouse smiled as though
she had arranged it all herself. Indeed, to Lottie's
surprise and Sean's grinning approval, the schoolteacher rose to her feet and invited everyone present over to the schoolhouse. "Mrs. Gardener and
some of the other ladies have prepared a wedding
feast," she said. "There's plenty for everyone."

Hearty applause greeted her announcement
and the congregation surged to its feet. Everyone,
it seemed, was eager to greet the bride and groom.

Michael, still on crutches, could barely contain
his glee, proudly introducing Sean to his school-
mates and making sure they called his mother Mrs.
O'Connor. In a few months, the bride thought, her
hand in her husband's firm clasp, everyone would
have forgotten about Crazy Lottie.

Amid a throng of well-wishers they hurried
across the frozen churchyard and into the warmth
of the schoolhouse. Long tables laden with sandwiches and pickles and cakes and cookies lined one
wall, just as they had on the night of the Christmas
party; and much to her amusement, Thelma Black
and Mary Jane Lewis were pouring tea.

"Take the battle to the enemy," Miss Douglas
whispered and handed her an overflowing plate.

She looked to the schoolteacher with a question
in her eyes and received a nod of encouragement
in reply. "Thank you," she said softly, "I believe I
will." Her gaze sought out Sean, deep in conversation with Abner Gardener and Jed Barclay. Sadie

was busy unloading more baskets of food, and Michael had loaned his crutches to Billy Jackson and leaned against the wall laughing when Billy toppled over with them. Holding her head high, she walked alone to where the two who had tormented her most huddled behind Sadie Gardener's best tea service. "Hello, girls."

"Miss Graham," Thelma mumbled while Mary Jane got very busy pouring more cream into a small jug.

"It's Mrs. O'Connor now."

"Oh, yes." Thelma's eyes were sullen but defiant. "It's hard to forget old habits."

"Yes, I remember." Lottie leaned over the table, fixing both girls with an unwavering stare. "Neither of you was particularly quick to learn. Perhaps it's that slowness that sees you both still single in a town teeming with bachelors, or"—she poured milk into her tea—"perhaps it's your sour tempers and bad manners." The haughty look left Thelma's face and Mary Jane looked as though she would burst into tears on the spot. "You could make a fresh start." Lottie set down the milk jug and waited.

Mary Jane was the first to crumple. "Let me give you my best wishes on your marriage, Mrs. O'Connor." She cast a shamefaced glance toward Thelma, and added, "We both do."

"Thank you." Lottie bent her head in a gracious nod, then turned her back.

"Everything all right?" Sean materialized at her side.

"Perfectly all right." She turned a beaming face to him. "Come and help me thank Sadie and Miss Douglas for all they've done today."

*   *   *

"Now then, Mrs. O'Connor," Sean said once they were back home. Michael had gone to Billy Jackson's for the night and the two of them sat together before a snug fire. "Have you started on my Christmas present yet?"

Her mouth dropped open in surprise. "What a question on our wedding night." She glowered at him, the mist of romance that had clouded her gaze all day clearing with dismaying speed.

"No?" His eyes twinkled in the firelight.

"No. And if I had I wouldn't tell you," she said tartly, but she felt laughter bubbling to the surface as he grinned at her. She would never be proof against her husband's sweet talk.

"Then I have a suggestion." He leaned over and whispered in her ear while his fingers tangled in her hair, removing the pins and combs, bringing it cascading down around her shoulders.

"Here?" she squeaked. A hot blush suffused her face and spread across her bosom.

"Why not here?" Sean's fingers touched the hot skin above the deeply cut bodice of her dress. "Come here," he invited, holding out his arms to her. "My darling wife," she heard him murmur before all rational thought fled.

On a warm spring evening in May, Lottie sat alone on the worn wooden bench beneath the Sweetheart Tree, gazing toward the mountains. She no longer searched the horizon for Patrick but she loved to rest here, on this spot, to dream and number her blessings.

Pine Creek Farm spread out below her. The creek, in spring flood, tumbled through newly greened pastures. The number of cattle grazing the meadows was nearly double what she'd had a year ago. New calves romped about their mamas or butted heads in an excess of playful energy.

She held a letter from Louisa in her hand, bearing the news that their father had died. *It was a release,* Louisa wrote.

His past years have been full of pain, and the debilitating weakness vexed him beyond bearing. He spoke of you at the end, Charlotte. I believe he regretted the harsh judgment he rendered when Michael was born. It's a pity you couldn't have come east for a visit, but I understand your reasons.

I'm so glad for you. Sean sounds like a fine man, and you deserve your happiness.

She folded the letter and tucked it into her apron pocket. She felt a passing sympathy for the man who'd sired her but no sorrow, either of anger or regret, burdened her heart. After so long it was almost like hearing of the death of a stranger. But Louisa would be lonely. Tonight she would write to her sister and invite her for a good long visit. They could be girls again and make the house rafters ring with their laughter. They would all go to a dance in Prospect. Who knew? Louisa might decide to stay. There was nothing to keep her in Toronto.

She sniffed the air and smiled, turning her head to gaze upward through the tree branches. After ten barren years, the Sweetheart Tree had at last come into bloom, filling the air above her head with the sweetness of its perfume and its promise of a rich harvest.

She heard a shout and looked to see Michael running at full tilt toward the creek, a fishing pole in his hand and Duke barking and racing beside him. His leg had healed as straight and strong as before, and he had lost the sullen attitude of last summer. Among the greatest blessings of her marriage was Michael's host of friends. It seemed she could never bake enough cookies to keep up with the stream of boys who passed through her kitchen on a Saturday morning.

She gave up trying to count her blessings. They were beyond number, and she owed them all to a stalwart, faithful man with brilliant blue eyes and a touch of Irish blarney on his tongue. She turned, reaching behind her to trace the faded initials Patrick had carved on this tree. The love of her youth, full of laughter and adventure. On the other side of the tree were a second set of letters, *LG* and *SO'C.* The love of her maturity, full of devotion and courage and steadfast strength.

"Darlin' girl, what are you doing up here alone?" Sean's voice called her from her reverie.

She turned her head, her heart lifting with delight as always at the sound of his voice. "Come sit by me." She patted the bench beside her.

"Ah," he sighed, sinking down and stretching out his legs. His arm went around her shoulders, a familiar gesture of contentment and tenderness. "It's a good farm, girl." He surveyed their acres with satisfaction. "Fertile and abundant. A man can be happy here."

"Even a gold prospector?" She couldn't resist teasing. "Tied to the soil, grubbing in the dirt?"

"Darlin' girl." He tapped her knee with his finger. "It's not polite to remind a man of the follies of his youth." He kissed the side of her neck and gently touched his hand to her bulging belly. "You'll teach the wee one disrespect."

She moved, leaning closer against him, resting her head on his shoulder, smiling secretly to herself, fulfilled and secure. "Tell me, Sean O'Connor"—

she challenged him playfully—"is it respectful to call the mother of your child, 'girl'?"

"Sure, and why not." He responded to her mood, giving full rein to his Irish tongue. "Mother, woman, love of my life, grandmother even. To me you'll always be my darlin' girl, full of sweetness and delight."

With Sean beside her, his hand in hers, his eyes filled with love, she felt as young as the girl she'd been when first she came to Prospect, ready to dance on the breeze or whistle up the moon. "I love you," she whispered.

"Don't ever forget it." He kissed her properly then, taking her breath away, reminding her that her passion for the land and his passion for the gold were but pale imitations of the true love they shared with each other.

The leaves above her head rustled lightly. Her lips curved in a smile against his. The Sweetheart Tree in bloom had bestowed its blessing on her for a second time.